WOODCUTTER

WOODCUTTER

SHAUN BAINES

THISTLE
PUBLISHING

This first edition published in 2018 by:

Thistle Publishing
36 Great Smith Street
London
SW1P 3BU

www.thistlepublishing.co.uk

CHAPTER ONE

Charles Bronson woke with a start. He was five foot five, thick set with wavy blonde hair. Like his namesake, he sported a handlebar moustache, but it wasn't so he looked more like the movie star or that lunatic in prison. It was to detract from the nervous tick in his cheek coming alive from the moment he rose to the moment he fell asleep.

He rubbed his eyes and gulped. "Are you still up there?"

The room was a bedsit in an abandoned block of flats known as the Devil's Playground, home to junkies and rat faced dealers. The tatty furniture was pushed against the walls, clearing a space for a tin bath filled with slurry. He'd obtained it from a farmer in Crawcrook who was paid enough not to ask questions. Above it was a naked man called Enoch, suspended by his ankles to a beam in the ceiling. His arms were either side of the bath, braced against the floor. Enoch's skin was slick with sweat as he struggled to stop his head dipping into the slurry.

Bronson checked his watch. "That's almost two hours. Sorry I nodded off, but if you're not going to talk, then there's nothing for me to do, is there?"

"I don't know anything," Enoch said, squeezing the words through gritted teeth.

"I wish I could believe that. You know, I've drowned two people in that tub so far and they all keep telling me the same thing. They don't know anything."

Bronson approached, smoothing out his moustache. His nostrils had become accustomed to the smell of the slurry, but he was annoyed about his clothes. This kind of stink couldn't be washed out and he'd binned two suits already. He lived on a budget and the organisation he worked for weren't the type of people to dish out clothing allowance.

"Enoch, I'm going home for a shower. Don't worry. I'll come back, but I live a fair distance away and I love long showers. Do you think you can hang around for me?"

He smiled at his own joke, though he'd used it before.

"Please, Bronson. Let me down. I don't know anything," Enoch said.

Who had scared these people so badly they would rather drown in cow shit than spill the beans? This was going to go wrong again, Bronson thought. His boss wanted answers, but no-one was talking. He'd be left with another dead body to dispose of and an awkward conversation to be had with his superiors.

"You pay the Daytons one hundred pounds a week, right?" Bronson asked.

Enoch nodded.

"What's it called? Your restaurant?"

"The Peking Lantern."

"Oh, I've been there. It's nice. Anyway, you pay money so your lovely restaurant doesn't get burned down with you in it, right?"

Enoch nodded again.

"Why would you stop paying?" Bronson asked.

"I don't know."

Bronson grabbed Enoch by his hair and stared into his frightened eyes. "You do know, but you're being very rude by keeping it a secret." He yanked downwards, forcing Enoch's head under the slurry. Enoch fought against him, but he was too weak to offer much resistance. Counting down the seconds on his watch, Bronson finally released him.

Enoch coughed and spluttered, choking on the slurry in his mouth. When he was able to breathe, his breaths came as whimpers.

"I. Don't. Know. Anything."

"Jesus Christ," Bronson said, wiping his dirtied hand down the side of his trousers. "That's bad for you and bad for me, isn't it?"

This was supposed to be his breakthrough. He figured Enoch would crack the minute he saw the bath full of shit, but he'd turned out to be a hard bastard. He would have admired that except his own head was on the line too. Someone was choking the money supply to the Daytons. If he didn't figure out who, Bronson's name was as much shit as the slurry Enoch was about to drown in.

A knock came at the door. The authorities gave the Devil's Playground a wide berth, refusing to pour resources into an unwinnable fight. They allowed the tower block to police itself. Knowing he was safe, Bronson opened the door and smiled.

Peter Pan Hands shook his coat from his shoulders as he entered. He was in his forties with tumbling locks of ginger hair. His green eyes sparkled with mischief no matter what he was doing at the time. The Irish lilt of his voice charmed women and gangsters alike.

"If it ain't the Magnificent One," Peter said. "I gather I've got a collection."

Bronson closed the door. Peter wrinkled his nose, but seemed unfazed by the scene in front of him. "Why do you always take their clothes off?"

"It's something Daniel taught me," Bronson said. "People feel more vulnerable when they're starkers."

Peter considered the idea until he was distracted by something. "I thought you said this guy was Jewish. Aren't all Jews circumcised?"

"Enoch runs a Chinese restaurant. How orthodox do you think he is?"

"Orthodox or not, it's obviously pretty cold in here, if you know what I mean?"

Bronson laughed, slapping Peter on the back, but Peter's face grew serious. "Listen mate, I only dump these bodies out at sea as a favour to you. I'm not dropping a live one in for anyone."

"I understand. I didn't think he'd last this long."

"I'm freelance and I need the money, but…"

"It's okay, honestly. I'll take care of it." Bronson pulled out a knife and waved it in front of Enoch's face. "This is my friend Peter. He's an arms dealer, but he also has a boat. He's going to drop your dead body in the North Sea if you don't give me the answers I'm after."

Despite his exhaustion, Enoch swung away from the blade and started to cry. "Okay. Cut me down and I'll tell you."

Bronson looked to the knife in surprise. Why hadn't he thought of this earlier? He'd carried that tub of shit up three flights of stairs for nothing.

He placed the knife under Enoch's penis. "Get talking or maybe you'll get circumcised after all. I ain't no doctor and this place ain't sterile. You don't want little Enoch to go green and drop off, do you?"

With his face purple and his eyes wide, Enoch spoke to the knife. "Someone sent a photo to my phone. It was of my wife. She was tied to a chair. She had a blindfold on. Her face was bloody, but she was alive. Then they sent a text."

"What did it say?" Bronson asked.

"No more money to the Daytons. Next time she dies. Tell no-one."

"That was it?"

Enoch nodded. "They released her. She didn't see anything, I swear."

"And you never saw anyone either, I suppose?"

"No, but when she came home, she had five hundred pounds with her."

"Jesus," said Peter to no-one in particular.

Bronson looked at him. "They're paying people to not pay us? That's crazy."

"Or really smart," Peter said. "Who's going to give you money when it pays more to keep it in their pockets?"

"And if they do pay, their loved ones die. Who are these guys?" Bronson rubbed his chin, hoping the answer might come in a blinding flash of brilliance.

Enoch snuffled back a sob. "That's all I know. Please cut me down."

The twitch in Bronson's cheek took on a staccato rhythm. It sometimes happened when he was worried. Enoch had told him all he knew, but it wasn't much. Aside from a text, Enoch had no contact with this new, mysterious gang. Bronson could check his phone, find the caller ID, but it was probably a throwaway and already smashed into several pieces. No-one this careful would be that stupid.

After hours of interrogation and buckets of cow shit, Bronson still knew nothing.

"Okay, Enoch, time to go home," he said, working his knife through the rope.

Bronson shivered as the temperature dropped and a voice spoke behind them. "What did you find out?"

Bronson and Peter turned to see Scott Dayton walk into the room. He was as tall as Daniel, but with none of his warmth. Scott's eyes were icy blue and his skin was white. He dressed in dark suits, tailored to limbs as thin as icicles. Sometimes he looked like a funeral director, sometimes like the corpse about to be buried.

He adjusted the knot on his silken tie. "I asked you a question."

Clearing his throat, Bronson recounted the little he knew and tried not to stutter. When he finished, Scott studied him for an uncomfortable amount of time before turning his attention to Peter.

"It looked like Bronson was letting Enoch go."

Peter shrugged. "He can do what he likes."

"No, he can't. Neither can you."

Peter pulled on his coat, evidently feeling a chill. In all the years Bronson had known him, he never backed down from a fight. He admired that in Peter, but hoped today might mark a change and if it didn't, Bronson was powerless to intervene.

"I don't work for the Daytons," Peter said, buttoning his coat, "and I'm not scared of you, either."

Scott gestured to Bronson. "Give me your knife."

"He didn't mean anything by it, Scott. There was no disrespect." Bronson looked at Scott's extended hand and turned to Peter. "Tell him you didn't mean anything."

Peter's mouth clamped shut. His eyes narrowed as Bronson presented the knife to Scott, who held it aloft like a trophy.

"It's time you learned who has the power here." Scott span on his heel, driving the blade into Enoch's chest. There was no escaping the strike and Enoch didn't scream. His strength had long been spent. He gulped in surprise and his arms gave way, his head sloshing beneath the shit. The body convulsed, spilling slurry over the floor and spattering Bronson's shoes.

"It's like that freaky cheek of yours," Scott said with a grin. "All that jerking around for no reason."

"You didn't need to do that, Dayton," Peter said, his big hands rising from his side.

"You came for a dead body, right?"

Bronson slipped between the two men. His back was to Peter, but his eyes were locked onto Scott.

"He didn't pay his debts, Peter," Bronson said. "He was protecting the gang trying to take us down. He deserved it."

"You Daytons are butchers." Peter placed a hand on Bronson's shoulder. "You're on your own with this one, pal. Give me a call if you need anything else."

They watched the Irishman leave. Bronson sensed the coldness emanating from Scott in waves. "He won't say anything," he said.

Scott punched Bronson in the stomach. He doubled over and Scott forced him to his knees. He held Bronson's face over the bath of slurry. The oily stain of Enoch's blood rested on the surface.

"You better start getting me some answers or you'll be the one hanging up there next time. Who's out there? Who's trying to take us down?"

"I don't know," Bronson said, immediately recalling Enoch's fateful words.

Scott pushed his face into the slurry. It was cold and drew itself up his nose. It's just water, he told himself as disgust clawed at the back of his mind. Just water. Not cow shit.

He was released, but didn't dare breath. He blew the slurry from his nose, wiping his face clean before gasping for air. He'd rather suffocate than have that stuff inside him. When his head stopped spinning and the gagging passed, he looked around the room to find Scott was gone. He was on his own.

"Bollocks," he said.

CHAPTER TWO

At six foot eight inches, Daniel looked more like the trees he chopped down for a living. His eyes were a deep hazel colour with an intensity that thrilled her, though she had to admit, his gaze could also be frightening. He had the broad back of an oak tree and a weathered face belying his twenty-three years.

Mrs Guptal watched from her kitchen window as he carried logs cut from her sycamore, placing them neatly in his van. His muscles strained and veins pulsed in his thick neck. His face however registered none of the effort. He was like a machine, as powerful and as impersonal as the chainsaw he used.

A stirring rose in Mrs Guptal she had not felt in years. The material of Daniel's work shirt stretched over his body. She wondered what it would feel like to be held in those powerful arms. He was a child compared to her thirty-seven years, but her eager imagination dismissed the age difference. She was attractive and he was a man.

She glanced at the clock on the kitchen wall. Three o'clock. Mr Guptal would not be back for another two hours. Their Quick Stop shop on the corner of Station Road was always busy. It was a focal point of a small village called Hounswood, but her husband wouldn't be there. He'd abandon his duties to their teenage shop assistant and slink into the Kingston Hotel, drowning sorrows he had no right to claim as his own.

Mrs Guptal blushed when Daniel caught her watching him. His back had been turned, but it was if he had sensed her curiosity. He gave her a brief nod before she ducked behind the curtains to spare her reddening cheeks.

Her husband had not always been so inattentive. As newly-weds, it was all she could do to get away from his wandering hands. She was blessed to feel so loved. They spent days in bed, not just lovemaking, but talking. They were close; two bodies with one soul her husband often said.

As the years went by and drink stole her husband away, she fantasised about an alternative world populated with what-ifs? What if she had married someone else? What if her husband had not become such a lush? What if another man offered himself to her? Just once, she thought dismally. Just one more time.

"I'm finished, Mrs Guptal." Daniel stood in the door frame, blocking light from a weak Scottish sun. His hands were clasped behind his back as he waited patiently for payment.

It was three fifteen.

"Why don't you come in, Daniel?" Mrs Guptal asked. "You'll need a cuppa after all that hard work."

***

Daniel perched on the edge of Mrs Guptal's brown leather sofa and looked about the room. The walls were beige. The carpet was beige too, though slightly darker in shade. There was a bookcase filled with books whose spines were unbroken. A television sat in the corner and a sideboard stood underneath a window obscured by freshly laundered net curtains.

Nothing here told him anything about the woman making tea in the kitchen.

"Are you all right, Daniel?" Mrs Guptal appeared in the doorway, her slender figure barely masked by a thin, yellow sari.

He accepted the proffered tea with a small smile of thanks and balanced the china cup and saucer in his clumsy hands. The smell of the tea was unfamiliar and Daniel looked to Mrs Guptal for guidance.

"It's green tea," she said. "You'll like it."

Returning his gaze to the moss coloured liquid, Daniel wasn't so sure.

"You haven't been in Hounswood long, have you?" Mrs Guptal asked.

He sipped from his cup, taking care not to embarrass himself by spilling any. The tea was bitter, but not unpleasant and he was thankful he wouldn't have to mask his distaste.

Daniel wasn't good at hiding his emotions.

"Nine months," he answered.

Mrs Guptal slid in next to him on the sofa, leaning back into the headrest. Daniel was a solitary man who didn't partake in village gossip, but it was a small place and even he had heard what they said about the woman wasting her life on the village drunk.

Taking in the soft contours of her face, her eyes were as dark as twilight, but typically he saw much more. Her pupils were dilated and the rise and fall of her breasts had quickened as her breathing gained pace. Her left eyebrow was raised two millimetres higher than her right and her lips were parted.

"There's not much to do for a young man like you in a village like this. Surely, you should be living it up in a big city somewhere."

"I came from a city, but it didn't agree with me."

She seemed lonely, he thought. Some wives, at least those from his hometown, relished the freedom of a dysfunctional marriage. They didn't necessarily seek comfort elsewhere, but they sought their independence and it made them stronger. Here was a woman who withered without attention and Daniel felt sorry for her.

Opening his mouth to speak, Mrs Guptal placed a finger on his lips. She let it linger, her fingertip exploring the soft flesh of his mouth. Daniel's heart hammered in his chest and he longed to kiss her.

He gently placed his cup and saucer on the carpet.

"Don't do that," Mrs Guptal said, leaping to her feet. She scooped the cup and saucer from the floor and found a coaster on the sideboard. She gave it a quick polish with her sari before setting the cup and saucer out of harm's way.

Daniel's quizzical look stopped her in the middle of a panic.

"My husband ..." she said. "He doesn't like anything on the carpet in case it's knocked over."

He rubbed his hands. "I better be going."

"Oh, no. Don't. Please."

Ignoring her, Daniel stood, casting a shadow over a woman who was suddenly so small in his eyes. Her veneer of confidence was brittle and as light weight as the layer of dust on her furniture.

Daniel didn't know much, but he knew people and he saw a fear in Mrs Guptal he didn't want to be around. There was enough of that in his past.

"I was just being silly," she said. "Stay a little while longer."

He moved toward her and embraced her in his thick arms. The top of her head barely reached his chest, but when they connected, she shuddered and he knew she was crying. Daniel let her tears soak his T-shirt.

"I'm such a bloody fool. I don't know why I put up with him, but he's in my head. I act like a crazy woman and know it's him making me be this way." Mrs Guptal gripped Daniel tighter and his heart raced. This was the first time he had touched a woman in over nine months. True, he was no longer attracted to her, but like Mrs Guptal, he craved the intimacy of human contact. He was pleased he had been brave enough to reach out. It was not his usual reaction, but his instinct had told him it was what Mrs Guptal wanted most and Daniel always trusted his instincts.

"What the fuck is going on here?" Mr Guptal staggered into the room. He was short, but with the drunken attitude of a bigger man. He'd been handsome once, but years of drinking had taken their toll. His face was gaunt while his stomach was round, rolling over a belt that struggled under the strain.

"Well, woman? What have you been doing?"

Mrs Guptal looked terrified and pushed from Daniel's grasp. "You're back early, darling. Do you want a cup of tea?"

"No, I don't want a cup of tea. I want to know why you've made a cuckold of me."

Daniel breathed slowly through his nostrils, attempting to control his rising anxiety. Had things worked out differently, Mr Guptal might have walked in on something he did have a right to be angry about. As it stood, Daniel was lending comfort to someone who needed it and he saw no reason for the idiot's agitation.

"I'm sorry, Mr Guptal. Your wife was upset. I was trying to make her feel better."

Mr Guptal jigged from one foot to another, snorting beery fumes like a bull. He stepped up to Daniel, his fists clenched and his jaw set in stone.

"You shut up. You come to stick your dick in my wife. Make her feel better, eh?"

"No, darling, no," Mrs Guptal said. "He's just a gardener."

Her words cut Daniel keenly. Just a gardener? His T-shirt was still damp from her tears and she'd dismissed him as if he were nothing. She was placating a drunken husband, but the sudden switch of attitude riled Daniel.

And her stupid husband had no right to be angry, either. Daniel tried to relax, but he knew this mounting tension too well. If it wasn't for Mr Guptal and The Kingston Hotel, seethed

Daniel, his wife wouldn't have been in such a state. He wouldn't be the innocent party forced into the middle of a fucked-up situation.

"Listen, I'm going to go," Daniel said, his hands bunched into fists. "You better work this out between the two of you."

He moved toward the door, but Mr Guptal blocked his exit. "You're not going yet. You insult me and take advantage of my wife. I'm going to teach you a lesson."

Before Daniel could reason with him, Mr Guptal swung a punch. He was too drunk and too short to land it accurately. It glanced off Daniel's brawny shoulder with the lightest touch, but it was too late. Daniel's anger flared like the beginnings of a volcano. He slapped Mr Guptal across the face, spinning him a hundred and eighty degrees. Grabbing him by the back of his head, he rammed his face into the wall. The blood from Mr Guptal's nose sprayed over the beige walls. The room finally had a splash of colour, thought Daniel.

"Get out, you animal," Mrs Guptal shouted. "Leave him alone."

She ran between the fighting men, folding her bleeding husband in her arms. He stood over them, his chest rising and falling, an all too familiar anger coursing through his body. They cowered from him, holding each other tightly, neither one of them daring to look into his eyes. Blood rolled down the wall. He could smell it. He could smell their dread. His instinct to maim, the one he tried so hard to bury, had burst free from a faulty dam.

He closed his eyes. "I'm sorry."

***

As he shoved the last of his clothing into a rucksack, Daniel thought of the harm he had visited upon the Guptals. It made him ill. He had been minutes from sleeping with Mrs Guptal and had then beaten her husband to a bloody pulp.

Whether they informed the police or not, his life here was over. It was a small village and word would spread. People would avoid him on the street, but he'd feel their eyes upon him, even with his back turned. Work would dry up. He would be ostracised and the place he hoped to call home one day would be gone.

He slung it over his shoulder and had one last look around the room. The walls were the same green they were when he moved in. The laminate flooring was still chipped. The sofa and bed he was leaving behind had been chosen by the previous tenant. There was nothing to say Daniel had even been here.

The doorbell rang and his chest tightened in panic. The Guptals had reported him to the police after all. He'd hoped Mrs Guptal might have forgiven him, but the small measure of comfort he'd offered clearly meant nothing. Perhaps the sins of his past overrode any kindness he showed in his present.

The doorbell rang again. It was insistent and echoed around his now empty home.

He dropped his rucksack and groaned. He'd got nine months of freedom and was surprised it had lasted that long. All he'd wanted when he arrived in Hounswood was to be forgotten. It was a stupid idea, really. Men like him were never faceless for long. Soon he'd be taken down to the station, identified as Daniel Dayton and his nightmare would start afresh.

With a deep breath, he answered the door.

Outside was a man he had not seen in a very long time.

CHAPTER THREE

"**E**vening, ladies. Make sure you behave tonight."

Scalper Brown was head doorman at Newcastle's Glitterball nightclub, a job he had held for eight years. The club was the biggest in the city, safely holding up to five hundred sweaty punters, though they routinely admitted more. It made his job impossible and Scalper often wondered if he was there for security or window dressing.

Most of the guys he'd started out with had gone on to better things. It was long tedious hours of vigilance interspersed with brief bouts of fire-fighting, like a sentry posted on a deserted border. It didn't suit everyone, but Scalper liked the hours and, considering the alternative was jail, he was happy to remain on duty.

Three young women tottered by him, heading down to the cloakroom. God knows what they were checking in, he thought. If he took their clothes and stitched them together, he'd be lucky to end up with a handkerchief.

Scalper was in his forties and average height, but his hard, round muscles made him look taller. If he wasn't working, he was working out. He shaved his head twice a day, not because he was going bald, but because he liked the feel of it. Years ago, someone had said he'd been scalped by Red Indians and the nickname stuck.

"Hey, Scalper, you ever seen anything like these?" Balancing on her five inch heels, a regular called Jackie exposed her large breasts.

Scalper laughed. "Put 'em away, love. My mother warned me about girls like you."

Fairbanks, the new starter, watched Jackie disappear into the steam of the nightclub. "Does that happen often?" he asked.

It was his first night. He was twenty, but looked younger. Skinny and pale, he seemed as threatening as a lollipop. Health and Safety prohibited doormen from wearing jewellery, but when Fairbanks refused to remove his diamond stud earring, Scalper hired him immediately. They were short staffed and if he was prepared to have that thing torn from his ear in a fight, then maybe he was tougher than he looked.

"Happens all the time, mate," Scalper said, "You might see a few more before the night is out."

Fairbanks grinned and scanned the queue for potential trouble makers.

When Scalper was his age, he was already running with Ed Dayton and his crew. Ed was older than Scalper and a natural leader. He charmed the birds and the branches they sat on. Scalper, a young, bare knuckle fighter at the time, fell under his spell so when breaking windows and stealing chocolate bars escalated into extortion and robbery, Scalper barely noticed. It wasn't until his beloved mother abandoned him that Scalper saw what he'd become. He was a thug; a petty criminal that disgusted and frightened her in equal measure. He knew he'd have to change.

But it wasn't the kind of job he could resign from. He knew too much. Standing in front of Ed, looking into his steel grey eyes, Scalper's stomach churned as he told him of his decision. Scalper was no fool. He made money for Ed and Ed had expensive tastes. Trying to hide the quiver in his voice, he expected the worst.

What he didn't expect was the hug. Ed wrapped his arms around Scalper's broad shoulders. He gave him the faintest Judas kiss on the cheek and offered him another job.

"Something more respectable," he'd said. "Family is the most important thing in the world. We need something to heal the wounds between mother and son."

Eight years later and Scalper was exactly where Ed Dayton wanted him. By the time he realised that, it was too late.

By midnight, there still hadn't been any trouble. Scalper stretched and yawned lazily. Everyone was happy to get in from the cold. It should be a good thing, but Fairbanks looked nervous. His eyes darted left and right, never settling on anyone for long. Scalper sighed. New bouncers liked to prove their metal. They started fights to show they could finish one. Scalper was capable of violence, but abhorred it when it wasn't needed.

As the queue died down, he pulled Fairbanks to one side. "You alright, mate?"

Fairbanks looked surprised. And embarrassed. "Kosher, mate."

"Listen, this job is about smiling, hand shaking and letting people have a good time. We never get into a ruck unless we can help it. If you're here for trouble, you'll get it from me first. Understand?"

Fairbanks swallowed, his protruding Adam's apple bobbing with the effort. "I'm not looking for a fight," he said.

"What did you say?" Scalper asked. Years of working in clubland had left him partially deaf.

"I'm not looking for a fight," Fairbanks said, raising his voice. "Ever since I saw those tits, I've had a hard on the size of the Tyne Bridge."

Scalper wasn't that deaf, but he couldn't help asking again. "What?" he repeated, cupping a hand to his ear.

Fairbanks took a deep breath as Scalper counted down the last few beats of Daft Punk's Get Lucky. It couldn't have been timed better. The DJ was useless and always left a gap between songs and in that brief moment of silence, Fairbanks shouted, "I want to see more tits."

The queuing punters erupted into laughter. Fairbanks went red from the tips of his ears to the base of his neck. He looked like the rubber at the end of a pencil.

Scalper grabbed him in a bear hug. "That was classic."

"Fuck you," Fairbanks said, pulling himself out of Scalper's massive arms. The crowd applauded and Scalper gave a bow and waited. This would be the moment, he thought. This was when he'd know if he could trust Fairbanks with his life. Scalper watched as Fairbanks studied the crowd, trying to determine what to do. At last, the penny dropped and Fairbanks gave them a curtsy. They cheered and Scalper cheered with them. He had his answer and finally felt safe in Fairbanks' presence.

Scalper's earpiece crackled into life. It was Grievson, part of the in-house security team. "We've got a problem in the third stairway. A girl OD-ing. No-one's called 999 yet."

He turned to Fairbanks. "Can you handle the queue?"

Scalper got a worried smile in response. Doormen were never left to handle a queue on their own, especially not a newbie like Fairbanks. The hardest of bouncers could be overrun by a drunken mob.

"I'll be as quick as I can, okay?"

Fairbanks nodded and Scalper ran through heavy doors into the club. The air was humid as revellers danced and sweated en masse. Heavy bass thudded inside his chest. Lights flashed and strobed as he fought his way to the stairwell.

He was almost there when he saw Mosely from the corner of his eye and his brow furrowed. Joseph Mosely was younger than Scalper, but prematurely greying. The hair at his temples was almost white while the rest of his curly, dark hair was peppered with grey. His expensive suits were tailored to a thin frame and housed a number of secret pockets where he hid pharmaceuticals.

He was leaning against the bar, shouting into the ears of two young women who appeared to be falling for his lies. If his charm failed, Scalper knew he'd spike their drinks. He'd often turned a blind eye to Mosely throwing a semi-comatose woman into the back of his BMW.

Scalper pulled him to a quieter corner of the club. "How many people have you dealt to tonight?"

Mosely smiled, his perfect white teeth shining blue under florescent lighting. He reached into his pocket and retrieved a pink pill, placing it delicately on his tongue. He swallowed and looked back at the girls waiting for him.

"Has it been cut with anything?" persisted Scalper.

Mosely rolled his eyes. "Why do we have to keep going through this? You look after the people outside. I look after them inside."

Scalper jabbed a finger toward the stairway. "There's a girl dying over there. You're the only dealer allowed in here. Are you saying you had nothing to do with it?"

"She could have brought it in with her." Mosley smoothed down the front of his suit. "Drug dealing is a nasty business, Scalper and the market is flooded with dealers. I do what I can to gain an edge. Honestly, I don't know what's in these pills. Could be talcum powder, could be lawn fertiliser."

"You're a scumbag. You know that, don't you?"

"Our money comes from the same place so don't come all high and mighty with me. Dayton pays me to deal and you're paid to let me. We're both feeding from the same trough."

"If Ed knew how much you cut your shit –"

"He'd what? Tell me to stop? Ask me to walk a straighter line?" Mosely asked.

Scalper hoped Mosely didn't see the doubt in his face. Ed Dayton was the kind of businessman untroubled by ethics. However, he was always troubled by a drop in profits. When Scalper started working as a bouncer, he saw it as a gracious favour granted by an old friend, but it didn't take long before he realised Ed saw it differently. Scalper was there to facilitate the needs of dangerous men like Mosely. His respectable role in the firm was a lie he swallowed night after night.

Mosely looked to the stairway and Scalper saw his concern. Maybe Ed didn't care what the drugs were cut with, but he'd care about Mosely killing his customers. And Mosely knew it.

"I don't want to cause you any bother," Mosely said, "so I'll leave early. It wasn't a bad night, mate. At least the bitch paid up front."

Mosely snatched the radio from Scalper's lapel and threw it against a wall. It shattered into pieces. "Don't want you radioing the Daytons and telling them I've been a naughty boy, do we?" said Mosely. "Now get on with your job. I'll see you tomorrow."

Scalper cursed as Mosely weaved his way through the crowd and disappeared among flashes of light. One day he'd see that fucking creep in a wooden box.

By the time Scalper made it to the stairway, Grievson was white with panic. He was average height with dyed black hair. He had a scar running down his face. He told everyone it was from a bottle fight, but Scalper knew it came from falling off his BMX when he was fifteen.

Scalper went straight to the girl. She was in the recovery position, but that was the extent of the help she'd been given. There was vomit in her hair and that was good. The less time the drugs were in her system, the better.

"Do you know who she is?" asked Scalper.

Grievson shook his head. "They all look the same to me."

Brushing the hair away from the face, Scalper recognised Jackie immediately. He tried to compose himself.

Her breathing was shallow and her face was a death mask; a poor imitation of the giggling young woman who had teased Scalper at the door. Typically, her so called friends were nowhere to be seen. It happened every time. At the first sign of trouble, friends were the first to leave. He hoped he'd witness more loyalty if he ever ran into trouble.

Slamming his fist into the floor, he hissed like an injured animal. Mosely was going to pay for this. He couldn't let the slimy twat out of the club like nothing had happened. Not this time. He needed to be taught a lesson. Ed would understand. If he didn't, then Scalper would cross that bridge when he was thrown off it.

"Are we dumping her out back, then?" asked Grievson.

Scalper took another look at Jackie. She was so fragile, as if someone had stolen the vibrant girl he knew and replaced her with a china doll.

"Yes."

"Sorry, mate, I didn't hear you. This bloody music –"

"Yes," shouted Scalper. "Do what we always do. Throw her in the alley and call for an ambulance."

Grievson nodded quickly, picking Jackie up under her armpits and dragging her downstairs. Scalper watched one of her silly high heeled shoes coming away from her foot. He picked it up and threw it down the stairs.

Leaving the stairway, Scalper barrelled through the club, knocking punters left and right, hoping to spot Mosely lingering in the shadows, but he was gone. He'd fled the scene of the crime, but he'd be back and Scalper would be waiting. He returned to the entrance of the club, barging the double doors open in anger. The cold air rushed to greet him and he saw the danger immediately. Five guys. A big man with acne restrained Fairbanks against a wall, his forearm pressed on his throat. Four others stood in a line. Three of them had bats. One of them swung a bicycle chain.

It was organised. It was a take down.

He reached for his radio, but Mosely had smashed it in a fit of pettiness; an action that was likely to get Scalper killed. There'd be no back-up. No friends. He would have to do this on his own and the prospect sent a shiver of fear down his spine.

He'd faced down bigger guys, but never five at once. He couldn't win, but he couldn't abandon Fairbanks and run away. The best he could hope for was to take a few of them out. If Fairbanks could get free, they could fight their way to safety, but he wasn't hopeful.

Hesitation would get him killed for sure and Scalper waded in, targeting the guy with the bicycle chain. He feigned a left jab, swinging a right fist into the guy's stomach. It connected hard and his opponent crumpled.

Something struck the back of his head. Adrenaline coursed through his system, blocking pain receptors, but his vision blurred and he lost his balance. He couldn't go down. He'd never get back up again.

He straightened and swung a blind left at the shapes around him. He hit nothing but air. There was a kick to his right knee and he heard his tendon pop. Scalper staggered, but kept his feet. The figures surrounded him, forcing him into the centre of their circle with kicks and slaps. There was no way out.

He made to grab the nearest guy, but he stepped out of reach with a laugh. Someone punched him from behind, driving their fist into his kidneys. He arched his back in pain, grunting like a whipped horse, exposing his stomach to the bicycle chain slashing through his flesh.

His strength washed out of him and he dropped to the pavement where he lay waiting for the finishing blows. Fairbanks' face swam into view and Scalper thanked a God he didn't believe in. The boy had fought free of that acne faced goon. He was a good lad. Stronger than he looked. Scalper blinked away blood from his eyes, glad it hid his tears of relief.

Fairbanks placed a gentle hand on Scalper's chest. "I'm sorry, mate."

Scalper shivered with shock, but managed a smile. "Hell of a first night. You came through for me in the end, though," he said.

Fairbanks laughed. "You were really kind to me, Scalper. I won't forget that."

Scalper tasted the coppery tang of blood in his mouth. He'd been around violence long enough to know he was suffering from internal injuries. Had Fairbanks called for an ambulance yet? He hoped so. He didn't know how much longer he could hold on. There should be one coming for Jackie by now. Maybe he could hitch a lift?

"Have you called for an ambulance, mate?" he asked Fairbanks, but when he looked at the boy, he knew no-one had called, least of all Fairbanks.

There was a cold detachment to his face that reminded Scalper of Ed Dayton whenever someone was about to die.

Fairbanks pulled a Stanley knife from his pocket. Bouncers aren't supposed to carry weapons, Scalper thought.

"It's just business," Fairbanks said. "I hadn't expected you to be so nice."

The blade was placed in Scalper's mouth and it cut swiftly, opening up his right cheek. Blood spurted from the wound. He expected it to hurt, but all he could feel was the warm sensation of liquid running down his neck. Gulping down air, together with mouthfuls of blood, Scalper was drowning, unable to catch a breath.

The last thing he felt was Fairbanks stroking his shaven head. It was a display of tenderness that wasn't reflected in his eyes.

CHAPTER FOUR

"I've got good news," said Detective Constable John Spencer as he pushed passed Daniel.

Spencer was tall and thin with oily hair tied in a ponytail. He wore a cheap suit that hadn't seen a dry cleaner since he'd pulled it off the rack and he was still wearing too much aftershave. No-one spoke to the detective without their eyes watering.

Daniel closed the door slowly.

One thing had changed about Spencer, though. He had grown a moustache. It was black and wiry, hiding a scar Daniel gave him when he had failed to pay his debts.

Spencer looked at the rucksack and stroked his chin. "Going somewhere?"

Staying by the door, Daniel watched the detective prowl around his empty home. Spencer tapped a cigarette from a crumpled packet and lit it with a disposable lighter. "You mind if I smoke?"

Daniel folded his arms over his chest. "What are you doing here?" he asked.

Spencer snorted blue smoke from his nostrils and ignored him. He wandered into the kitchen and returned looking unimpressed before inspecting Daniel's only bedroom. "Shit, this place is small."

He came back to the room, flicking ash onto the carpet. "I've got to hand it to you, Daniel. You hid yourself well, which is no mean feat given your size. Nine months on the run is more than most people could manage."

"You're not here to arrest me for what I did to the Guptals, are you?"

Pushing the cushions from a worn sofa onto the floor, Spencer flopped into it with an exaggerated sigh. His ponytail wrapped itself around his shoulders like a greasy snake.

"What makes you say that?"

As Daniel eased away from the front door, he noticed a flicker of concern in Spencer's eyes. "Because you work for Northumbria Police and live in the pocket of the Daytons. Neither of those things have anything to do with the Guptals."

Spencer smiled and twirled the end of his ponytail with his fingertips. "Okay, then. It's time to lay my cards on the table. What do you want to know first? Why I'm here or why I'm here in your house?"

Daniel stiffened. He already knew the answer, but he wasn't about to play so easily into the detective's hands. He kept quiet. Spencer was sly and could trick him into revealing too much.

"I'm here because I've made some terrible mistakes in my life. The biggest of which was consorting with your father. Actually, the biggest mistake was getting in too deep with your father's bookies and allowing your father to cover the bill. From there, I've been forced to make a lot of compromises."

Daniel glanced at his rucksack. Could he grab it and run? The van keys were in his pocket. He could be on the road before Spencer even had a chance to fart, but he couldn't leave him here. Not alive at least.

"I know what you're thinking and all I'll say is don't," Spencer said. "Firstly, the guys at the station know I'm here. Secondly, I've called your father with your exact whereabouts. He'll have men on the A69 heading your way already."

Daniel's mouth turned dry with fear. His suspicions were correct. This was about his father. It was always about his fucking father. He couldn't stand to see Daniel free from his control. "I'd rather be in handcuffs than back in Newcastle."

"Stop being so melodramatic. It's not like he's going to kill you. I don't think."

Daniel rounded on Spencer and he leapt from the sofa, his palms open in a gesture of peace. "Do you remember when I questioned you over the assault of a bar tender at the White Ensign pub in Gateshead?"

Daniel shook his head.

"I keep forgetting you're not very smart," Spencer said, taking a step back. "He refused to serve you and you beat him with a pool cue. It took fifty-two stitches to put his face back on and he still looked like the Elephant man."

"What's your point?"

"If you could do that when you were thirteen, what could you do to me now? All I'm saying is I need you to calm down. Let me explain why I'm here and you can make your own decision."

Daniel walked silently around the room, circling the detective. Spencer followed him with his eyes, a thin sheen of sweat on his forehead. He stopped pacing and cracked his knuckles. "I'm seconds from digging a hole out back with your name on it."

"You have to know this was never going to last," Spencer said, trying to keep his voice calm. "Your Dad was never going to give up looking for you."

"I'd rather be dead than face that man again."

"Be careful what you wish for, Daniel. Those guys on the A69 might not be as reasonable as me."

Daniel stepped closer. "Tell me why you're here?"

"I told you I had good news, didn't I? If you calm down, I'll tell you. Just back off, okay?" Spencer placed another cigarette in his mouth. As he went to light it, he caught Daniel's eye and slid it back into his packet.

"Your father is worried sick. He wants you back. There are guys like me –"

"Bent coppers," Daniel said.

Spencer breathed deeply, steadying his nerves. "There are guys like me in every station in the UK waiting for a word, anything, to track you down. I got transferred to Dumfriesshire Area Command, the arsehole of the world no-one ever bothered to wipe. Then I hear about a disturbance; a giant of a man assaulting two victims in their home. There aren't many giants around, Daniel. I showed the Guptals your photo and it was a positive ID."

"I wasn't assaulting him. He was a wife beater."

"Wife beater or not, you almost killed him. I persuaded them to drop the charges. You're in the clear. That's the good news."

Spencer attempted a smile, but it looked crooked on his worried face. "Between you and me," he added, "I think there was something messed up going on in that house, but that's the countryside for you. They marry their cousins out here, so what do you expect?"

Whipping his rucksack back onto his shoulder, Daniel moved to the door.

"Where are you going?" asked Spencer.

"Somewhere else."

"What about your father?"

The straps of the rucksack cut into Daniel's shoulder and he paused to get more comfortable. "You said it yourself. I'm a free man. Dad has spent nine months looking for me. If you keep your trap shut – which you will if you know what's good for you – it'll be another nine months before he finds me. You're not expecting me to wait for them to come, are you?"

Daniel reached for the door handle.

"Someone is making a move on your Dad's patch."

Daniel stopped and Spencer continued. "I'm stuck in Scotland and I don't know all the details, but it looks bad for him."

"What are you talking about?"

Looking around Daniel's empty cottage, Spencer shrugged. "Look, I'm sure Scotland is great. There's enough whisky and enough men in skirts to make anyone happy, but I have a family in Newcastle and I haven't seen them since you disappeared. Whoever finds you gets guaranteed passage back home. I get to start again. No more working for the Daytons. You of all people should appreciate that."

"So it's my freedom in exchange for yours? You're not the only one who wants a new beginning." Daniel readjusted the rucksack. It was weighing him down. Inside were clothes and a poster of the Tyne Bridge he had never mounted. It was still in the cardboard tube he had purchased it in. The bag was almost as empty as his cottage so why did it feel so heavy?

It was getting late and the light was dying outside. A purple ray of sun beamed through the window, settling on Spencer's troubled face. "I know you won't come with me. Christ, I couldn't even fit you in my car, never mind persuade you to sit nicely." He tried to laugh, but it sounded like he was retching. "When I spoke to your Dad, he told me things were going from bad to shit and his family was being attacked."

"Good," he said. "My family deserve it."

"Not all of them, Daniel."

The rucksack slipped from his shoulder. There was so little in it, there was barely a sound when it hit the floor, though it was enough to make Spencer jump. He swallowed before resuming. "Whoever is attacking the Daytons doesn't care who gets hurt. Your daughter was targeted. I'm sorry, Daniel, but Eisha's in a coma."

CHAPTER FIVE

The party was held in the function room of The Amen Corner, an up market bistro owned by the Daytons. The building dated back to 1893 and was originally the offices of a shipping magnate called Sir Malcolm Arnott. It reflected Sir Arnott's lavish taste with stained glass windows, marble pillars and a fluted archway entrance. On purchasing the property, the Daytons had installed a revolving dancefloor and sound system.

Ed Dayton sipped from a glass of ice cold Feuillatte champagne, hoping to wash away the bad taste in his mouth. Smiling faces filed into the room. Some headed straight to the bar while others found seats among the shadows to continue their secretive whispering. Ed had arrived before his guests so they knew he wasn't afraid of them.

Silver balloons filled with helium were captured in nets hanging from the ceiling. They would be released when the guest of honour arrived. The Glitterball DJ prepared his set while waiters carried hot food from the kitchen, arranging it on a central table made from maple wood. It was going to be the party of the year. Ed insisted on it.

He needed this, he thought. It had been the worst time of his dubious career so far and Ed had had his fair share of dicey moments. His empire was being dismantled before his eyes under a shroud of smoke and mirrors. Ed understood gunfights and he knew how to use a baseball bat. What he didn't understand was Fairbanks.

Ed was in his early fifties, standing six foot tall with an athletic build he worked hard to maintain. His grey eyes and long lashes softened a face lined with harsh experiences. He was dressed smartly in a dark blazer and light coloured chinos, but kept the knot in his silk tie loose. It reminded him too much of a noose.

"Looks like it's gonna be a helluva night, Ed."

John 'Smally' Washington sidled up to him, a pint of bitter in his hand. John was in his early twenties with short black hair brushed forward and made crisp with gel. His nickname always confused Ed. Although Smally barely made five foot tall, he was also close to thirty stone in weight and anything but small.

He was a made man in the Network, a Glasgow based gang who made most of their money from drugs and women. Ed forced a smile and slapped Smally on his shoulder. The room was cool, but his shirt was damp with sweat. "I like to treat my friends, Smally. You know that."

Smally took a mouthful of his bitter and looked at Ed over the rim of his glass. "From what I hear, you're running out of friends fast. 'Course, this isn't my patch, pal. I've only heard rumours."

"Well, this *is* my patch, mate so why don't you stop acting cute and tell me what you know?"

Pulling up a nearby stool, Smally squeezed between the wooden arms. His bulbous stomach rested over his wide thighs. "We heard you're bringing in your snitches, trying to find this Fairbanks guy, but no-one knows anything about him."

"It's only a matter of time."

"We also heard you even reached out to the Maguires and Curly's crew. I thought you had an ongoing turf war with those guys."

The Maguires were a family firm like the Daytons, operating out of the West End. The rumour was they got their first big break when Nanna Maguire performed abortions during the war for unwed mothers. Curly's Crew were a newer outfit, born out of the rave scene in the Nineties when everyone was off their heads on ecstasy. The three gangs weren't at war. They had an uneasy alliance. Ed approached them, looking for answers and was assured they weren't behind the attacks. He was just as sure that if Fairbanks succeeded, the Maguires and Curly's Crew would sink their teeth into his twitching corpse like the tracksuit wearing hyenas they were.

He took a gulp of Feuillatte. "I haven't spoken to them. It's not that big of a deal."

Smally finished his bitter and gestured with his empty pint glass. "Better go get another one."

As he stood from the stool, it came with him, pinched around his wide waist. He looked for assistance, but Ed merely grinned while Smally waved his fat arse left and right before finally plucking himself free.

Smally hid an embarrassed face by wiping his sweaty brow with the sleeve of his shirt. His piggy eyes narrowed when he saw Ed's amusement. "You know who it could be?" he said. "Those Eastern Europeans. They bring in smack through Liverpool. They use cats and dogs because it's easier to get them passports. Can you believe that? Somewhere in France, a vet fills their stomachs with drugs. They sail through Customs and go to a farm in Herefordshire. Only there's no vet waiting for them there. Just a fish knife and a bonfire to get rid of the remains."

"Sounds to me like you've heard a lot." Ed's iPhone chirruped, alerting him to a text message. "I have to take this. Get a drink and don't worry. We'll be eating soon."

He watched Smally waddle to the bar, catching a backward glance of undisguised malice, before he checked his phone.

It read: 'Mr Brown in stable condition. Still unconscious. Brain damage likely.'

Ed signalled a waiter to bring him another glass of champagne. He'd slap Dr Hilltop the next time he saw him. He was being well paid to keep Ed informed of Scalper's condition. He might have employed a little bedside manner. Brain damage likely? Was that anyway to tell someone one of their oldest friends was a vegetable?

Whatever Scalper needed, he'd get. Private nursing home. Round-the-clock care. Scalper's Glitterball colleagues would visit regularly. Ed wouldn't be able to make it himself, but maybe he'd pay the nurses to wear extra tight uniforms to make up for his absence. It was the least he could do. Scalper was practically family.

And that was what tonight was all about. A family celebration that included his most trusted of friends. Daniel was returning home, uniting a fractured family. Ed allowed himself a smile and he relaxed.

Bronson ushered in guests by the entrance. He'd told him to take the night off, but the guy never stopped. It wouldn't have been so bad, but Bronson was the last person Ed wanted to greet the guests. Squat and toad-like, he was more likely to scare people away than be any kind of a welcome. The facial tick didn't help either.

He shook off his irritation, letting his eyes wander around a room that was filling up nicely. Mr and Mrs Maguire lingered in front of a black and white mural depicting ship workers dismantling a tanker of some sort. Neither held a drink in their hands. A local MP weaved drunkenly through the crowd, accidently bumping into a woman called Stacey Flowers, Newcastle's biggest slum landlord. They were here for him. Doing what they were told, being where they should be.

His glass almost slipped from his fingers when he saw Mosely by the bar. The dickhead should have been collecting money at the Blue Tiger pub. While it was a job anyone could have handled, Ed had ordered Mosely to do it. After the debacle at the Glitterball, Ed didn't know how long he could hold his temper in Mosely's company.

The drug dealer ordered a Jack Daniels and Coke at the bar and downed it in a single gulp. At least he was smart enough to be scared, thought Ed. Mosely smoothed down his dark suit and ran a hand through his hair. Searching the gathering crowd, he was startled to find Ed watching him.

Mosely approached, like a man walking to the gallows. He stopped at a distance. Ed let him wait and then finally beckoned him closer. Alcohol fumes reached him before Mosley did. Clearly he'd had more than one drink tonight.

Ed placed a hand on his chest and moved him back a step. "Why aren't you at the Blue Tiger?"

"It's done. I've been. All taken care of."

Scott watched them from afar. Ed looked in his direction and Scott stood from his table, circling slowly toward them.

"It's a great party, boss. When's Daniel arriving?" Mosely asked.

"Should be here soon."

"How long has he been gone? Nine months? Long time to be gone. Where did you find him?"

As Ed finished his drink, a waiter appeared at his side with another tray. There was champagne, single malts and wine from his own cellar. He should have been feeling drunk. He pulled at his tie and reached for another glass of champagne. "Would you like a drink, Mosely?"

Mosely waved away the offer, retrieving a strip of pink tablets from inside his jacket. He popped one in his hand and swallowed it dry. "Like I said, great party and I wanted to say how sorry I was about Scalper. He was a good man and we worked together a lot. Have you heard anything from the hospital?"

"You're talking about him like he's already dead."

Mosely continued, as if he hadn't heard Ed speak.

"I mean, it's a dangerous job, but no-one could have seen it coming. That Fairbanks kid cut him open like a fish."

Ed grabbed him by the throat. Before he knew it, Mosely was propelled through a set of doors. He struggled to keep his feet as he was marched backwards down a corridor. More doors clattered open and Ed threw him to the floor of the men's toilets. He kicked him in the face, briefly regretting it when he noticed blood on his six hundred pound Santoni brogues.

Scott locked the door with a clunk.

The walls were decorated in polished black stone flecked with silver. Black and white diamond tiling finished the floor and by the ceramic washbasins were vases of fresh flowers. Ed had never tortured someone in a nicer room.

"You really fucked up, Mose," he said. "I came up with Scalper. He was one of mine. Where were you? You must have seen what they did to him? Why didn't you call the boys?"

"I was long gone when it happened. I wasn't even there, I swear it. I wouldn't have wished that on my worst enemy."

Scott kicked Mosely in the mouth. His head snapped backward and he spat bloody saliva on the floor. Ed saw a broken tooth in the pool of red liquid.

Mosely coughed, wiping his chin clean. "I've made you hundreds of thousands of pounds over the years. Why are you acting like I'm the one to blame? So what if Scalper got the shit kicked out of him? That's his job, isn't it?"

Ed growled at his son. "Give him a Japanese flag."

Scott flipped Mosely onto his stomach before he had a chance to react.

"No, Ed, please. I'm sorry. I didn't mean to say that."

Scott pressed his knee into the base of Mosely's spine, pinning him to the ground while Ed restrained his wrists. Reaching under Mosely's groin, Scott undid his trousers and yanked them down to his knees. He splayed open his arse cheeks.

Crying out, Mosely's legs slapped uselessly against the tiled floor. "Please don't do this. I'm sorry."

Ed handed Scott a lighter. It was a limited edition Zippo; a birthday present from his first wife. Sapphires in the shape of a heart decorated the casing. It was tacky, but it reminded Ed of better times.

He nodded to his son. "This is how we get rid of arseholes, Mosely. We burn them shut," Ed said.

Mosely screamed at the sound of the lighter being struck. His cheeks were spread wider. He wriggled, twisting left and right, but Scott's large hand had him secured.

The flame was lowered.

"Don't. Don't ..." he shouted.

Scott looked to his father for the final confirmation. When he shook his head, the lighter was snapped shut. Mosely was released and he crawled naked to the farthest corner, his designer trousers around his ankles. He sobbed against the wall while Scott washed his hands.

Ed's shadow fell across Mosely and he shrank backwards.

"The only reason you're alive is because you make us so much money, but I'll be speaking to Scalper when he wakes up. If I find you had anything to do with it, Scott will come looking for you and I won't be there to stop him. Do you understand?"

Mosely nodded, wiping snot from his face with the back of his hand.

"Good," Ed said, as Scott unlocked the toilet door. "Enjoy the party."

CHAPTER SIX

Daniel had driven his van from Scotland, resisting Spencer's advice to take the train for comfort. While it was true that his large frame was unsuited to long periods behind a wheel, Spencer was not to be trusted. If he wanted Daniel to take the train, it wasn't out of concern for his well-being.

Traffic was light and he arrived in Newcastle within two and a half hours. He parked in a side street and walked to café called Mag's Pies and Peas. It had been there since his childhood and he recalled the smell of pastry with fondness. He was desperate to see his daughter, but Spencer had told him of the home-coming party at The Amen Corner and he needed to know how cordial his invite was.

The café was glass fronted and opposite Newcastle's Central train station. He pretended to read the menu on the wall while watching the station entrance. It was night time and the streets were busy. Party goers staggered along the pavement and when the pavement became blocked, they staggered out into the road, heedless of traffic. Taxis swerved to avoid them, honking their horns. Buses belched exhaust fumes as they dropped off and picked up. It was movement and noise, something he was no longer accustomed to.

The place was swamped by vehicles and pedestrians, but it was two motionless men, watching the crowds spill out of the station that caught Daniel's attention. They wore dark coats, their faces hidden behind scarves. Spencer was supposed to deliver him into the hands of these men. Whether he attended the party or not, his father wanted to see him soon.

Leaving the restaurant, he slipped in behind a shrieking hen party dressed as superheroes. He was too tall to remain circumspect for long and he flagged down a taxi.

"The Queen Anne, please."

The driver pulled sharply out into the road, narrowly avoiding a man dressed in a Newcastle United top.

The soft drum of the tyres on tarmac reminded Daniel of the day he abandoned his daughter. It was raining and she wore her pink anorak with yellow flowers. Daniel had forgotten to bring her hat. Her long, dark hair was soaked and plastered down her face.

He'd told his sister-in-law Lily he needed a babysitter. She often looked after Eisha when he was busy and didn't get suspicious. As he stood on her doorstep saying goodbye, Eisha smoothed her wet hair away from her face.

"When will you be back?" she asked.

"Soon."

"Tonight?"

"I'm not sure, honey."

"Tomorrow then?"

He remembered the sense of choking loss. It was like a hand around his throat. "Why are you asking all these questions? You always stay with Aunt Lily and Uncle Scott. What's the problem?"

Eisha made to grab him and he pushed her away. There were tears in her eyes, but he pretended it was rain. "I'll be back soon. Okay?"

He turned around and walked down the driveway, picking up his pace when he heard his daughter's desperate pleas. He didn't look back. He plunged on through the rain until out of sight, he ran to his car and climbed inside. His body trembled and he waited for the nausea to pass. Steam obscured his view through the windows. He was cocooned and the world he knew was gone.

He'd either done the best thing for his daughter or the worst, but there was no going back. Eisha was better off without him.

Starting the engine, he wiped the windows clear to check his blind spots and saw Eisha waiting on the pavement. She tried to get in, but the handle was too cumbersome for her small hands. When her efforts proved futile, she banged on the door, her eyes wide and despairing.

She shouted for him, saying something Daniel couldn't hear over the sound of the rain and his idling engine. He almost opened the door then, almost pulled her into the car and drove far away together, but he knew he couldn't and he knew he wouldn't be able to stand to hear her final words.

She placed her small hand on the window, but Daniel left, the sound of the drumming tarmac filling the car.

"Are you alright, mate?" the cab driver asked over his shoulder.

Daniel hadn't realised he'd been crying. He wiped his tears away with the heel of a hand and watched the lights of his city stream by in ribbons.

When they reached Queen Anne's, a pallid looking receptionist gave him directions to the Children's Ward. He had never been there before and was surprised by how quiet it was. It was long and narrow with beds down the left and right of the room. Some of them were behind plastic curtains. Those he could see had frail children lying in them staring up at the ceiling. Some read tattered comics, others dozed, but no-one spoke, not even the nurses, who hovered in corners and whispered between themselves.

Eisha was in a room of her own at the farthest end of the ward and Daniel was thankful for that at least. He passed a waiting area with hand drawn copies of Disney characters sello-taped to the wall and children's wooden chairs painted in primary colours. He stared straight ahead, trying not to notice the abandoned toys littering the floor.

His daughter's room was closed, but he peered through a circular window in the door. He saw a heart monitor and some sort of ventilation machine, its bellows forcing air in and out of her lungs. There was a wall mounted defibrillator and a red plastic panic button. A single bed with a duvet covered in cartoon characters he didn't recognise was pushed against the wall, but he couldn't find Eisha. She was in there somewhere, hidden under the machinery.

He gripped the door handle, feeling the coolness of the metal in his hand. He closed his eyes and counted up to five. When he got to four, he opened them again to see a young WPC at his side. She slapped his hand away from the door.

"Excuse me, sir, it's family only." She was average height with a heart shaped face and stern blue eyes. Taking a deep breath, he narrowed in on the details. Protruding jugular. Rapid heart rate. Bleached skin tone. She was nervous. Straight posture. Shoulders back. Locked stance. Nervous, but in control, he thought. On her duty belt, he saw handcuffs, pepper spray, torch and baton in the blink of an eye. All present and correct, but no radio. Why wouldn't she want a radio for back-up?

"Come on, Godzilla, shake a leg before I have to shake it for you," she said, her voice steady.

He stared not at her, but through her. He was numb. There was something wrong, but he was too tired to work it out. His body had left Scotland, but his head was somewhere else. It'd been a long journey and all he wanted was to see his daughter.

Exasperated, the WPC snapped the handcuffs off her belt. "Sir, I need you to come with me."

She placed a gentle, but certain hand on his chest. He grabbed it and hauled her skywards. Her feet left the ground. Her legs kicked against his. She reached for her spray, but Daniel grabbed her other hand and twisted it behind her back. They almost looked to be dancing.

"Are you a real police officer?" he asked.

"I didn't rent this uniform for the night, big boy. Let me go before you land yourself in proper trouble."

He shook her like a rag doll and brought his snarling face so close to hers their foreheads touched. "How much did he pay you?"

"I was supposed to lock you in the car, okay? That's all. Wait for someone to collect you."

He let go of his grasp and the officer dropped to the ground. She rubbed her tender wrists and looked at him accusingly.

"They told me you were a handful," she said, "but I didn't expect Frankenstein."

Daniel took her identity card and waved it in front of her face. "I know who you are. You tell anyone I'm here, you'll be back in this hospital as a patient."

The threat was unsubtle and it worked. The officer walked away, her head down. "Sorry," she said, as she knocked elbows with a young woman coming in the other direction.

"It's not me you should be apologising to." If the WPC heard her, she didn't show it and marched on toward the exit.

The young woman stopped in front of Daniel, her lips full and smiling. She was tall with weight around her hips and thighs. Her shoulder length chestnut hair gleamed under the hospital lights and her eyes were olive green.

When Daniel remembered he hadn't seen Lily in nine months, he realised it was far too long. She hugged him, pressing her face to his chest as he willed his heartrate to slow down.

"What was that all about?" she asked, pulling away, leaving him with the scent of her hair.

"My Dad."

"Thought so. Scott told me about your party. I take it you're not going?"

He stopped looking at her mouth and shook his head.

"It's not like we haven't seen it before." She checked her watch. "Your Mam will be drunk by now."

"Dad will be greeting his guests, plotting their downfall while they shake his hand. He won't know it, but they'll be doing the same thing to him."

Lily smiled. "And what about Ma Dayton? Will she be there?"

"She'll be there alright. St George couldn't finish that dragon off."

They laughed. Lily's husband – his brother – would also be there, skulking in the shadows, pretending to be somewhere else. He didn't mention it and neither did Lily.

She looked through the window into Eisha's room and the joy fell from her face. "I guess we're better off here."

He followed her gaze. "I haven't been in yet. I …" Lily took his hand and led him to Eisha's bedside where he saw his daughter at last. She was lying on her back, her eyes closed, her skin ashen. He flinched at how small she was, lost in the bed sheets. Lily's grip tightened and he squeezed back.

Up close, Eisha looked asleep. He could have been checking in on her before going to bed himself. Her mouth was open. In the past, it was a sign of her dreaming, but Daniel didn't know if people dreamed in comas. He didn't know about her condition, her medical history or know why she was attached to so many wires.

Reaching out, he cupped Eisha's head in his hand.

"She's tough like her old man" Lily said. "Tough as bullets. Dr Hilltop comes in every hour or so. He's keeping a close eye on her."

He brushed Eisha's face with the back of his hand and kissed her forehead. "Sorry, I've been away so long."

Plastic seats were staged against the wall. He sat in an orange one. Lily sat in the blue one. She dropped his hand and the warmth of her touch grew cold.

"How have you been?" she asked.

"Okay."

"Have you been working?"

"Not the kind I used to do."

Lily's chair creaked in the silence. She was frustrated. He sensed anger, too. He only cared about two people in his life. One was in a coma because he abandoned her. The other he'd used in order to escape.

"Where have you been, Daniel?" Lily asked.

He shrugged and stared at the floor.

"You left your daughter on our doorstop and disappeared. Why didn't you say something? Were you in trouble?"

"No more than usual." Watching from the corner of his eye, he saw her neck was flushed. Hands splayed open and rigid. Fidgeting in her seat. A bouncing knee. It was painful to witness.

"I didn't walk away from my daughter for nothing," he said. "You have to know it was important that I went away."

"She cried every night for months." Lily pulled a crumpled tissue from her pocket and dabbed green eyes that were turning red. "And Scott? Scott went ballistic. I've never seen him so pissed."

"Did he hurt my daughter?"

Lily hurled her spent tissue into the waste basket. "Of course not. He was pissed at you. I barely saw him for three weeks and when he came back, he wouldn't say what he'd been doing. All he said was he was looking for you."

Eisha's blankets were tangled around her legs. Daniel jerked the duvet free, smoothing it over her bare feet. They looked bigger. He wondered if Scott and Lily had bought her new shoes while he was away.

"Scott changed, Daniel," Lily continued. "He wasn't exactly talkative before you left, but he got worse. Darker somehow. What did you do to him?"

"To him? Nothing."

"Then what? Tell me why you left."

Daniel kicked the waste basket, sending it clattering to the wall, startling the nurses on the ward. They peered at him, but couldn't meet his stare, finding other things to do. He dropped into the chair beside her.

Jumping to her feet, Lily jammed her fists into her hips, her green eyes blazing. "You've got no right to be angry, Daniel Dayton. You left that poor girl. You abandoned her to God knows what. We should be thankful she only ended up in a coma. I'm sorry to say it, but it's the truth. She needed a father and at least Scott tried."

"I'm her father. Not him."

"Then act like one."

He reached for his cheek as if he'd been slapped. Lily towered over him and he shrank in his chair. She was on the verge of tears, but they were hot, explosive tears. The kind that heralded an avalanche of recrimination. There was nothing to say in his defence. He was furious too, but didn't know why. He'd been protecting Eisha, but looking at her frail body, he realised how wrong he had been. He should have been with her. That was the only way a father could protect his daughter.

Daniel stared at the floor and Lily placed a hand on his head. "I understand the Dayton family more than you know. If you aren't going to tell me why you left, at least tell me why you came back."

An alarm sounded in the ward outside, high pitched and insistent. He heard voices shouting and nurses scrambling into action. Somewhere a child was in trouble, maybe even dying. His eyes fell on Eisha's sleeping face and he took Lily's hand. There was no other way around it.

"I'm here to fucking kill someone," he said.

CHAPTER SEVEN

E d tried to compose himself as he walked back into the function room where the party had begun without him. There were bodies and designer labels everywhere. Glasses clinked, voices rose and fell. He waved at familiar faces and they lifted empty glasses in his honour.

Searching the crowd for Daniel, his chest tightened. Where the bastard was he?

His mother held court with some of the lower ranking thugs in his organisation. She was in her sixties with curled white hair yellowed by the cigarette permanently wedged in her mouth. Ed had given her money to buy a new outfit and was dismayed to see her wearing the same old purple frock she always wore to parties. He'd have words with her later, too.

Liz and Monica hovered by the edge of the dancefloor, waiting for the DJ to start the music. Liz was in her early forties. Her blonde hair was natural and her body was gym tight. She towered over Monica, who was only five foot five in heels.

Monica was the fizz in his champagne and somehow complimented Liz's more graceful presence. Her dyed black hair was spikey and unruly. At twenty-four years old, her slim body was a gift of youth rather than one born of diet and exercise. Like Liz, her clothes were always this season's.

To outsiders, their friendship was a mystery, but knowing Liz was Ed's first wife and mother to his children while Monica was his second, made the coupling ever more unusual. There was plenty of speculation, but no-one dared mention anything to Ed. Still, rumours were powerful things and he heard more than a few regarding Liz and Monica.

The silent figure of Scott appeared at his shoulder. "Do you think Mosely had anything to do with what happened at the Glitterball?"

Ed nodded at the DJ and the music began. It was loud with a heavy bass, making him wince. Monica squealed in delight and pulled Liz onto the dancefloor. They took centre stage. Monica wrapped her slender legs around Liz's and they gyrated to the song. They had rhythm, he thought. Maybe that was what drew them together.

He glanced at Scott. "Mosely hasn't got the balls for it."

Scott stood with his hands clasped behind his back and watched his mother and step-mother writhe against each other.

"Where's your wife?" his father asked.

"She's at the hospital. She doesn't like to miss visiting hours."

"Why's Lily visiting Scalper?"

Scott looked down at his father, perplexed. "She's visiting Eisha."

Jesus, thought Ed. How could he forget something like that? His only grandchild was a victim of Fairbanks' terror campaign like everyone else. The only difference being she didn't deserve it.

He had been there at Eisha's birth and never missed a birthday celebration. Daniel had recorded a clip of her first steps on his iPhone. On the night Eisha was taken to Queen Anne's, Ed had watched the clip until dawn.

"How's she doing?"

"Lily doesn't talk about it."

A disco light lanced through the air, shining briefly on Scott's face. His mouth was set in a thin line and his skin shone like early morning frost. He was upset and Ed knew why.

He took his son's hand in his. "We're going to catch whoever did that to Eisha."

"By throwing a party?"

"You know how fast rumours spread. We have to show these people that it's business as usual. It's important they know we're not scared of this Fairbanks character."

"I'm not scared of him," Scott said.

Ed smiled. "I didn't think you would be, but this is a way of announcing that the Daytons are united again. It's a welcome back party for your brother."

"He hasn't earned any welcome back."

"He shouldn't have run off. I know that, but we have to put it behind us. With him, we can take care of Fairbanks and move on."

Scott pulled his hand free. "You don't need him. You have me."

"I couldn't run this business without you, but your brother has something special. He can read people. No-one can sniff out a rotten apple like Daniel. He's like one of them mystics. We need him in this fight."

"Are you expecting me to roll over and be happy about it?"

Rubbing his temples, Ed squeezed his eyes shut. He saw Daniel turning his back on him, leaving without a word. He remembered the bitterness and what drove them apart. When he opened his eyes, Scott was leaving too.

He grabbed him by the arm. "When Daniel disappeared, he left a hole in us. It was a fissure Fairbanks exploited. It was how he got in and gained control. Only your brother can plug that gap."

Scott's implacable face told Ed he wouldn't be persuaded. He let go and Scott lingered for a second. His face clouded over and with a final glance at the dancefloor, Scott pushed his way through the crowd and was lost in the melee. If Ed didn't know better, he'd think he'd hurt his feelings.

The party was giving him a headache. Liz and Monica waved from the dancefloor before being swallowed up by fellow revellers.

Lights flashed. The music banged. What was intended as a good time was beginning to feel like a scene from a war movie. Ed battled on. It would be good for the family and good for business. People would talk and word would spread, quashing doubts over the Daytons' future. It was all part of the job.

As his eyes roamed the room, they stopped at the sour face of his mother. Sighing, he approached her table. Ma Dayton puffed angrily on her cigarette.

"The bloody music is too loud," she said. "I can't hear myself think."

"It's a party. It's supposed to be loud. Where have all your friends gone?"

"Your friends, you mean? They're up there with those hussies." Ma Dayton stabbed her cigarette toward the dance floor. "They only listen to me because I'm your mother."

The waiters and waitresses lined up behind the buffet table, arms behind their backs, signalling it was time to eat.

Thank God, thought Ed. "Let's get some food, Mam. Everyone will be waiting for you. Shall we see what they've got?"

It was a tradition at every Dayton get-together that Ma Dayton was the first to be served. He helped her to her feet, allowing her to lean on his arm as he guided her around the table. While she lit another cigarette, Ed glanced at her shoes and wished he hadn't.

Leading her to the buffet table, he kept his chin high as his mother shuffled by his side in her frayed sheepskin slippers. She nodded regally at his guests as she went, passing Smally who nodded back, dipping low to hide his smile. On reaching the table, she turned to the room and gave a little curtsy to a small gathering waiting with their plates.

Ed glowed when he saw the array of food on offer. Fresh flowers in crystal vases were interspersed between silver dishes of sumptuous food. There were red lobsters stewing in butter, poached turbot with truffles, roast duck fillets, venison medallions with parsnip ribbons and more. Each dish was garnished with a flourish turning it into art.

This wasn't about food. It was about power and all those invited to sit at Ed's table knew it.

"What would you like, Mam?" he asked.

Peering into the dishes, cigarette clamped between her teeth, Ma Dayton looked overcome by choice. "It looks bloody gorgeous."

"What about some soup? You always start with soup."

Ma Dayton granted her consent and a waiter darted forward, lifting the lid off a silver tureen. Pea soup was on the menu at every party Ma Dayton attended. She always chose it and it never failed to placate her.

The waiter ladled the green liquid into a deep white bowl. Ma Dayton stamped out her cigarette on the table and lifted the bowl to her beaky nose, breathing deeply. Her eyes narrowed as something bobbed to the surface.

"I'm not eating that," she said, pulling back quickly.

Ed looked at the soup and his heart fell. "It's nothing, Mam. Just eat the bloody stuff."

"It's a lump. In my soup. I don't like lumps in my soup. How many times do I have to tell you?"

He snatched the bowl from her gnarled hands. "Give me a spoon," he said to a waiter before turning to his mother. "If I take it out, will you eat it?"

She lit a cigarette from her packet and blew smoke into her son's face. "Yes," she said finally.

Ed took the spoon and fished around in the soup. He sensed the eyes of his guests burning into his back.

"Can't you find it? I saw a lump."

"I'll fucking get it, Mam. Wait a minute." This was all he needed, he thought. What a fucking life. His business was going under. His friend was in hospital. His granddaughter was in a coma. People were losing faith in him, scared of getting caught in the maelstrom of his downfall.

And his own son was fucking late for his own fucking party. "There," he shouted, finding the lump. "There. I've got it."

He thrust the spoon under his mother's nose. She gasped and clasped a hand over her mouth. "What's that?"

It was cylindrical and three inches long with a flattened end oozing a watery grease. Alarmed, Ed picked it out. It was soft under his touch with a brittle centre.

"I have no idea," Ed said quietly, but Ma Dayton recognized it and her legs went weak. She held onto the table for support, but it was too late. Ed watched her clatter to the floor, pulling the tablecloth and the fine dishes of food on top of her. The dancing stopped. Everyone on the floor froze to the sound of smashing plates. Some crept closer, eager to discover what the fuss was about. No-one checked on Ma Dayton.

Taking a serviette, Ed wiped the object clean. He gagged when he identified a knuckle. It was a severed finger, grey and slightly warm from the soup. And everyone in the room saw it.

CHAPTER EIGHT

ive Oaks was a five bedroom, detached house in the leafy confines of Gosforth, a well-to-do suburb of Newcastle. It was a
red brick new build with wooden double doors at its entrance
and large lead lined windows. It was set in six acres of formal
lawns, pasture land and a man-made lake big enough to have
an island at its centre. In the summer, there were garden parties
where Newcastle's elite gathered to crow about their portfolios. In
the winter, there was a thirty-foot Christmas tree imported from
Norway and a Santa's Grotto where Santa gave deserving children
iPads and hover boards.

Inside was a billiard room with mahogany panelled walls
and its own bar. To the rear of the property was a period sun
room overlooking the fields of Northumberland. In the wine cellar was a collection of wines purchased from a bankrupt minor
royal and a secret entrance to a soundproofed room and a bloody
gurney.

It was a monument to his achievements, but to Ed, it was
where he had brought up his family. Returning from work, all
the troubles of his day were left on the doorstep. Liz would press
a glass of wine into his hand and peck him on the cheek. They'd
retire to the front room and curl up on the sofa, watching Scott
and Daniel bicker over computer games on their sixty-inch TV.

Ed shuffled uncomfortably in his leather chair. The joy-
ful days of his past felt like eons ago. Faceless men roamed the

corridors outside, their Glock pistols barely concealed. The house was guarded and secretive. Five Oaks was on lock down and his home was stifled in panic.

The office was on the second floor. The walls were lime-washed bare brick supporting a gallery of paintings of the Tyne Bridge. Two Chesterfield sofas sat in front of Ed's oak desk and a row of reconditioned gas lamps lit the room. There were no windows, only a single porthole with lead lining in the form of a cross. Sitting behind his desk, Ed pictured the sighting of a rifle and shuddered.

A closed meeting had been called for a handful of men in an attempt to clamp down on the rumours. He had lost face at Daniel's party. The jokes about 'finger food' and 'getting the finger' were making the rounds already. It needed to stop before it gathered momentum.

"Shall we begin?" he asked the others in the room.

There were three other men present and they looked at each other nervously. Scott was perched on the sofa, his arms folded over his chest and his eyebrows knitted tightly together.

"No-one saw anything at The Amen Corner," he said. "All the food was prepared on site and there were no new starters."

"What are you saying?"

"The kitchen is a busy place. It wouldn't be hard to slip in and out again without anyone noticing. The issue is the food. I got the chef to go through every other dish. He didn't find anything. Either Fairbanks chose the soup and got lucky –"

"Or he knew it was mam's favourite and chose it specifically."

Drumming his fingers on his desk, Ed stared at Mosely standing on the opposite side of the room to Scott. His face was swollen with purple bruises and his hair looked unwashed. It looked like his swagger had been left on the floor of the toilets. Good, thought Ed. It would remind him who had the real power in this room.

Mosley stumbled forward. "I'm sorry, boss. It's exactly the same at The Glitterball. No-one saw a thing. It's like he wasn't there. He didn't speak to anyone and no-one spoke to him, except Scalper."

Ed leaned forward. "And we all know what happened to him, don't we?"

Casting his eyes to the floor, Mosely continued. "I went through the CCTV footage at the entrance. He stayed out of sight the whole time, but the rest of his gang weren't so smart."

He reached into his jacket, but instead of his favourite pink pills, he pulled out a sheaf of photographs and placed them in front of Ed. They were black and white and grainy, but Scalper's assailants were clearly visible. He adjusted his jacket while he waited for a response.

Ed studied the images, his heart quickening. Finally, they had something to go on. He only had to find one of these men. After an hour in his secret room downstairs, they'd know everything they needed to about Fairbanks – location, weaknesses, inside fucking leg measurement. And then it would be Fairbanks' turn in the wine cellar.

He smiled and Mosely's face lit up. His desperation sickened Ed and he threw the photographs at him. Mosely scrambled to catch them, but they fluttered to the floor.

"They're no good sitting on my desk," Ed said. "Get them to the boys. I want those scumbags found."

Mosely dropped to his hands and knees, stuffing the pictures into his jacket.

The fourth man in the room was Walter 'Noodles' Reeceman. He was as old as Ed, though the years were less kind. He had a stooped gait and his rounded shoulders looked like the carapace of a beetle. His skin was so pale, it was tinged blue and his long thin fingers twitched constantly. Wherever he went, he carried a battered leather briefcase he never opened in company.

Noodles thought his nickname came from the gangster played by Robert De Niro in Once Upon a Time in America. It confused him because he wasn't a gangster. He was a barrister acting under the name Reeceman and Co. and working solely for the Dayton family. He advised on business matters and potential grey areas of the law, but the truth was no-one knew where his nickname came from. No-one really cared.

"What about you?" Ed asked, pointing his finger at Noodles. "You must have found something under those rocks you inhabit?"

Noodles gave him a thin lipped smile. "Following all we have found out here today, I have additional facts that might have a bearing on our current situation."

Ed and Scott rolled their eyes while the barrister cleared his throat. "Firstly, I spoke to Liam Kircher, who hired Fairbanks to man the doors at Glitterball. He claims to have never met him and hired him purely on the strength of his CV, which he had received one month previously. This wouldn't be his usual practice, but following a spate of resignations at Door to Door Securities Ltd, he was short staffed and needed individuals asap."

"How long have we been short staffed?" Scott asked.

"I don't deal with human resources," said Noodles, pulling at the sleeves of his shirt. "It's my conclusion that Fairbanks threatened door staff into leaving to guarantee a place on the rota. Given he was smart enough to avoid the extensive security system at said club, I believe he was also smart enough to orchestrate such a manoeuvre."

Ed rubbed his forehead with the heel of his hand and sighed. "He's had us under surveillance. Working in the shadows. Waiting for the right moment to strike and in all that time, we had no idea there was a bomb waiting to go off."

Scott got to his feet. "We're the fucking Daytons. He can't do this to us."

The room was silent in response. Ed avoided the glare in his son's eyes while Noodles clicked his fingers together. With no-one willing to agree with him, Scott sat back down.

"I also spoke to DC Spencer," Noodles said. "He didn't want to talk at first. He's intent on pursuing the 'fresh start' you granted him, Mr Dayton. Eventually, he informed me of a break in at the mortuary of Queen Anne's Hospital. Someone took the fingers from the corpse of a homeless woman. There are no leads, but it is likely that these were the very same digits that made their way into the buffet at The Amen Corner."

Ed slapped his hand on the desk. "But, why? I get that he'd want to make me look like a dick, but why do something like that?"

"Perhaps he was showing you how close he could get, like the attack on Scalper," Noodles said.

"Maybe he was just showing us how clever he is," added Scott.

Noodles adjusted his shirt sleeves again, tugging more firmly than before. "It's more likely he wanted to use the rumour mill against you. The fastest way to undermine authority is to damage a reputation. Once they begin, it's like King Canute trying to hold back the tide."

"What if this isn't about us?" Scott asked. "What if it's about Daniel? It was his party. His daughter is in hospital."

Ed paced behind his desk, lost in a jumble of his thoughts. Fairbanks was mounting a clever campaign and had been for a while, right under their noses. He should be angry, but what alarmed him was that he wasn't angry enough. There was a bottle of whisky in his desk drawer, but decided to wait until his men had left. He was at sea, bobbing in the middle of the ocean with something unknown swimming beneath and it unnerved him. Whisky couldn't help him with that.

His men wanted a leader, a strong arm to steer them into conflict. Scott in particular ached for war. He always did, but this wasn't Scott's kind of problem. It wasn't a doorstep shooting or back alley beating or any of the things his son excelled at. This required someone whose violence was measured and targeted; someone more like him.

He stopped pacing, fixing his men with a steely glare. "We have to find Daniel," he said.

Scott jumped from the sofa. "I can deal with this."

"You heard what I said, Scott."

Picking up his briefcase, Noodles placed a hand on Scott's arm. "Your father is correct. Daniel was always more calculated in his response with these types of things."

Snatching his briefcase, Scott whacked it across the lawyer's head, sending him sprawling. He emptied the contents over him as Noodles scrambled to his feet. Two apples and a sandwich fell out. Mosely sniggered, but fell quiet under Scott's glare.

As his other son stormed out, Ed wondered where Daniel was hiding.

CHAPTER NINE

Daniel lay low behind a laurel bush at the side of the driveway. It had been his favourite place when playing hide and seek with his brother. There were scores of hiding places at Five Oaks, but for some reason, Scott never checked the most obvious. When his brother gave up his search, Daniel would linger and watch the birds flutter in and out of the laurel.

He was bigger now and his hiding place wasn't as convenient. Leaves crunched under his feet as he searched for a more comfortable position. There was a string of cars parked outside his former home. Something was going on and he didn't dare make his move while the house was so heavily occupied. Two hours passed before Mosely appeared through the front doors, his hand rummaging inside his jacket. He popped something in his mouth and climbed into his silver BMW 4 Series. The tyres sprayed gravel behind him as he sped down the driveway to his next meeting. A white faced Noodles appeared, climbing carefully into his BMW 5 Series. He didn't start the engine for several minutes. When he did, he drove purposely to the exit. Scott's military grade Hummer H1 Wagon sat idle. Daniel guessed he'd be next to appear, but after twenty minutes, he didn't show.

Daniel shook the cramp from of his legs. It was time, he thought and crawled closer to the house.

There were two sentry guards posted by the entrance. He recognised one as Bronson. The other was called Bear, an overweight ex wrestler known for breaking people's toes for fun. They were dangerous men. Bronson in particular never backed down in a fight. Daniel prepared to rush them, thinking the element of surprise might count for something when Monica stepped outside. He smiled instantly. She was exactly how he remembered her and he half raised his hand to get her attention before forcing it into his pocket. She wore a golden summer dress, patterned with poppies and leaned into Bronson and Bear as she spoke.

Daniel couldn't hear what she said, but they left their posts and walked down the driveway toward him. He dropped out of sight and held his breath. Their crunching footsteps grew louder as they approached.

"I wonder how much the poor cow knows," Bear said.

"Best if she's kept out of it. She doesn't need to know about Fairbanks. It's enough to give anyone nightmares."

And then they passed, presumably off to patrol the fence line at Monica's request.

Spencer had been telling the truth. The Daytons were in trouble. He'd presumed his father's search for him was fuelled by anger over their last meeting, but now it smacked of desperation. He picked a fallen leaf from the ground and crushed it in his fist. He'd find out everything soon enough.

He watched Monica skip to the jetty by the lake. The water was grey and choppy, the waves whipped by a wind turning them to froth, but she didn't appear to feel the cold. She had her back to him, her dress dancing around her legs and seemed content to watch the water. Daniel doubted she knew how many bodies were under the surface.

There was movement from the house and Scott emerged, following Monica's path to the lake. He took her into his arms. His shoulders quaked. He looked to be crying. They stayed in the clinch until Scott's hands slowly snaked around the small of Monica's back, his fingertips massaging her buttocks. Something was said and Monica twisted out of Scott's grip. Her fists were clenched and Scott wiped his eyes clear. He watched her flee back to the house, his shoulders slumped. A sudden wind tore at his clothing and Scott turned to the lake, hands jammed in his pockets. Daniel wanted to see if he would throw himself in, but he didn't have time.

Keeping low and out of sight of the cameras, Daniel ran to the house. He leapt up the front steps and skidded to a halt in the great hall, the first room that greeted his father's guests at Five Oaks. A spiralling oak staircase curled to the second floor and a labyrinth of rooms and corridors beyond. It had been built from a tree in the grounds felled by a lightning strike. There were marble statues of nymphs and goddesses and oil paintings of kings and princes. A five foot wide crystal chandelier hung from the ceiling, cleaned annually by specialist contractors so friends could admire its sparkle on every visit.

Monica sat on the first step of the stairway, hugging the newel post for comfort. Her mouth dropped when he entered and she got to her feet. Leaving the stairs, Monica jogged toward him, smiling the way she had when she had announced her engagement to his father. Daniel placed his hands on her shoulders, spinning her violently around and clamped a hand over her mouth. She stamped on his foot, sending pain up his leg and he fought to control her. Writhing and kicking, she clawed at his arm.

"Stop struggling," he whispered in her ear.

But Monica wouldn't. She slammed the back of her head into his chest. She pushed one way and pulled another, drawing from an endless well of energy. How long would it take Bronson and Bear to complete their inspection of the grounds? He dragged her to the front doors and kicked them shut. Releasing her, he locked them inside.

Monica spun on her heels, anger in her face, then confusion, then hurt. Monica slapped him hard. He lurched and she rushed at him, wrapping him in her arms and burying her head in his chest. He gently pulled her from him, wishing the embrace could last. When her open smile was met by his hard stare, she lowered her head.

"All I have to do is scream," she said.

"I hope you don't."

She looked up the staircase to the second floor. "If you're here to hurt your Dad, I will. I swear it. They'll get you before you get anywhere near him."

"You still love him?"

Monica nodded. "Ever since he came into the restaurant."

It was her first night as a waitress in Ed's new restaurant called Spaced. His father was unusually drunk and demanding, shouting at the staff so that they became too afraid to serve him. Monica, her hands shaking with nerves, brought out his first dish, accidentally spilling it on his lap. Ed erupted in a drunken fury, firing her instantly and threatening much worse. Daniel led Monica into the kitchen and told her to remain there while he calmed his father down. He was amazed when she came marching back out with a glass of white wine and threw it into Ed's lap.

"That's to take the stain out of your trousers, you knob," she said.

Daniel laughed while his father fumed, leading him away before Ed could do any more damage, but Monica kept her job and received a bouquet of spring flowers the next day. She received many more after that and Ed spent more time and money in that restaurant than he ever saw as profit.

Seeing Monica for the first time in nine months, Daniel recounted a thousand tender memories.

"I need you to get out," he said, but Monica stood her ground, her face set like stone. He didn't want to hurt her, but he didn't want to be caught either.

"Why are you doing this?" he asked.

"There was a time you would have done exactly the same."

"A lot of things seem to have changed since then. What were you doing by the lake with Scott?"

She wrapped her arms around her stomach, her face flushing with shame. "You don't know anything."

Monica broke into a run for the staircase. Daniel pursued, catching her easily. He lifted her off the floor, carrying her on his hip while his hand covered her mouth again. Opening the door to a large storage cupboard, he threw her inside. She slid along the floor and came to a rest at the far end. Monica opened her mouth to scream. Daniel slammed the door shut, barricading it with a statue of the goddess Athena.

He felt bad, but he had a plan and he intended on fulfilling it.

Daniel took the stairs two at a time. He knew where to go. Everyone called it the Office and no-one stepped inside without an invitation. But the Office was more than a room. It was the centre of a spider's web whose strands spanned the globe. Engineered over decades, Daniel's father had placed himself in the middle of a criminal enterprise that included thousands of players.

The door was covered in padded, black leather with studs arranged in a diamond formation. As heavy as it was, it opened easily on well-oiled hinges and Daniel slipped inside.

Ed sat behind his desk, his head in his hands. Although he was handsome, worry had aged him. It brought Daniel no comfort to see how low his father had sunk, but neither did he feel any sympathy.

Sensing a change in the room, Ed lifted his head and Daniel absorbed the information emanating from his father. Reddening of skin. Raised chin. Arched eyebrows. Relaxed jaw. Open posture. He saw the shock and the relief, but he was surprised to notice how much his father still loved him.

Standing from his desk, Ed opened his arms. "You're back," he said with a wide grin.

In four large bounds, Daniel covered the distance from the door to his father, drawing out a Heckler and Koch VP70 gun from his inside pocket. It was a gun he had taken to Scotland; a gun he had kept for the sole purpose of killing his father should the need ever arise.

He levelled it at Ed's forehead. "Who hurt my daughter?"

CHAPTER TEN

S tanding on the shores of the River Tyne, Fairbanks cast another line into the slow moving current of an eddy. He had insisted on renting a warehouse in the town of Wylam so he could fish in peace. It was eight miles west of Newcastle, close enough for his raids on the Dayton empire, far enough away for some perspective. The sun was high, warming his pale skin and catching the ripples in the water. Trees lined the shore. The sound of the nearby motorway was masked by the flowing of the river. He was isolated and it calmed him down.

His red and white float bobbed merrily, but the bait underneath went unnoticed. He wound in his line and cast a little further out. He heard the snap of twigs behind him and he was joined by an elderly dog walker and his Labrador.

"Nice cast," the old man said. He was balding with a protruding nose and large ears. When he smiled, his teeth were straight and white. Fairbanks assumed they were dentures. He stood by Fairbank's side, his dog sitting obediently by his and admired the two perch lying dead on the ground.

"Looks like they're biting today, son."

Fairbanks nodded, but kept his eyes on the float. "Would you like to take them? I don't really like fish."

The old man scooped them up with a groan, stuffing them into the pockets of his wax jacket. "Why are you fishing then if you don't like fish?"

"I like knowing that because of me something is dead." He glanced at the shocked expression on the man's face. "I like your dog though. What's he called?"

"It's my daughter's dog," the old man said by way of an answer, taking a step back.

The float was almost out of sight when Fairbanks reeled it in. "I wasn't allowed a dog when I was young. My father was a drunk. He would drink bottles of beer all day and spend the evening throwing them at me."

"That's an awful way to grow up."

Fairbanks shrugged, pulling his line out of the water and lying his rod on the shore. "I left when I was ten. Took my books and as many sandwiches as I could carry. I thought life on the streets had to be better than a life ducking behind sofas. And in a weird way, it was. Even when the paedophiles got me."

The old man dropped the perch back on the ground. "I'm sorry to hear that. I really am. I better be going, though. It doesn't seem right for me to take these. Look after yourself, son."

Fairbanks produced a fish knife, plunging it into the belly of the perch. The old man watched as he slit it open and reached inside for its guts, tugging them free. He offered them to the Labrador who sniffed them and gulped them down in two hungry bites.

"You didn't tell me the name of your dog," he said, as the animal licked his fingers clean.

"I don't want to tell you." The old man backed away, yanking on the leash causing his dog to yelp.

"I like people who know how to keep quiet," Fairbanks said. "If you see me here again, keep walking. I don't like my down time interrupted."

The old man fled, pulling the dog behind him. Fairbanks watched them go, rolling his earring between his fingertips. It was thanks to the local paedophiles that Fairbanks had grown to appreciate the loyalty of dogs. Old men, like the one scurrying away, would seek him out. He'd take their hand, skipping by their side as he was led somewhere secluded. Fairbanks preferred it that way and it didn't take long for things to turn nasty. Sometimes it was probing fingers, sometimes exposed genitals. He allowed their confidence to go so far before he whipped out a pocket knife and sliced at whatever body part was closest. They begged him to call an ambulance as he ransacked their belongings. He never did of course and would go to his favourite restaurant for a pizza instead, sitting outside with the owner's dog.

It wasn't long before Fairbank's reputation reached the ears of a street gang called Orphans' Eleven, despite the fact there were only nine of them. They found him in Tipton Park where Fairbanks slept in the summer months. The park was around fifty acres with playgrounds and petting zoos for children to enjoy.

It was deserted at night, save for those who preferred the shadows. He was dragged from his hideaway and pulled to the edge of a boating lake. In front of him stood Marcus Dougherty. He was fifteen years old with a pig-like face encrusted with acne. His hand was forever down the front of his dirty tracksuit bottoms and he smelled of sour milk.

The rest of the gang formed a circle, jeering and tormenting from a distance. One of them held a Jack Russell on a length of rope. It yipped excitedly.

"Do it to him. Do it to him," they chanted.

Dougherty pushed Fairbanks to the ground. A body sized mailbag was pulled over his head. For the first time Fairbanks could remember, he began to cry.

"Please let me go," he asked between sobs. "Please. I'm sorry."

The bag was briefly opened and the Jack Russell fell on top of him before it was sealed shut again. The animal, trapped and scared, howled against its incarceration. Fairbanks howled with it.

Hands nipped at him and he was towed along the ground. His stomach lurched as he was thrown into the air. He was weightless before he heard a splash. The cold water of the boating lake engulfed him. Desperate for freedom, the Jack Russell bit and scratched, scrambling for the last breath of air. Fairbanks held the dog by the throat, throttling it while its hind legs gouged at his throat.

The water swallowed them both. They kicked upwards, the dog frantic, digging its claws into Fairbanks' face. He pulled at the opening of the sack, but his fingers weren't strong enough to undo the binding. His head ached from a lack of oxygen. They sank amongst the sludge. The Jack Russell quietened its efforts and snuggled under Fairbanks' armpit. His lungs burned. It wouldn't be long before he too drowned.

He heard splashes and his body sloshed around the bag as he was hauled out of the water. The bag was opened and he spilled onto the ground. The dead body of the dog rolled out ahead of him. He gasped for breath, drawing air into his tiny body, like he was a new born baby. Retching, he vomited dirty water as Dougherty's gang laughed. He heaved until he was empty, but found enough strength to crawl over to the Jack Russell, cradling it in his arms.

Dougherty dragged him to his feet. "I want half of what you make from the nonces. You're working for us now. Understand?"

Fairbanks nodded and Dougherty pitched him back into the icy waters of the boating lake with a sharp laugh. When he swam to the surface, the Orphans' Eleven were gone.

The memory of it stung. For all of his achievements, for all the millions he had taken from gangsters, crooked businessmen and corrupt politicians, Fairbanks would always be the little boy in the lake. He carried the stain of its dirty water with him.

A chill settled over Wylam. There was no point in casting out again. He'd been disturbed too many times, firstly by a nosey old man and then by his own demons. He gathered his rod and landing net, kicked the dead fish back into the river and headed up an embankment to the warehouse.

Dougherty leaned against a chain link fence. His acne never failed to disgust Fairbanks. Though he was in his late twenties, it showed no signs of relenting. The spots were red and capped with yellow pus, as angry as the man they inhabited. "I was looking forward to fish fingers tonight," he said.

"You know I don't keep them."

"Guess it's another kebab then." Fairbanks went to pass him, but was stopped by a hand on his arm.

"Are you sure this is going to work?" Dougherty asked with a sneer.

"My plans always work."

"You've got a gift. I'll grant you that, but this one seems dangerous. You might be the brains, but I'm the boss. You better remember that."

Fairbanks shrugged his arm free. "Does everyone know what they're doing?"

"I've gone over the plan with the boys a hundred times. We're ready to go in at five am," Dougherty answered, picking at a boil on his neck. "The Daytons won't know what hit them."

CHAPTER ELEVEN

H
e had been told he was in the Queen Anne's Primary Care Unit. He was told not to move. He was told to relax and he was told it was serious. He remembered the female doctor speaking to him, but he couldn't remember what she looked like. In his first few hours of consciousness, Scalper floated above his bed in a drug induced haze and waited for gravity to pull him back down.

A parade of strangers visited his room. Some examined him, others sat by his bedside and wished him well. Twice he saw Fairbanks leaning over him, a Stanley knife in his hand. When his visitors left, Scalper listened to the sounds of the hospital until he drifted off into a restless sleep.

When the haze was lifted, there was a terrible toll to be paid. Pain flooded his body, occupying the space left by the opiates. His left knee was shattered. He would never walk again without a stick. The cuts to his face were closed, but the wound to his stomach had become infected. Necrotising flesh was removed and the wound re-sown. The remaining scar was so deep, it would tie Scalper into a stoop and force him, together with his walking stick, to hobble like an old man.

The blow to the back of his head caused a fracture two centimetres in length. While the consultant was confident it would cause no long lasting side effects, it was also his duty to list them. Scalper counted ceiling tiles as the consultant rattled them off.

He didn't want to know. The injuries he'd sustained gave him nightmares. He didn't need to know what horrors lurked around the corner.

The consultant was a professional and stopped when he saw the first of Scalper's tears roll down his cheek.

He was lucky in lots of ways. The love he'd invested in his friends and family had been returned to him tenfold. He was in a private ward. He chose his meals from a menu of twenty different options. There were bouquets of flowers and baskets of fruit everywhere. When visiting hours came, his room wasn't big enough, forcing people to wait outside, though there was always space for his beloved mother.

As the clock ticked to the first visiting hour of the day, his expectations rose and he welcomed a break from his worries. He kept his eyes trained on the door. When it opened, all expectations were dashed. Mosely ran a hand through his curly hair, looking over the beds. He spotted Scalper watching him and jumped, though Scalper didn't know if it was the shock of being watched or the state of his broken body.

Mosely was overtaken by a patient on crutches as he slowly made his way to Scalper.

"Private room, eh?" he said, taking a seat. "Ed's looking out for you, I see."

It was too painful to move, but Scalper's eyes followed every twitch in Mosely's face.

"I heard you can't talk with the stitches in your face. Is that right?"

He waited for a response and then slapped his forehead. "That was stupid. Sorry, mate, but it's good for me, uh? I doubt you have very nice things to say about the way I acted."

This wasn't the Mosely Scalper knew. His hair was greasy and his suit was crumpled. Scalper saw stains on his lapel. As Mosely sat gazing at the flowers, he folded his thin arms and crossed his legs, as if he was trying to disappear into himself. He was the Dayton's biggest drug runner. What had happened?

Mosely wiped his face with his hands. "This Fairbanks guy … Ed thinks that I …" He shook his head and took a deep breath. "What I'm trying to say is I was a total dick … Smashing your radio … I mean, if you'd still had that, you could have called for back-up. You could have run those scumbags into the ground. You wouldn't be lying here like some rotten vegetable."

Scalper teared up, but fought hard against it, blinking rapidly. His vision of Mosely blurred and came back into focus. There was no way he was going to let the man who put him here see him cry.

"Everyone thinks I set you up," he said, "and when I say everyone, I mean Ed. You can guess what that means. The only reason I'm alive is because I make him enough money to waste it. Shit, I bet I even paid for this room."

Mosely's hand went to the pocket of his favourite pink pills, but he stopped himself. Scalper saw him struggling with his urge. They were the same opiates Scalper was avoiding. He didn't care if Mosely swallowed a few pills. At least there'd be a chance he'd choke on them.

"Maybe you don't believe me, Scalp, but I wanted to clear the air. I don't know how long I've got so while I am still here, I want you to know I had nothing to do with this."

All he could do was watch the words come out of Mosely's mouth. He was trapped in his body, unable to ask questions, unable to shout. He had never heard Mosely apologise for anything and Scalper was starting to believe him. Was it a trick? Was he being genuine?

Picking lint from his sleeve, Mosely suddenly remembered something. "How's your friend doing, by the way?" he asked.

Scalper closed his eyes, shame washing over him. He hadn't thought of Jackie once since being here. He was no better than

Mosely. In fact, he was worse. At least Mosely was here trying to make amends. Had she made it? Was she dead? She could be lying in the same alley she'd been thrown in for all he knew.

Mosely shifted in his seat. "Ah, Jesus, sorry for bringing that up. Sorry, Scalper. How are you going to know? I'll find out for you. I'll let you know. How's that?"

He opened his eyes. It hurt, but Scalper nodded slowly.

"Then that's what I'll do," Mosely said, slapping the palms of his hands on his legs. "I know you'll have other visitors on their way – one's you'd much rather see, so I just wanted to say sorry again. No-one should have taken the beating you did, but you took it and you're still here. I feel terrible; a complete prize prick, Scalper."

His chair scraped on the floor as Mosely stood to leave. He got to the bottom of Scalper's bed before he turned back. "Let me know the minute you can speak. I'll come back and you can give me a proper bollocking. Okay?"

Scalper hadn't meant to, but he smiled and the pain rippled from his face to his spine.

"I wish I knew if you believed me or not," he heard Mosely say.

The pain rolled on, spreading southwards to the angry scar in his stomach. One tiny gesture and his body was wracked in agony. He felt like throwing up, but he hardened his resolve. There was no way he was going back on those drugs. He'd have to ride this one out.

As the pain subsided, he caught the dejected look on Mosely's face and realised he was waiting for some sort of assurance. Scalper hated to admit it, but he had a new found respect for him. His apology was clumsy and insensitive, but it came from the heart.

Mosely patted the bottom of the bed. "Listen, I've got to go. We can't find this Fairbanks anywhere. You're the only who can identify him and you can't say a word, can you?"

Scalper tried to speak, but it was too painful. Resigned, Mosely nodded his goodbyes and left the ward. Scalper hoped his guilt wouldn't weigh him down.

***

Outside, Mosely marched to his car, the fresh air washing away the medicinal smell of the hospital. It felt better to be out of there at last, but not better enough. He retrieved a pink pill from his pocket and gulped it down.

Finding his phone, he pressed speed dial and waited for an answer. "It's me … No, he hasn't given a description of you yet … because his mouth is sewn shut, for fuck's sake … I don't care what you said. You never said you were going to tear him up … Is everything still set for …? Okay, okay, just remember our deal."

The line went dead. If the Daytons didn't appreciate his work, then he'd go elsewhere, he thought as he slipped into the driver's seat and slammed the door shut.

Waiting for the numbing effects of his pill, he tapped the steering wheel. Mosely was in deep and he was very scared indeed.

CHAPTER TWELVE

The gun was so close to Ed's face, he smelled the grease of its innards. He rarely got this close to guns anymore. He was too well known to carry one and generally too powerful to have one pointed at him. It was an oddity of criminal life, he thought as he looked down the barrel. Although his career started with a gun, the longer he stayed alive, the less important they became. He'd forgotten about this one though. It was special.

"Why didn't you come to your party?" he asked.

Daniel pressed the gun into his left eye. "I asked you a question."

He made himself comfortable, breathing slowly through his mouth. "I asked you one back."

It was painful to see the confusion in his son's face, but not unexpected. The boy was an idiot. "Try and remember who you're talking to. Things will move faster without that gun in my head. You have questions. I have them too. Let's get on with it."

The gun wavered in Daniel's hand.

Ed forced a smile on his face. "You look healthy," he said. "Scotland must have agreed with you. Why don't you put the gun down?"

"Who hurt my daughter?"

"Damn it, Daniel. You're my son and I love you, but think about what you're doing. What's your plan? Shoot me in the head and fucking ask me questions afterwards?"

Ed reached for a drawer in his desk. Daniel tightened his grip on the gun.

"I'm going to get a bottle of whisky. I have two glasses in here. Why don't we have a drink?" Ed pulled out a bottle of Glenfiddich. "Eighteen years old. Only the best." He placed a crystal tumbler next to it and rummaged through the remaining contents of the drawer. "There's another glass in here."

"I don't want to drink with you."

"Wait a minute, will you? It's in here somewhere."

Ed emptied the drawer onto the floor. Notebooks, dead mobile phones, rolls of fifty pound notes. He took a silver framed photograph, standing it on the desk so Daniel could see it and continued his search.

"Oh, well. I can't seem to find it," he said, sitting back in his chair, but Daniel didn't notice. He'd lowered his gun and was staring at the photo.

"Do you remember where we were when that was taken?" he asked.

Daniel nodded.

It was a beach in Marbella two minutes' walk from their villa. Daniel and Scott were in their early teens. They stood side by side, their skin golden from the sun, their arms wrapped around one another. Ed and Liz stood behind them, hands on their shoulders. They were smiling, even Scott. It was the last holiday they took together as a family.

"It's my favourite photograph in the whole world," Ed said. "I don't know what happened to us after that. It's like the tide came in and washed us away."

"I didn't come here to stroll down memory lane, Dad."

He sipped on his whisky, enjoying the smoky heat as it travelled down his throat. "I didn't think you'd ever call me Dad again."

"It was a mistake. It slipped out. You lost the right to be my father a long time ago." Daniel dropped into the sofa. "Are you going to tell me who hurt my daughter?"

"We've been chasing our tails here, but I've had time to think on it. If I tell you what I know, are you going to hunt this guy down for me?"

"Not for you. For Eisha." Daniel's face was hard, his eyes narrowed and piercing. Ed was glad. It didn't matter who he did this for as long as the moron could finish what he started. Judging by the look of him, it wouldn't be a problem.

"Honestly, the pieces didn't start to fit until you walked in that door. How much do you know?"

"Nothing. A guy called Fairbanks is making a move on you. That's all."

"That's pretty much all anyone knows, except me and like I say, I've only just figured out who this guy is."

Daniel folded his arms, settling into the sofa.

"Power breeds arrogance," Ed said. "I thought the Daytons were untouchable so I never saw the threat coming. Not long after you left, one of our guys was found dead. Can't remember his name. Anyway, in his pocket was a note demanding ten million pounds. Ordinarily, I wouldn't even have been told about it. Stuff like that happens all the time, but I think it was Fairbanks trying to get my attention."

"Why?" Daniel asked, leaning forward.

"The guy had been shot, but he'd been left with a fish lodged in his throat. Pretty weird, right? It's the sort of thing that requires extra consideration."

"But you didn't do anything about it, did you?"

Ed shrugged and swirled the dregs of his whisky around the tumbler. "I'm a busy man, Daniel. I can't do everything."

"What happened next?"

"One of our internet businesses was hacked. When the punters logged on to get an eyeful through the webcams, all they got were re-runs of M.A.S.H. We had an outfit knocking off post offices in Liverpool, but they went missing. The next thing I hear they turn up in an animal crate. Someone had posted them to Merseyside Police."

Ed stopped when Daniel's laughter finally drowned him out. He waited impatiently, pouring another drink, cursing when he spilled it on his desk.

"Are you finished?" he asked.

Daniel held up his hands and regained control. "You're right. It's weird, but anyone could have done that. Why do you think it was Fairbanks?"

"Because you know what wise guys are like. They can't keep their mouths shut. They'd be bragging all around town if they'd taken the piss like that, but no-one said a thing. Just like now."

While Daniel deliberated over what he'd been told, Ed got up from his desk and joined his son on the sofa. "I'm not worried, you know? I was before, but I'm not now."

Daniel snapped his head around to face him, as if he'd only just realised he was there. "What are you talking about, Dad?"

He placed a gentle hand on his knee. "You'll catch this guy. I'm sure of it. You're an extraordinary man, Daniel. Despite your faults."

"My faults?" Daniel asked, his eyebrows arching.

"It slipped out. It's the drink talking." Ed tried to stand, but Daniel pulled him back down.

"I need to know everything if I'm going to catch Fairbanks. That's what you want, isn't it?"

Ed nodded.

"So, keep talking. You said the pieces didn't start to fit together until I walked in. What did you mean by that?"

"Let go. You're hurting me."

Daniel looked down at his hand circling Ed's arm and then back into his eyes. "If you think this hurts, wait until I really get started."

"I don't know what I meant. Just let go, will you?"

His muscles screamed as Daniel's fingertips buried deeper. He tried to prise the fingers free, but they were like steel. "It was the gun. It's a Heckler, right? VP70? The one I gave you before you ran away?"

Daniel released him, studying his face. "I kept it to kill you, if I ever needed to. I thought that would be better than its original purpose."

Rubbing his arm, Ed stared at the floor. "The gun was for a very specific job, which you refused to do."

The gun was back in his face so fast Ed barely saw Daniel move.

"Do you want to talk about that job?" he asked.

He shook his head. "Let me tell you this and you can get the fuck out. Okay?" Ed felt the embarrassment creep over his face. No doubt Daniel noticed it too. He wasn't accustomed to feeling shame. Not with the career he had, but when he saw Daniel's gun and realised he'd brought this whole thing down on himself, it was something he couldn't deny.

"It had to be completely untraceable and no-one could know you had it. I went outside the firm and found this kid who had what I wanted. He asked me what it was for. I lied and he knew I was lying."

"It was Fairbanks?"

"I think he took a closer look at us after that. Found out you'd disappeared. That Scott was obsessed with finding you. They were weaknesses he could exploit. I brought him here as sure as blood in the water attracts sharks."

"You're unbelievable." Daniel stood, pacing the room. He stopped to peer through the porthole into the grounds outside.

Bear and Bronson wandered by the lakeshore. "I need you to call off your dogs. No more men waiting for me at train stations or coppers at the hospital."

"Okay."

"When I call, you come running with whatever it is I ask you to come running with."

Ed nodded.

"I didn't hear you."

"Okay," he said.

Turning away from the window, his son held the gun by its barrel. He approached softly. "You think you're in control," Daniel said, "but you're not. You invited Fairbanks in and now you have no idea how to handle him. If it wasn't for Eisha, I'd sit back and let him tear you apart, but no-one hurts my daughter and gets away with it."

"What are you going to do?"

Daniel whipped the gun across Ed's face. There was a wet crunch as the handle connected with his nose. Blood streamed over his lips and mouth. He pressed his hands over his face, feeling it pulsate with pain.

"Take my revenge," Daniel answered. "You may not have laid a hand on my daughter, but you're behind it. The only reason I'm not using this gun to shoot you is because I might need you in the future, but be warned. There's a very real chance it's on the cards."

Tears blurred his vision, but he watched as Daniel turned to leave. "Wait," he shouted and Daniel paused. "You won't be able to do this without my help so make sure you keep me in the loop."

"Why should I bother?"

Ed spat blood on the floor. The pain radiated down his jaw and around the back of his head. "Because you're stupid, Daniel. You're gifted, but you're also so dumb, you can't see what's right in front of your eyes."

Daniel made to strike him again and Ed cowered. "What are you talking about?" he asked.

"Guys like Fairbanks never do the heavy lifting themselves. He has help. Ask yourself why Fairbanks is so good at killing people, but he only manages to put your daughter in a coma. He can off some of my toughest guys, but he messes up when it comes to a little girl?"

Daniel didn't look convinced, but Ed didn't care. He'd given Daniel all the information he could, even the unpalatable truth that he was the cause of his own downfall. Leaning forward, he allowed the blood to flow freely from his nose. It pooled around his expensive shoes.

The office door opened and slammed behind him. He glanced at the round window that looked like the scope of a rifle. Ed had set his best weapon against Fairbanks. All he had to do now was wait.

CHAPTER THIRTEEN

L iz lived in a luxury apartment on the Gateshead side of the River Tyne. It was on the fourteenth floor and afforded her an unrivalled view of the Newcastle cityscape. There was a fifty-inch plasma screen on her wall, but it was seldom on. She preferred to watch the city where vehicles scuttled like ants or people no bigger than dots ambled along the promenade oblivious to her attentive eye.

It had been part of her settlement in her divorce with Ed. Noodles contested it, but her ex-husband signed away the deeds without a whimper. He wanted her to have a place of her own, somewhere the boys could visit and where he would be welcome from time to time. She often joked Ed was the perfect ex-husband. It was the husband part he struggled with. Sitting in her lonely vigil, it was a joke she made less often.

Unlike most new builds, her apartment was large and spacious. Her sitting room had floor to ceiling windows with enough room for two green leather sofas, a wing-backed chair in zebra print and a glass coffee table. The kitchen was state of the art with a double door fridge freezer, granite work surfaces and an oven she had used twice since moving in. There was her main bedroom with walk-in wardrobe, a guest room, two other bedrooms and a bathroom with a sunken bath and whirlpool shower. There was a communal gym on the ground floor where she spent an hour every day.

Despite the open invitation, Ed rarely visited. In fact, she had few visitors. She occasionally entertained male friends, but not so often that they felt comfortable dropping by and her female friends never saw her outside of a restaurant or night club.

It was a surprise to see Monica sitting outside her door, her arms wrapped around her knees.

Offering her a seat and a drink, Monica perched on the edge of the sofa, watching the remaining drops of wine run into one another. Liz glanced at the round faced clock on the wall. It was ten o'clock in the morning.

"Do you want another?" she asked.

"Better not," Monica said, sliding her empty glass away on the table in front of her.

Liz was fresh from the gym. She desperately needed a shower, but when she saw Monica, she knew it would have to wait. The sweat on her body was cold and made her shiver.

"Is there something up, Mon?"

Monica looked longingly at her empty wine glass. Liz's instinct was to get her a refill. They were kept women after all. Who would care if they got loaded before noon? It's not like either of them had responsibilities, but something told her to delay her generosity.

She sat next to her on the sofa and listened to the dull roar of the city outside.

"It's all gone wrong," Monica said at last.

"What has, darling?"

Monica examined her fingernails. They were bitten down to the quick. Liz placed a comforting hand on the small of her back. "I know what it's like living in that house, babe. You can tell me."

Monica took a deep breath. "I'm pregnant."

Something grabbed Liz by the throat. Her hand shrank away from Monica. She went to the kitchen. It was all she could do to disguise the sick feeling in her stomach. Her legs felt like rubber.

With another bottle of Chardonnay in her hand, she returned to her seat. Liz took Monica's glass and poured herself a generous measure.

The girl was talking, but Liz wasn't listening. She guzzled her wine, but it went the wrong way and she choked. Spluttering, she saw Monica's pretty face wet with tears, looking at her quizzically.

"Are you okay, Liz?"

Liz steadied herself with fortifying gasps of air. "How could you be pregnant?"

"What do you mean? You might live like a nun now, Liz, but you must remember how it works. How do you think I got pregnant?"

Fixing the girl with a hard stare, she saw Monica wither in her seat.

"I'm sorry, Liz. I'm sorry. I'm just so upset. I didn't think this would happen."

Liz had been prepared for someone like Monica to come along. Men were weak like that. They needed a woman in their life to feel virile. She never begrudged Ed re-marrying. After he gave her this apartment, it seemed petty.

"Does Eddie know about this?" Liz asked.

"Not yet. When we first got together I told him I didn't want kids. I think that was one of the reasons he married me. He never wanted more than the family he already had and now Daniel's back –"

"Daniel's back?"

The question was met with silence. Monica stared at her open mouthed. That should have been the first thing you told me, you dopey cow and you know it, thought Liz.

"I haven't seen my son in nine whole months," she said.

Monica moved to pick up her wine glass when she remembered it had been taken. Liz clutched it to her body and leaned back into her chair to wait. Monica related the story of how Daniel had broken into Five Oaks, how he'd locked Monica in a cupboard and the murderous look in his eyes as he closed the door.

"I screamed and screamed for help," she said. "My voice got hoarse."

"Where was Bronson? I thought he was doing security."

Monica glanced toward the kitchen. "Do you mind if I get myself a drink?"

"It's not good for the baby," Liz said. "So, where was he?"

"Oh, I don't know. All I know was that I was in that cupboard for what seemed like hours. Eventually Daniel let me out, but he had a face like thunder. I love the boy. You know I do, but he's changed."

Of course, he's changed, thought Liz. He's been without his family for the best part of the year. How can a boy survive without his mother?

"By the time I got to my feet, he was gone. I ran up the staircase and into the office."

Monica expected to see the worst. Ed was on the sofa, his back to the world. She looked around for some clue as to what had happened. When she saw the blood, she rushed to his side. He was breathing, but something was wrong. "Ed? Ed? Are you okay, baby?"

At the sound of her voice, he reached for her hand. She tried to get him to talk, but he wouldn't say a word. Climbing onto the sofa, she lay beside him, her arm draped over his shoulder. They stayed that way until dark. Only then did he reveal his broken nose.

The cool wine slipped down her throat. Liz was cold, but knew it was her son who had frozen her insides. If he was back, then he was back for a reason. She had visited Eisha, but it was too difficult to see her connected to all those machines. The flowers she sent in her absence were from the best florist in Newcastle. They would suffice.

Daniel was out for revenge, which meant whoever had hurt his little girl was in serious trouble. He would dig and scratch away until he found what he was looking for.

She tapped the side of her glass, worried if he dug a little too deep, he might find something else.

"What am I going to do?" Monica asked.

"Are you going to keep it?" she asked.

The words were out of Liz's mouth before she could stop them. Monica was horrified. "Jesus, Liz. Are you mad?"

She couldn't believe she'd just said that. It came from the worst part of her; the part of her that had driven her to leave the family home.

"I'm sorry, Monica. I don't know why I said that."

Monica picked up her handbag. "Are you jealous of us?" she asked, getting to her feet. Liz looked up at the haughty expression on her face. For the first time since meeting Monica, Liz saw more than Ed's piece of skirt.

"Don't you get silly on me, girl. I've got everything I want right here. Why would I care about you and your life?"

"Because it was the life you once had. I'm not stupid," Monica said. "I know Eddie still loves you in some sick, twisted way and I think you might love him too, but I'm his wife and I'm going to be the mother of his new child. You're scared this might be the thing to push you out the nest completely."

Liz was heavy in her seat, as if gravity was clutching her shoulders and forcing her down. She was gobsmacked. Monica had never spoken to her like this before. If she'd had, she'd have been gone long before now. "You're talking out of your arse," she said.

"Am I? Monica asked, storming off into Liz's bedroom. She returned moments later brandishing the photograph Liz kept by her bedside.

"I thought I'd find something like this. Ed has the exact same photo in his office. The Daytons pretending to be a normal, happy family." Monica threw it at Liz and it landed by her feet. "You're anything but normal, Liz. That's why Ed is married to me and you live here, all alone, like the dried up old spinster you are."

Liz could only watch as she marched to the door. As Monica reached it, she turned back to Liz one last time. "Did Ed ask your blessing to marry me?"

"What has that got to do with anything?"

"I know you, Liz. I know what you're capable of. You wouldn't have let me in if you thought I was some kind of threat. Did Ed ask for your permission?"

Liz drained the last of her wine and twirled the stem of her glass in her fingers.

"Your time is over, Liz." Monica sniffed back an angry sob and left, slamming the door closed.

She looked at the view from her window. The city had changed. The buildings and traffic were the same, but her place within it felt different. She had given up being Ed's wife, but Liz never relinquished her claim as a mother. She was still the matriarch of the Dayton family. It was the most important thing to her in the world and she wouldn't give it up for anyone. By getting pregnant, Monica was wrestling the power from Liz's grasp. Or at least thought she was.

Because Liz knew something Monica didn't.

Ignoring her glass, she gulped from the wine bottle. She loved Monica in her own way, but she'd been a silly, little girl. She had been right about the Daytons, though. They weren't a normal family. She'd thought she was marrying a man, but she'd been marrying into a house of vipers.

She'd have to play this one carefully, she thought. Liz could tell Ed about the pregnancy, but he'd think she was out to make trouble. He'd never really believed they were friends. Just like a man to be so short sighted.

Instead, she'd wait for Monica to tell Ed herself. It would test her limited patience, but it was the only way. There couldn't be any doubts in his mind. Only then would Ed realise his darling, young Monica had slept with another man.

CHAPTER FOURTEEN

Daniel tried to understand why his daughter's doctor was suddenly off sick.

"I'm sorry, but I can't tell you why he isn't here," the ward sister said.

She was in her fifties with tightly bound greying hair and a bosom swelling against her uniform. She reminded Daniel, not of the sexy nurses he fantasised about as a teenager, but of a drill sergeant with a chest full of medals.

The nurses' station was opposite Eisha's private room, comprising of a long work surface supporting two computers, one of which had a sign on its screen reading 'Do Not Use. Maintenance Requested.' Behind the desk, harried looking medical staff in crumpled lilac scrubs consulted files and sipped coffee from paper cups.

Had it been any other doctor, Daniel would have begrudgingly accepted their absence, but the Daytons had been topping up Dr Hilltop's salary for years. He was theirs to call on night or day. If his daughter's condition didn't warrant Hilltop's undivided attention, then Daniel wanted to know what did.

"I'm her father," Daniel said. "I haven't seen Hilltop anywhere near her."

"I can assure you that *Doctor* Hilltop has been diligent to the upmost. Your daughter is in very good hands."

"If I can't see him, then I want to see her medical charts."

The ward sister's face reddened and Daniel knew something was wrong. She might have been able to bluff her way around a missing doctor, but now she was rattled.

She turned to seek support from the staff members behind her, but they were gone, off on their rounds. It was her and Daniel. The ward sister seized a sheaf of leaflets on mental health and fanned them out on the desk. "Mr Dayton, I could show you her charts, but with all due respect, would you be able to understand them? They are very complicated. It takes years of education that I don't think –"

Daniel made to grab the Sister's hair, but she jerked away. She stood in shock, open-mouthed and then remembered her training, reaching for the panic button. He leapt over the desk in time to sweep her hand away. She looked for an escape, but the area behind the desk was small and Daniel was large.

"You're lying to me, Sister. I want the truth." He bared his teeth. "What aren't you telling me?"

She took another step backwards. "Members of the public aren't allowed in the nurses' area."

"I'll get it out of you one way or another, Sister."

When she sighed, he felt her breath on his face. The ward sister dropped her gaze. "We have mislaid Eisha's medical files. I've ordered all the nurses at my disposal to search for them, but it will take time. Until then, you are welcome to have a seat in the waiting room."

"I don't understand," he said, looking about the ward. The place was tired, but clean. The patients were sick, but happy. As far as he could tell, the ward was well ordered and running efficiently.

"Like I said, we're looking into it," the ward sister said. "I have every confidence we'll have your daughter's information within the hour."

"No, I mean, you don't strike me as the kind of nurse who mislays files," he said, but the ward sister remained quiet.

"It wasn't you, was it? It was Hilltop."

"Dr Hilltop is an accomplished physician. There is no way –"

Daniel held up his hand to silence her, trying to stop it turning into a fist. His father had been right. Well, up to a point. He'd known the doctor all his life. There was no way he was behind the attack on Eisha, but this was too much of a coincidence. Why would he hide her files?

"Why don't you just get her records off the computer?" he asked.

"He's password protected them. No-one can see them but him. We have a paper copy for the nurses and a computer record for Dr Hilltop. They are both inaccessible and without them, we can't treat your daughter."

"What do you mean?"

The ward sister moved the leaflets around the desk. "I'm sorry, Mr Dayton, but without her records, we don't know what medicines she's previously received. We could accidentally give her an overdose or give her something she's allergic to."

"How could you be so fucking stupid?" Daniel asked.

He paced back and forth, feeling claustrophobic. Lifting the hatch, he slammed it aside, waking the dozing children and causing one of them to cry. If only Eisha would wake so easily, he thought.

The ward sister bustled past him and went to the young boy sobbing into his blankets. "There's been a mistake, Mr Dayton, but upsetting these children won't fix that."

Taking a tissue, she dabbed the boy's cheeks. Daniel stood at the end of his bed. The boy was thin with dark circles under his eyes. A book he had been reading lay on the floor. He picked it up and gave it to the ward sister.

"What's wrong with him?"

"Kidney failure," she answered as she tucked him under his blankets.

He was quiet now and trying to sleep. Daniel glanced in Eisha's direction and then down at the nurse.

"Get me those files, Sister," he said.

The waiting area wasn't a room. It was a corner of the ward with mismatched furniture and the hand drawn pictures of Disney characters he had noticed on his first arrival. The toys were piled in a wooden trunk decorated in flaking yellow paint. He took one out. It was an old Barbie dressed as a nurse. He threw it back in the trunk.

He shouldn't be sitting around doing nothing. One phone call would get him Hilltop's address and one taxi ride would take him to the doctor's door. What happened after that would be up to Hilltop. If he was ill, it would depend on how ill and if he had simply fancied time off, his feet wouldn't touch the ground until Daniel threw him at the foot of Eisha's bed.

Dr Hilltop delivered his daughter into the world. Daniel wouldn't allow him to be responsible for her death.

He had been a child himself when Eisha was born. He was sixteen and Tawnee, Eisha's mother, was younger still. They had met at the Bigg Market, an area of Newcastle known for its raucous pubs and drunken fighting. The streets were filled with music and littered with broken glass.

Daniel had been collecting money owed to him by a doorman called Charlie Dumpster. The same doorman was attempting to bar an inebriated Tawnee from his premises. Her innocent face and big, blue eyes were in direct contrast to the litany of abuse she was hurling at Dumpster. Daniel intervened and their teenage romance began. It was passionate and short lived. On the day of Eisha's birth, Tawnee and Daniel hadn't spoken for five months.

Ed drove his son to the hospital, a private, secretive building where the rich paid to hide their mistakes. Daniel got out of the car and waited for his father, but Ed remained in the car and

Daniel understood without having to ask. Ed had handed over the mantle of fatherhood to Daniel. It was up to him to take it forward.

Tawnee's parents were at the birthing suite and ignored him as he entered. Tawnee's father was in his forties with a receding hairline and pronounced jowls. Her mother looked like an older version of Tawnee with a beehive hairdo and glossy red lipstick. Daniel couldn't help but shudder. They stood either side of their daughter's headboard like sentinels, urging her to push. The sooner it was out, the sooner it was over.

Tawnee acknowledged him with a string of curses he had become accustomed to. Her pink eyes bulged in pain. Her face was red and streaked with matted, sweaty hair. He stood with hands clasped in front of him and noticed a smell in the room he couldn't place until he saw that Tawnee had shat herself.

The midwife appeared, smiling and nodding her head as if everything was going according to plan. She was in her sixties, about five foot three with white, permed hair and a ruddy complexion. Her round stomach jiggled under her uniform as she worked. Gathering the soiled paper sheets from under Tawnee, she noticed him watching. The smile dropped from her face.

"I've heard all about you, young man. It's all very acceptable for fathers to be present at the birth of their children these days, but you're not welcome at this one. Kindly remove yourself. I'm sure you'll be more comfortable outside."

They turned their backs on him, apart from Tawnee, who shot venom at him through her eyes.

"I want to be here for the birth of my child," he said, surprised at how quiet he sounded.

"This is no place for the likes of you," Tawnee's father said.

It was four against one; odds he could manage in a street fight, but at his baby's birth, they were overwhelming. God knows what Tawnee and her parents had told the midwife, but he didn't want things to escalate and sloped off to wait on a bench in the hallway.

Dr Hilltop passed Daniel several times as he inspected the mother's well-being. He was a small man with a brown, shrivelled head sitting on scrawny shoulders. His white medical coat almost reached the floor and he seemed to glide along without making contact with it. He said nothing to Daniel, but Daniel caught him glancing in his direction more than once.

Tawnee's screams filled the long hours of waiting. He tried to block them out, but each one sounded worse than the last. Dr Hilltop made a final appearance as Tawnee's yells reached a crescendo. "Perhaps if you come inside, you'll learn the consequences of sex without control," he said.

The baby was out and bawling. Daniel stood slack jawed as the midwife cut the umbilical cord and cleaned up the new arrival. The baby was weighed and swaddled and placed in the waiting mother's arms.

"It's a girl," Dr Hilltop announced.

After the drama of childbirth, the baby fell swiftly asleep, happy to be warm and close to her mother. The doctor congratulated everyone without meeting their eyes and departed to update his records. The midwife followed, shooting a withering glance in Daniel's direction as she left.

After ten minutes, Tawnee was tired. The unnamed child was taken to the baby unit while she rested. Daniel and Tawnee's parents left the room to be greeted by Ed Dayton and Noodles Reeceman in the hallway.

Tawnee and her parents had agreed to sign over custody of the child to Daniel. She had played her part and would regret it for the rest of her life. The baby was Daniel's and he promised to protect her forever, even if that meant they couldn't be together.

Watching nurses scurrying around the ward looking for missing paperwork, seeing the angst on the ward sister's face as she made repeated calls on the phone, he wondered if he had lived up to that promise. His daughter lay behind a closed door, unattended and untreatable. Would it have been better if he had asked his father, not to arrange for custody, but to drive him back to Five Oaks?

He retrieved the Barbie doll from the trunk and wrung it in his worried hands.

Lily walked into the ward and found him in the waiting area. As she approached, he accidentally snapped the doll in half and quickly hid it before she noticed.

"Have you been here long?" Lily asked with a smile. Her hair fell in curls, framing her face. She wore a faded leather jacket over a cashmere jumper and tight jeans. He drank in her appearance, feeling his heart lift for the first time in nine months.

Lily loved his daughter almost as much as he did. Maybe more. She was as close to a mother as Eisha would ever have.

Her face flushed when she looked into his eyes. His love life was a legion of mistakes and he didn't want to make another by taking his brother's wife.

"Would you like to go for a coffee?" he said.

CHAPTER FIFTEEN

Phoney Tony picked the last of the scab from his knuckle. It was infected. "Here, look at this."

He waved his dirty hand at Rickman and Sticks. Rickman was forty-two and had spent most of his criminal career cleaning up after Tony. He was thin with the kind of streaky tan that came from a bottle. Sticks was slightly younger and twice as fat. He had a tattoo of his baby boy over his heart and burning skulls on his elbows.

"You know who that's off?" Tony said, squeezing pus from his hand. "Remember when I beat that gypsy kid for welching on his dues? I hit my knuckle on his teeth. Bet the little bastard gave me something."

Rickman and Sticks looked at one another and shuffled their feet. Neither seemed interested in their bosses' sores. Unknown to Tony, they'd held long discussions on the subject. If Tony was septic, it was because he didn't wash until he got caught out in the rain. He was five foot three, overweight with a stomach that lay like melted wax over his knees. Phoney Tony was a millionaire several times over, but he hid it well.

Disappointed with his men's lack of interest, Tony went back to counting mailbags full of cash or whatever passed for payment at the time. He was a collector for the Daytons, a role requiring an accountant's lack of imagination and an honest heart. Tony had neither of these attributes, but if a penny went missing, he had to answer to Scott and that instilled dedication in anyone.

Reaching in for another roll of notes, his fingertips brushed against something unusual. He pulled out a watch, hefting its weight in his hand before holding it high so Rickman and Sticks could witness his find.

"Breitling. Cosmonaute," he said.

Rickman whistled. "Lovely, ain't it? Belongs to Achy Dave. Couldn't afford repayments on his new Range Rover."

What came out of the bags came out of Newcastle. Loans, drugs, girls, extortion, blackmail, back room bookies and armed blags. The rest came from rental properties, a nod toward legality that allowed the Daytons to claim back tax from HMRC. The money flowed as freely as the Tyne and was just as dirty. It worked like a beautiful machine and Phoney Tony loved it.

His crew made collections every week and used several safehouses around Newcastle to make the count. They never used the same site twice in a row. Each house was wired with a panic button that alerted Scott through his mobile phone. Any trouble and the Iceman would cometh, usually with a baseball bat.

This week, Tony and his crew were at Nail Fantastic in Walker, a salon run by a Chinese family, who had long since retired to bed. They left the back office open for Tony to do as he liked, together with a plate of dumplings and fried rice. The room was on the second floor, windowless and narrow. It was reached by a metal staircase outside, on which was posted a wide and heavily armed man called Paulo. The door to the room was reinforced with steel and deadlocks impossible to open from the outside.

The room was safe, but Tony hated it. The only thing that said office was the desk he sat at while he counted. Everything else said storeroom. Wooden shelves lined the walls, stacked with varnish removers, paints and lacquers. The air was toxic. He'd have a headache tomorrow and wouldn't be able to taste his food for days.

Tony finished the count, squeezing his tired eyes with his thumb and forefinger. He entered the amount into his iPhone and pressed a button. The money would be delivered to a second safe house where it was re-counted by Scott himself. His final job was to smash the phone and buy a new one later in the week.

"Has the car arrived?" he asked.

Rickman stopped admiring a recent manicure he'd received gratis from the Chinese couple and jolted to attention. "I'll go outside and check."

"Don't go outside and look, you fucking foetus," Tony said. "How many times do I have to tell you? Give him a shout. What if some fucker's outside waiting to jump us?"

"No-one's ever outside, 'cept Paulo."

"Saddam Hussein could be waiting outside with an AK-47 for all you know. What do we always say?"

Sticks chimed in with his boss. "Don't open the door without the say-so."

Rickman muttered something he didn't want Tony to hear and took out his phone. When the line was answered, he whispered hurriedly into the handset. Sticks checked his sidearm and waited for his colleague.

Rickman snapped his phone shut. "Phil says we're good to go. He can see Paulo on the stairs. Everything's fine."

"Why did you call Phil and not Paulo?" Tony asked, pressing the last greasy dumpling into his mouth.

"I never call Paulo. He's from Brazil or something. I can't understand what he says."

"Jesus Christ, Rickman. Let's just get out of here. I want my breakfast, you tool." Tony looked to the door and stood slowly. He gave Sticks the nod and the locks of the door were undone with two loud clunks.

Paulo leaned against the wall, his eyes closed in contemplation. Sticks nudged his shoulder to wake him and saw Paulo's shirt soaked with blood. His throat was cut, not sideways, but lengthways so the skin flapped like bloody curtains in the wind.

"What's going on?" Tony asked.

Sticks searched for Phil in the darkness. He was stood by the car with a shotgun pressed against his groin. He looked apologetic. The man next to him unleashed both barrels and Phil was blasted in half.

As Sticks turned to warn his boss, his head exploded, a high velocity bullet showering Rickman in shards of skull and brain matter. Tony ran to the panic button, pressing it repeatedly. Rickman stumbled back into the room, wiping bloody tissue from his eyes. Blindly, he reached for the gun holstered by his thigh. A bullet tore through his elbow. He screamed as his forearm waved loosely, blood jetting from the wound. A second bullet blew away his jaw and a third ended his misery, burying itself deep within his chest.

His lifeless body dropped at Tony's feet when a voice came from outside. "No-one else has to die. We just want the money."

Tony took a gun from the drawer of his desk. It was a .38 Super from Astra. Each of his safety houses had one, loaded and filed clean of their serial numbers. It trembled in his hand as he pointed it at the door. "Do you know who you're robbing?"

"We know everything about you, Tony. I want you to go to the shelf on your right."

He glanced at the tins of nail varnish on his right hand side.

"That's it. That's the one. On it you'll find a micro camera that's been recording your activities for the past five months. I'm looking at you now. I know you've pressed a panic button and I know you're pointing a gun at the door."

"Who are you?"

"My name is Fairbanks and I'm either going to be your boss or your executioner. I'll give you the option. Put the gun down and come work for me."

Tony's double chin quivered. He'd heard the rumours. Everyone had. Tony was loyal to the Daytons, but that was before Fairbanks had killed four of his men. Judging by the steadiness in Fairbanks' voice, he had done it with ease. That eerie tranquillity scared him more than being shot.

"How do I know you'll not kill me the minute you step inside?" he shouted through the door.

"It's not good business, Tony. You're the Dayton's bag man. You know where the money comes from. I kill you and I wouldn't know who owed me what. I can't make a living without you."

The logic was sound. It appealed to the mathematician in him, who was just as scared shitless as the rest of Tony. He placed the gun on the table and smiled into the hidden camera. The rumours about Fairbanks were linked to talk of the Dayton's demise. Although he had dismissed it, Tony had spent time planning a way out. Luckily for him, Fairbanks had recognised his importance. He controlled the revenue streams, making Tony indispensable.

Just before a bullet tore through his chest, Phoney Tony wondered if he should have held on to his gun just in case. His hands pressed around the ragged wound, desperately trying to stem the flow of frothy blood that bubbled down his clothing. He fell with a thud. The last thing he saw was a young man with a hunting rifle waving him goodbye.

***

Fairbanks shouldered his rifle, smoke curling from its barrel. Dougherty was by his side. They watched silently as their crew grabbed the money and ran for the waiting car.

"How long before the Daytons get here do you think?" Dougherty asked.

Picking up the Breitling watch, Fairbanks checked the time. "It won't be long. We better be quick."

Snatching the watch from him, Dougherty admired it on his wrist. Fairbanks touched his earring. He had all the jewellery he needed, he thought. He could always take the watch back later if he wanted to. Walking to the shelf, he retrieved the micro camera. It had been purchased in cash from a man who knew better than to remember the names of his customers, but Fairbanks hadn't got this far without being thorough.

He looked over his shoulder and saw the guys waiting in the car with the engine running.

"Are you sure we should have shot this guy?" Dougherty asked.

"I think it was the best move."

"Yeah, well I think different. He could have been useful."

"Tony knows where the money comes from, but there's only one man who has access to what we need."

Dougherty shoved his hands in his pockets and stuck out his lower lip. It reminded Fairbanks of the greasy adolescent who had forced him to kill an innocent dog just to survive.

"You're not thinking far enough ahead. I let you get away with a lot because you're smart, but you're not smarter than me," Dougherty said.

"Really? And what would you have done, boss?"

"There might have been more money," Dougherty said, picking at a spot on his cheek. "Tony could have led us to it."

Fairbanks rarely carried a hand gun, preferring the range of his Remington rifle, but it was necessary for the next part of his plan. He produced a Colt Eagle from his pocket and pointed it at Dougherty, who barely had time to register he was in trouble before his left kneecap disappeared in a mist of blood and bone. He crumpled to the ground, growling in pain, hissing and spitting as he tried to keep the agony under control.

"It's time I got rid of you. Too many questions, Dougherty. Too much petulance. You've been useful, but I need to take charge now. Men like you can't take orders and men like that can't work for me."

"You can't do this. I run the Orphans. Not you."

"Things change." Fairbanks' gun was raised toward Dougherty's face when he heard a phone ringing. It wasn't his or Dougherty's. The sound came from Tony's corpse. Keeping his gun trained on Dougherty, he went through Tony's pockets until he found it. The screen was smeared with blood, but he saw Scott Dayton's name in green.

He had spent years fantasising about killing Dougherty. He'd thought of hanging him, gutting him, setting dogs on him, burning him alive. The choice was endless, but a chance encounter with Ed Dayton provided the answer. It would be his biggest score yet and Dougherty held the key.

"This isn't over, Fairbanks."

"Course it is. You just don't know it yet. See you later, boss." He snapped his heels together and gave Dougherty a fake salute before running to the door.

The world was spinning for Dougherty. His leg wept blood and he was light headed. Pressing his hands into the floor, he prevented it from revolving out of control. His anger fuelled his consciousness. He wasn't finished yet, he vowed. He'd stay alive. He'd use the last of his strength to wait for the Daytons. He'd tell them everything. He'd betray his crew, if it meant Fairbanks paid for his treachery.

Dougherty fixed his eyes on the open door. His final breath would be spent on revenge.

CHAPTER SIXTEEN

It was early morning and the hospital canteen was busy. Doctors and nurses squeezed between white Formica tables, sipping coffee or carrying breakfast trays. As a seat became vacant, there was a rush toward it, like the first empty space in a car park. The canteen staff stood behind the serving area in hairnets, their faces damp from hot bacon or curdled eggs. Like the doctors, their coats were white, but theirs were stained with food.

Daniel and Lily waited for a free table. He had told her about the missing medical charts on the way to the canteen. A group of four nurses pushed away their plates and gathered their belongings. An office manager in a pressed linen suit strode forward. Daniel caught his eye and he diverted left, depositing his cornflakes in a swing bin before swiftly leaving.

"But Hilltop's been so good to her, Daniel," Lily said as she sat down. "He's looked after every one of us at one stage or another. Has someone stolen them? What about her mother? What was her name again?"

"The last I heard of Tawnee, she was burning her way through the money Dad paid her to keep quiet. I doubt she even knows her daughter's in hospital, much less cares about it."

Daniel tipped two sachets of sugar into his coffee and stirred slowly.

"Hey, since when did you have a sweet tooth?"

Lily smiled at him. She tucked a strand of hair behind her ear and his heart raced.

"People change," he said.

"Do you remember the present you got me for my fifteenth birthday?"

Daniel remembered all too well and lowered his head.

Lily laughed, tapping her finger on her chin. "What was it again?" She reached over and took his hand in both of hers. "Oh, yes. A basket of fruit. For a fifteen year old girl. And what did you say?"

He cleared his throat. "Chocolate rots your teeth."

"I can still picture your face. Big Daniel Dayton like a love-sick puppy."

A flush rose in his cheeks and he sipped his coffee, his face twisting at the taste. "Too sweet," he said, pushing the cup away from him.

Lily rubbed her fingers over his knuckles and he tried not to look at her.

"I was right, though" he said. "You have a beautiful smile."

A young nurse carrying a slice of toast approached and indicated one of the free seats next to them. "Are these taken?"

"Yes," they said in unison. They watched her go and Daniel turned to Lily. "You knew I was in love with you?"

"Everybody knew."

Her hands were warm and soft. They were the right size for his, he thought. He saw a sliver of pale skin on her wedding finger and realised her ring was missing. She caught him looking and placed her hand under the table.

"Scott and I are over. He worked all the time and when he came home, I could tell he'd rather be back out on the streets. He's great with Eisha. He really is. It's me he doesn't love any-more. He moved out months ago."

"Is there anyone else?" Daniel asked.

"No," said Lily. "Not for me, anyway and Scott would have told me if he was seeing someone. He owes me that much."

Lily didn't know about Scott and Monica, but then that was hardly a surprise. He doubted anyone knew, least of all his father. The Daytons thrived on secrets, but if that one was discovered, it would go nuclear. His father's legacy would be reduced to a radioactive wasteland.

"Scott knew I was in love with you?" he asked.

"I don't think so, Daniel. Human relationships don't really compute with him. They're too hard to understand."

"Why did you marry him then?"

"Isn't it obvious?"

He looked around the canteen wondering what other people were talking about. Their day ahead? The one before? Their future and their pasts?

She reached out for him again, but he withdrew his hand and stared at the table.

"I'd bought you fruit, but he got you that necklace. I remember how you looked at him when he put it around your neck."

Stiffening in her chair, a look of realisation dawned on Lily's face. "That's why you stopped coming around, isn't it? It's why you stopped talking to me. You thought I liked Scott more than you? I was fifteen, Daniel. You bought me a stupid ass present. He got me a necklace. Of course, I was pleased. Why didn't you say anything?"

Daniel shrugged, feeling like an awkward teenager.

She tied her hair back, fastening it into a knot, revealing to Daniel the face he had fallen in love with all those years ago. "You think you see everything with your 'magical powers,' but you're as blind as the rest of us. It took one look to cut me out of your life."

"But I was right. You were engaged in under six months."

"Because of you, Daniel, you fucking moron. You were disappearing. I couldn't think of any other way of keeping you near."

There was a crash as a member of the canteen staff dropped a pile of plates on the floor. White shards shattered outwards in a star formation followed by sardonic applause by a handful of doctors. Daniel watched as brushes were found and the mess hurriedly swept away, feeling Lily's gaze upon him with every passing minute.

She sighed. "You're just like him, you know? Scott keeps everything hidden away, afraid that if he shows even a glimpse of himself, it's a weakness."

When she finished talking, there were tears in her eyes.

"What was it like being married to him?" Daniel asked.

"He never raised his voice to me. He never laughed or cried or joked or sulked. Humans are supposed to be spontaneous, aren't they? But not Scott. Giving me that necklace was the only time I feel like he showed himself to me."

On the way to the party, Scott noticed the present Daniel had bought for Lily. It hadn't occurred to him to bring a gift so he mugged a young mother pushing a pram two streets from Lily's house. He took her necklace and threw a hundred pounds at her feet. That was Scott's true self. Not the man Lily had pinned her dreams on.

But it had been his own foolish pride that pushed her into his brother's arms. All that wasted time, he thought. If only he had said something. If only he could make her see now.

He took her hand, lightly caressing the white band of her missing ring.

"Don't do this to me, Daniel. Not again," she said, drying her eyes.

"Lily, I –"

Daniel's iPhone trilled from his inside pocket. He looked at the screen and frowned. Lily retracted her hand and he excused himself with a scowl. It was his father, his voice stern, but excited. There was no need for Daniel to speak. It was a one-sided conversation. When his father hung up, he returned to Lily, but didn't take a seat. "Can you look in on Eisha for me?"

"What's going on?"

"Nothing. I just have to go."

"It's not nothing, Daniel. You don't have to protect me from everything."

"Keep on at that nurse to find her records. I'll be back as soon as I can." He tried to give her a reassuring smile, but judging by the look on her face, he failed.

"That's what you said nine months ago," she said, standing from the table. "There's nothing more important to you than Dayton business, is there? Just like Scott."

And he watched her leave, like he did on the night of her fifteenth birthday.

CHAPTER SEVENTEEN

y the time Daniel reached Nail Fantastic, the place was crawling with criminality he didn't want to associate with. A man in cotton overalls and neoprene gloves scrubbed and cleaned the stairs outside. Daniel stepped over him to get inside where two more men rolled a body in black plastic sheeting. They sealed it shut with duct tape while they chatted about a recent Newcastle/Sunderland derby game.

"The problem with Mackems is they don't know how to take a beating," said the young man with a centre parting in his hair.

The other looked up from his task. "My wife's a Mackem, dickhead." Daniel pushed passed them, walking around more bodies wrapped and sealed before he arrived.

Ed signalled him over to a group of men standing around Phoney Tony's desk.

"What happened?" asked Daniel.

Mosely took Daniel's hand. "Glad to have you back, mate," he said, casting a glance at Ed. Daniel pulled his hand free, resisting the urge to wipe it clean on his trousers.

"Looks like Fairbanks hit Tony and his boys," Ed said. He hadn't shaved and his bristles were flecked with white. "Blew his driver in half with a shotgun. We reckon a sniper took out Paulo, Rickman and Sticks."

"A sniper?"

"Someone good with a rifle anyway. He made off with fifty thousand pounds."

Scott stood next to his father, staring straight ahead. He was dressed in another tailored suit. As he adjusted his silver cufflinks, the light lanced Daniel's eye making him wince. Bronson greeted him with a nod from behind Tony's desk while a thick neck black guy Daniel had never met ignored him completely. The group waited in silence while the clean-up crew departed, heaving the bodies down the stairs and into a waiting van. They would be weighed down and dumped into the Tyne later.

"Is this place going to be clean enough if the police come sniffing?" asked Bronson.

Scott waved his concerns aside. "The lads have done a good job. Even if they did find something, all they'd know was that Tony and his boys were here."

"We'll torch the place just in case. It's not worth anything now," Ed said.

"Does anyone live above the shop?" asked Daniel.

"It will look better if they burn too," Scott said, finally deigning to look at him.

Daniel returned his gaze, stony faced. "Have you brought your big boy matches or will you get one of your minions to get their hands dirty for you?"

The temperature dropped and Bronson shivered. Scott moved toward Daniel, who turned on him, his fists clenched. Ed stepped in between. "They're good people. They know not to get involved. We'll get them out before we start the fire," he said.

Daniel winked at his brother.

"What's the matter with you, knob face?" Scott shouted at Bronson as he warmed his hands under his armpits.

"What am I doing here?" Daniel asked his father.

"We want you to talk to this guy."

No Neck guy moved to reveal a man gagged and bound to Tony's chair. His eyes brimmed with fear.

"What happened?" Daniel asked, indicating the ruptured knee cap. Someone's belt was tied tightly around his thigh. It stemmed the flow of blood, but it seemed like there was more out than in. "Who applied the tourniquet?"

"I thought it was a good idea to keep him stable," said Mosely.

"He was passed out when we got here," Scott said. "Maybe Tony or one of his boys got off a round before they went down?"

"He's one of Fairbanks' gang. We recognise him from CCTV outside The Glitterball," Ed added.

"I found the footage," Mosely said to no-one.

"He did Scalper?" Daniel asked. The guy was big enough, but he didn't have the heart to face a man like Scalper Brown.

"He was the guy who pretended to have Fairbanks up against the wall while his mates did the dirty work," Ed said.

"You want me to get him to rat on his boss? Could be he's more scared of him than he is of you. I would be."

Scott stepped around his father and pushed Daniel in the chest. "If you're so scared of Fairbanks, why don't you fuck off back to Scotland? You ran off before. Why don't you run off again, you little nancy?"

"Will you fucking put a sock in it for two seconds?" Ed pinched the bridge of his nose. "In case you two fuckheads hadn't realised, this is the first chance we've had to get some real intel. This guy can tell us where he is. We get some tools and finish this up before lunch."

Ed turned to Scott, gripping him by the shoulder. "You and Daniel have things to sort out, but this isn't the time. I know you feel like I've stepped on your toes by bringing Daniel here, but he can get this information quickly and without a fuss. We've already had to clean up a bucket of blood this morning and I don't want to have to call the guys back. If he can't get him to talk, then we'll resort to your methods. You've got your pliers?"

Scott nodded.

"Good boy," he said, before looking to Daniel. "The quicker you get him to talk, the quicker you get the guy who hurt your daughter. Are you ready?"

His father was right and, not wanting to spend any more time with his family than he had to, Daniel closed his eyes and breathed slowly. He opened them and observed. Dilated pupils. Taut neck muscles. Forward posture. Fear, certainly, but there was more. Daniel circled him, drinking him in, consuming him. Flexing fingers. Flared nostrils. Set jaw. It was anger. The man strained against his bonds, but it wasn't an attempt at escape.

"You don't need me here," he said.

"I said that from the start," Scott said.

Daniel ignored the comment. "He'll tell you anything you want. Something happened. This guy wants to talk."

Daniel nodded at Bronson, who ripped off the gag. The man winced and took a deep breath. As the air hit his lungs, he coughed, frothy saliva gathering at the corners of his mouth.

"Give him some water," Ed said.

Mosely lifted a bottle of water to his lips and he finished it in three messy gulps.

"My leg. I need something for the pain," he said.

Daniel wasn't inclined to ease his pain just yet, but Mosely produced a small vial and drew out its contents with a syringe.

"What's that?" Scott asked.

"Morphine. It will clear his head so he can focus on your questions."

"Why are you carrying morphine?" Ed asked. "It's not exactly a street drug, is it?"

Mosely plunged the syringe into a shoulder and watched as the man's face relaxed. "You'd be surprised what people take these days."

Ed shot a look at Scott, who gave a small shrug of his shoulders.

Daniel pushed Mosely aside and positioned himself directly in front of their prisoner. He wanted to be this man's whole world for the next five minutes. Anything this guy wanted, he had to know it was going through Daniel first; a classic interrogation technique.

"What's your name?"

"Marcus Dougherty."

"Have you been working with Fairbanks long?"

"Since we were kids. We were a tight bunch until he turned up."

"What do you mean?"

Dougherty licked his lips, leaving a trail of wet that turned Daniel's stomach. "People came and went. The ones who went didn't like Fairbanks. They thought his ideas were stupid. They didn't believe in him."

"How many are in your crew?" Ed shouted over Daniel's shoulder.

"Six, including me."

"Only six? Against us?" Scott asked, pressing a hand over his heart. Daniel knew there was a gun holstered there. His brother was feeling threatened.

"It's like the SAS," Daniel said. "The smaller the team, the faster they can strike and the quicker they can get away."

And it made taking over the Dayton empire almost impossible, he thought. Of all the things Daniel had surmised about Fairbanks, he knew he wasn't a gangbanger making a power move. It seemed too clumsy for someone that eloquent.

"What did you mean when you said 'they didn't believe in him?'"

"In his plans. His schemes. He doesn't like to be questioned. Anyone who did, disappeared. We never saw them again."

"His men were scared of him?" Ed asked.

Dougherty's eyes widened in response. "They were my men," he said before pausing to correct himself. "I run that crew. They *are* my men."

Daniel swallowed his disbelief. This guy was a thug, a chess piece to be moved around the board by a smarter man. If Dougherty was in charge, it was only because Fairbanks let him think that way.

"So what happened?" he asked, nodding at the wound in Dougherty's leg. "You stopped believing in him?"

"No, I always believed in him. I just hated him. He was a conniving bastard from the start. Whispering behind my back. Turning my boys against me. He bought them with easy jobs and easy money. All he asked for in return was complete obedience. I guess I didn't give enough."

"Why aren't you dead?" Scott asked, stepping forward so Daniel had to lean to one side to get out of his way. "I would have killed you. Stamped my authority all over your face. He's taken over your crew and he lets you live? It doesn't make sense."

As much as he hated to admit it, Daniel agreed with his brother. Leaving Dougherty alive was a liability. Had Fairbanks assumed he would bleed out before they got here? Was he relying on Dougherty's misplaced loyalty to keep quiet? Whatever the answer was, it was the mistake they were waiting for, but instead of feeling hopeful, Daniel was uneasy.

His father pushed passed him. "What does Fairbanks want with my business?"

Dougherty shrugged.

"What's he got planned next?"

"I don't know. He never told us anything."

"You don't know where he is?" Scott asked.

He shook his head. "That's how he works. We each get a part of the plan and we follow it blindly. It's why he demands complete faith. Do you think I go around cutting off women's fingers for fun?"

Ed turned to Daniel. "Is he telling the truth?"

He watched Mosely feeding Dougherty another bottle of water and nodded.

"It explains why Fairbanks shot him in the knee and not the heart," Scott said. "It doesn't matter if he's alive or dead. He doesn't know anything."

Daniel knocked the bottle from Mosely's hand. It landed in a pool of Dougherty's blood where the remaining water sluiced it between the cracks in the floorboards. "Even if you were one hundred percent sure he couldn't give you up," he said, "you'd double tap him just to be sure. Shit, Scott would do it for fun so why take the risk?"

Dougherty straightened in his chair. "I might not know his plan, but I know him. Know your enemy, Fairbanks always said. It's why we studied you for so long and I know plenty about him. He's an orphan, like the rest of us. He likes fishing and hunting."

"Hunting? Tony was shot with a rifle," Scott said to his father.

"And he wears a ridiculous stud earring he refuses to take out. It looks like a diamond, but it's not."

"What is it then?" Daniel asked.

"I don't need to know about his fucking fashion sense," Scott said. Daniel ignored him and focused on Dougherty.

"When he was younger, he killed a dog. It was an accident, but he never really got over it. He prefers dogs to humans. It's a loyalty thing."

"Get on with it," Scott said.

"Pet cremation services can compress your dog's ashes into glass and set it in jewellery."

"He's got a dead dog in his ear?" Bronson asked, laughing.

Scott shot him an icy glance and he fell quiet. "That's doesn't tell us a God damn thing."

"It tells us he has a sentimental streak," Daniel said. "Useful thing to know when you're dealing with a psychopath."

"Has he got money?" Ed asked.

"We all have. His plans go like clockwork. He conjures money out of thin air. I can tell you where it is." There was a collective intake of breath. Dougherty brightened at the flush of excitement they all saw in Ed's face. "He's probably shipping it to a new location as we speak. Get me out of here. Fix up my leg. I'll tell you everything."

Ed rubbed his hands together. "Let's get to work."

Immediately, Scott was on his phone, organising a gang of hard men to go in as Dougherty gave No Neck the address.

Ed paced the floor. "Bronson, go with Scott and pick up the shooters. Make sure you've got blades and bats, too. Go in two cars. Then if one of you gets pulled over, the other car will still get through. I don't want anything to go wrong."

"What about me?" asked No Neck.

"Stay with Dougherty. He's started talking and I don't want him to stop now. Find out everything he knows."

"I'll stay with him," said Mosely. "You need all the men you can get. I've got the morphine. I'll take him to Five Oaks. He can't go much longer without medical attention."

Scott placed a hand on his father's shoulder. "Hurry up, Dad. The longer we wait, the more chance Fairbanks has of getting away."

Mosley circled around Dougherty. "I want to help, boss. Please trust me."

"Get him sorted, Mosely, but if anything happens, it's your head on the plate, understand? And don't forget the couple upstairs before you torch the place."

Ed turned to Daniel. His father's face glowed, panting in anticipation. "Scott will go in with his guys and bring Fairbanks out. You can talk to him afterward."

"You're not going to kill him?"

His father ran his fingers through his hair. "Not right away, no. I want to talk to him first and I want the money he stole."

"You're after his money. This had nothing to do with your granddaughter, did it? As soon as Dougherty mentioned there was cash, you wanted it."

Ed might have been talking to Daniel, but his eyes watched Scott on the phone, waiting for good news. "You can't expect me to ignore the fact Fairbanks could be worth millions. There's a bigger picture here."

"I want that fucker to pay for what he did to Eisha."

Scott came off his phone and nodded at his father, who grinned in return. It was a large smile that split his handsome face in two. He patted Daniel's cheek. "He will, he will. As soon as I get his money, he's all yours."

Daniel watched his father walk away, too stunned to stop him.

"Sorry, mate," Bronson said, as he slipped by him.

Daniel threw his hands in the air. "You talk about family like it's oxygen to you, but it's really money that keeps you breathing."

No-one answered. Mosely wheeled a bleeding Dougherty to the door, his eyes trained on the floor. No Neck followed him, paying as little attention to Daniel as he had when he arrived.

"What did you expect, brother?" Scott said, his fingers tapping over his phone. "This is our chance to get back on top. Do you think Dad would sacrifice that for family? He never has before."

Daniel grabbed a can of lacquer and hurled it against the wall. It bounced and rolled impotently under Tony's desk. He hung his head, feeling exhausted. "He's like Fairbanks. When his men become redundant, he casts them aside, except with Dad, it's his own sons he uses."

Scott walked to the door. "Mosely will be back in a minute with the petrol. You're welcome to stay."

"Doesn't it bother you? How Dad treated us as kids? Training us to be animals?"

Standing at the top of the stairwell, Scott shielded his eyes against the morning sun. "Dad is a hardened criminal. So am I. So are you. You can't have all that in a family and expect love too."

He left without turning back. Daniel heard his footsteps on the metal stairs as he made his way onto the street. His brother was lying, of course. Like an iceberg, his words were part of a much bigger, complex whole. Scott expected his family to love him. It was why he constantly sought approval from their father and when it wasn't forthcoming, some twisted part of him sought it out in Monica.

Mosely appeared carrying a green plastic petrol can and sloshed liquid around the room. Together with Nail Fantastic's flammable stock, it would be ablaze in seconds, sending scorching heat into the roof above and molten flame dripping through the floorboards below. There would be nowhere to run. It would consume everything in its path, reducing it to ash and hazy memory.

Daniel hoped to be as deadly.

CHAPTER EIGHTEEN

Scott's heart pattered as he pulled the ski mask over his face. It was a signal for his men to do the same. The wool scratched his skin and he yanked a loose thread away from his mouth. Underneath the mask, he was smiling, trying to control his breathing. These were the moments he treasured. Most people took feeling alive for granted. For Scott, it was a state he worked hard to attain.

Pulling on his latex gloves, he looked over his Smith and Wesson one last time. It had been cleaned and oiled earlier. There were no fingerprints, no serial numbers and no chance it would jam. If Fairbanks was still there, he wouldn't come easily. Scott wanted to be certain that when he raised his weapon, someone's head was going to be blown off.

Their vehicles rolled into the car park of the Wylam warehouse. Scott and two doormen from the Glitterball got out of a rusting white Transit van. The doormen, who were called Jake and Marblehead were there in support of Scalper and by support, they meant revenge. Bronson and a man called Harvey climbed out of a Ford Mondeo, popped the boot and handed out a cache of weaponry.

Scott took Bobcat aside, the driver of the Transit van and reiterated his earlier instructions.

Night had arrived. The street lamps in the car park were broken and there didn't appear to be any signs of life in the warehouse. They could barely see and all they heard was the invisible water of the Tyne rumbling in the darkness. Scott edged to the warehouse, followed by his silent crew.

The building was a single storey with a pitched roof and walls of corrugated iron. There was one entrance and one exit. Scott had used similar warehouses in the past, but had always ensured they had multiple exits. One exit risked getting trapped under a hail of bullets. He breathed slowly, stymying his excitement. Like shooting fish in a barrel, he thought.

Scott and the doormen stood on one side of the entrance. Bronson and Harvey on the other. They raised their weapons. He scanned the surrounding area for witnesses or signs of an ambush. Seeing nothing, he readied himself to give the order when he felt the vibration of his iPhone in his pocket.

"Not again," he whispered, fishing it out. His anxious father had been texting all day. In between answering his messages and devising an assault strategy, Scott just wanted to get on with the shooting.

He hid the glow of the phone's screen under his coat and checked the message. It was from Monica.

"Pls call asap. Love, M. xxx."

There'd been no time to call her as he had done every day since their time together had ended. She rarely picked up. It was rarer still for her to call him. He read the message several times, wondering at the urgency and her motive for sending it. Bronson coughed gently and he switched off the phone, pressing too hard on the button so that it glowed back into life moments later.

"Fucking hell," he said, launching it into the darkness where it landed with a distant thump.

Scott placed the mask of his respirator over his face and breathed deeply. The air tasted stale and the visor fogged when he exhaled. One exit was a problem for Fairbanks, but one entrance was a problem for him. For all he knew, the Mexican army could be waiting on the other side of the door. Unlike Butch Cassidy and the Sundance Kid, Scott was prepared and he trusted in his abilities to kill.

He tugged the handle on the warehouse door. It was unlocked.

Bronson handed him a CR gas canister and Scott waited until everyone attached their respirators. He pulled the pin. Smoke rose from the diffuser. Opening the door, he skidded the can along the floor and followed instantly, keeping low, his gun trained ahead of him. There was no defensive gun fire. No Mexican army. His men fanned out, wafting the toxic gas around the warehouse.

Boxes were stacked neatly on floor to ceiling shelving units. The flooring was poured concrete and despite the layer of noxious gas crawling over its surface, Scott saw it had been swept clean. He heard nothing other than the rasp of his breathing through the mask.

No guards? An unlocked door? Scott's heart sank. They were too late. Fairbanks was gone.

Bronson caught his attention and pointed at an office in the rear of the warehouse. It was lit by a dull glow. Raising their guns, they inched toward it, their feet kicking up swirls of CR gas. Scott motioned for them to stop when they got within twenty feet. The office was a simple box shape, built from stud walling. The door was shut. The single window was smeared with grime, making it impossible to make out any details, other than confirming the light came from a desk lamp.

Voices and gunfire exploded behind them. Scott and his men ducked and ran for the office, diving inside, slamming the door shut. They swept their weapons around the space. It was empty. The gunfire stopped and they looked at each other in shock.

"What the fuck happened?" Bronson asked Scott.

Ignoring him, he looked around the office. It was unremarkable, just a room with a metal desk covered in chipped green paint. The lamp that lured them in had a canvas shade imprinted with leopard spots. The walls were bare, except for a handful of invoices pinned by the door.

Bronson pointed at a calendar with the picture of a topless woman. "Take a look, Scott."

"I think I can hear them coming," someone said.

"I'm not in the mood for your stupid jokes," Scott said to Bronson, wiping his hands down his trousers.

"We're sitting ducks in here," Jake the doorman said.

Bronson yanked the calendar down from the wall and threw it at Scott. "That doesn't look like a joke to me."

The blonde reclined on a deck chair wearing tight, bikini bottoms. Her large breasts were oiled and glistening in the sun. Where her face was supposed to be, someone had glued a picture of a skull, its yellow teeth bared in a grin. Today's date was circled in red with the inscription, 'The Day Scott Dies.'

Scott swallowed. "I have to get out."

Cleaning the window with the cuff of his shirt, he peered outside. There was no sign of Fairbanks, but he could see the exit. It was a five second sprint. Sweat stung his upper lip, but didn't dare take off his mask to wipe it away.

He reached for the radio on his belt. There were more shots and more shouting. Scott ducked involuntarily, expecting the flimsy walls of the office to explode under gunfire.

He needed to speak to the man on the other side of that exit. "Bobcat, can you hear me? We need you to move the van. Bobcat, it's Scott. Can you hear me?"

"What are you talking about?" Bronson asked.

"I told Bobcat to block the van against the exit door to stop Fairbanks from escaping." Scott turned back to his radio. "Bobcat, are you there?"

Everyone was quiet, waiting for an answer. After seconds of static, Scott clipped the radio onto his belt and stared at the floor. "Bobcat's dead."

"Jesus Christ. What's going on?"

"They must have followed us in," Bronson said. "We thought we were trapping them inside, but they were trapping us."

"Like fish in a barrel," whispered Scott.

"What're we going to do, boss?" asked Jake.

The pressure of their expectations weighed heavily upon him. Scott shook his hands free of the trembling that had gripped them. He tried to tell himself it was just adrenaline, like his father had told him countless times before. He wasn't convinced. Fairbanks had outmanoeuvred him so easily. He was out of his depth and Daddy wasn't here to bail him out.

"Look, we're going to make a run for that exit, but we have to be fast and hit the door at the same time. With any luck, we'll create enough room to squeeze through."

"That's madness, Scott and you know it." Bronson hoisted the gun in his hand. "We'll be cut into butcher's meat the minute we step outside."

"Have you got any better ideas?"

"What about if we just surrender?" Jake discarded his gun and held up his hands. "They might take mercy on us."

Bronson spat on the floor and snatched up the spare gun. "I'd rather be shot to shit than give them the satisfaction." He smiled at Scott, his cheek twitching. "Ladies before gentlemen, though."

At that moment, Scott didn't know who he hated more; Fairbanks or Bronson, but now wasn't the time. He crouched down, his long legs bunched into coils. "It's not far and I think we can make it. If we can't shift the van, then run. Start firing and run."

They all looked at each other, scared and vulnerable. Jake was white with panic.

"Okay," said Scott. "On the count of three."

He counted down quickly before doubt paralysed them all. They surged through the office door, their legs and lungs pumping. CR gas rose in plumes, wrapping around their feet like poisonous seaweed. The door loomed ahead.

Scott prepared for the impact of the door when it opened before him. He threw himself to the ground. Bronson fell over him, followed by the other men. Regaining their senses, they whipped their guns toward the exit. A light shone into the warehouse and a figure emerged to greet them.

There was a gunshot. They saw a rifle in the man's hands. They opened fire with a deafening roar, all five guns emptied into the silhouette. It danced under a barrage of bullets. Cordite mixed with the smoke of the CR gas and created a blanket of fog that settled over them. Their guns clicked dry. They couldn't move. They hid in the mist and waited for return fire, but nothing came. A hush descended over the warehouse.

The figure was standing deathly still, a spectre in the smoke. As the mist cleared, Scott saw its clothing was torn to bloody shreds. The head lolled to one side. Half of the skull was missing, exposing a brain that dripped in spongy globules to the floor.

It wasn't a figure. It was a body, strapped to an upright gurney with a rifle taped and mounted in its hand. Another band of tape covered the mouth.

"Shit, you know who that is, don't you?" Bronson asked.

The lifeless eyes of Dougherty stared at them. He wore the makeshift tourniquet Mosely had tied around his leg. He'd been riddled with bullets and, although it was Scott and his men who shot him, Scott recognised the hand of Fairbanks.

"That's the guy from the mugshots you've been showing around," Jake said. "What is he doing here?"

"Facing an execution squad," Bronson said, desperately wiping his gun free of prints.

Bronson had guessed correctly, but there was no point in cleaning down their weapons, thought Scott. Fingerprints or not, they were getting convicted. He pulled off his respirator and ski mask and welcomed the sting of the CR gas on his skin. They had been framed for murder with such eloquence, Scott almost smiled.

He wasn't surprised to hear police sirens outside.

***

Ed threw his night vision binoculars into the back seat of his BMW. He watched in astonishment as police cars surrounded the warehouse, their blue lights flashing. Armed tactical support jumped from an unmarked van, their bulky Kevlar vests giving them the look of mountain gorillas. Uniforms swarmed about like bees while POCT – the Priority and Organised Crime Team – dressed in shabby plain clothes, ordering each other about. It was chaos and his son was in the middle of it.

His car was parked behind a billboard advertising life insurance. Ed was too high profile and too old to be part of the action. With the arrival of the authorities, even at this distance, he was being drawn in closer than he liked. The BMW roared into life and Ed ran away.

Everyone in the warehouse would be fitted for handcuffs. When the police finished with that, they'd search the surrounding areas. Scott was going to prison. There was nothing he could do about that, but he had no intention of following him. Slipping into the anonymity of the A69 traffic, Ed drove back to Newcastle looking for somewhere to hide.

He jumped when his phone vibrated. Fumbling inside his jacket, he pulled it out to see another text from Monica. He didn't bother to open it.

"Can't you leave me alone for five minutes," he said, dropping his phone into the passenger seat. He'd been dodging her all day. It was always one of two things with her. His wife was feeling insecure again and wanted him to comfort her or some such shit, or she wanted money.

Ed drummed his fingers on the steering wheel. "Sorry, love, but I'm fresh out of both right now."

They'd taken a massive loss tonight with consequences he didn't dare to speculate on. It was supposed to be about turning the tables and taking back his dignity. Instead, he had slipped down another rung in the ladder and he had no idea how.

"Get a grip on yourself, man," he said.

His phone rang. Glancing at the screen, he saw it was Noodles and put it on speakerphone. "Noodles, we've got a problem."

"I know, sir. That's why I'm calling. The money stolen from our safe house was destined to several high ranking members of the Police Executive. It was due to be paid today. They want to know why it wasn't."

"What did you tell them?"

"That you were in the process of getting it back."

Ed chewed at the corner of his thumb, spitting a sliver of skin onto the passenger seat. "We haven't got it, Noodles. We got royally fucked."

Noodles drew in a calming breath. Ed heard it rattling in his lungs. "How fucked, Mr Dayton?"

"Like 'we're going to need stitches' fucked. They'll have to wait until we can free up some cash. There's nothing I can do about it now."

"I suggest you try. My earlier warnings of safeguarding one's reputation have come to pass. No-one knows who Fairbanks is, but they know he's usurping our power. Our friends in high places are squeezing us while they can."

"They're asking for more?"

"Fifteen percent."

"On top of what they already get? What if I refuse?"

He heard Noodles pacing. "All previous protections are withdrawn."

Ed took a roundabout too fast, swerving into the wrong lane. A housewife in her silver 4x4 honked her horn. Ed gained control of his BMW and flipped her his middle finger.

"Is there any other good news?" he asked.

The sun was rising. A pink halo lit the city rooftops and the streetlamps blinked out as he passed them. Ed worked late most nights. He hadn't seen a sunrise in years. He'd forgotten how peaceful they were.

"Tony sent Scott the count before it was stolen," Noodles said. "It was half what we'd usually expect."

He disconnected the call and detoured into an estate in Blaydon. Parking in an anonymous street of terraced housing, he watched as families closed the doors to their homes and went about their day. Mothers and fathers went to work. Children went to school. They'd return later, talk about what they did, have tea, watch telly and go to bed. A normal life to be repeated when the sun rose again tomorrow.

Withholding payments or demanding more would become the norm. He kidded himself that people obeyed him out of respect. It was fear that made them compliant. No-one was scared anymore and the Daytons lost power because of it. In a way, Fairbanks' job was already done. If he did nothing else, the rot had set in. The timbers of Ed's empire were crumbling, together with his resolve.

He didn't want to go home. Dougherty was waiting to be interrogated. Mosely would be stoned. Favours needed to be called in. It was too much business and too many problems to face. At one time, closing the doors at Five Oaks kept his troubles at bay. This morning he feared he'd be trapped inside with them and unable to escape with his sanity.

A young mother and her two sons walked toward his car. She had blonde hair and wore a slim fitting trouser suit. Her children were around two years old dressed in matching dungarees and strapped in a harness each. Their unsteady legs pulled mercilessly against their restraints, their faces red with the effort. He smiled as their mother leaned back to take the strain. She noticed him and smiled back.

Starting his engine, he slowly pulled away and headed to Gateshead where he was sure of a warm welcome. On his way, Noodles called back with grim tidings.

CHAPTER NINETEEN

Afrer his father burned him at Nail Fantastic and Mosely burned down the building, Daniel was uncomfortable. He couldn't explain why Dougherty was left behind as a loose end. The question was like an itch between his shoulder blades and it wouldn't go away.

Following the receptionist's directions at the hospital, he was surprised to receive a call from Lily. Calming himself down, he attempted to smile when he answered. His forced joviality didn't last long. Her name was still down as Scott's emergency contact and she outlined the details she'd received from a sympathetic policeman. They kept their chat brief and Daniel ended the call more confused than ever.

He sat quietly by Scalper's bedside, reluctant to wake him while he pondered over what Lily had told him.

Scalper woke with a start. "Jesus, I'm thirsty," he said.

"You can talk?" Daniel asked.

"Isn't that a line from Pinocchio? I can talk, but I've been warned about over doing it."

Scalper winced as he reached for a glass of water. Daniel got it for him and pressed it to his lips. Scalper slapped his hand away and took the glass for himself.

Daniel sat down and searched for something to say. "Don't think I've ever seen you with hair."

Scalper rubbed a tentative hand over his skull, feeling the prickle of his returning hair. "Can't bring myself to shave. Just the thought of a razor ..."

Scalper trailed off and a silence fell between them. Daniel looked around the room, impressed by the number of flowers and Get Well Soon cards on display. "You could open your own shop with all of these, mate."

"What are you doing here?" Scalper asked.

Daniel admired Scalper and his loyalty to the Daytons, but he didn't really know him and there was no point in pretending. Just like his phone call with Lily, some situations couldn't be forced. Best if it was kept to business.

"You know Lily? Scott's wife?"

"Sure. There's a card on there from her. I'm sorry I was too busy flying the light fantastic to thank her."

"She called this morning. Scott's been taken to Ponteland station. He's been charged with the murder of Marcus Dougherty."

Scalper stared blankly at Daniel.

"Do you remember the guy who pretended to have Fairbanks pinned against the wall?"

"The spotty one? Face like a pan of smashed crabs?"

Daniel nodded, but Scalper still looked confused. "Scott killed him for me?"

"I'm not sure. As far as I knew, Dougherty was at Five Oaks. He was a loose end for Fairbanks. I'd been wondering how it was going to get tied up. I guess Fairbanks found a way of getting Scott to do his dirty work for him. I don't know how he got to the warehouse."

"Warehouse?" Scalper sat upright, ignoring the pain in his body, though it was plain to see on his face.

"I don't know the whole story," Daniel said. "There's been a lot going on and I haven't got time to give you all the details."

"Wait a minute, Daniel. I take the beating of a lifetime and you're keeping me in the dark, like a fucking mushroom.

No-one's said shit to me since I woke up here. My body might be broken, but I'm not. I don't need protecting."

"I'm not trying to protect you."

"It's bloody typical. You're like that dick Mosely."

"What?" Daniel blinked twice. He was the unlikely visitor. He wouldn't have been here at all if he didn't need something, but Mosely was the last person he expected by Scalper's bedside.

"He came by and apologised for what happened at the Glitterball," Scalper said. "He felt guilty for smashing my comms, but it wasn't really his fault."

Daniel had been told what happened. He didn't think it was Mosely's fault either. He blamed Fairbanks for everything and saw his work everywhere, from Eisha's coma, Dougherty's death to Scalper's scars. He was the puppet master and they all danced to his tune.

Scalper continued. "He said he'd let me know what happened to a friend of mine called Jackie, but he never came back. I knew I shouldn't have trusted him."

At Nail Fantastic, Daniel focused on his interrogation with Dougherty, making a special effort to ignore Mosely, a man he *did* know, but didn't like. He hadn't questioned his possession of morphine like his father. He wasn't into the drug scene and had accepted Mosely's explanation without much thought, but he had wondered over the tourniquet. It was basic first aid, but for a self-centred prick like Mosely who didn't help anyone but himself, it was pretty advanced.

There was only one conclusion. Mosely knew about Dougherty and his exploded knee cap beforehand. Begging his father to be the one who took him to Five Oaks, Mosely delivered him to the warehouse as per Fairbanks' instructions so he could be executed by Scott. When the trap snapped shut, Fairbanks was rid of his treacherous boss and his enemies were sent to jail. It was genius.

"What did you and Mosely talk about?" Daniel asked.

"He did all the talking, as per usual. I couldn't speak. I would have torn my stitches."

"You didn't tell him anything?"

Scalper shook his head.

"Just as well. He's been playing both sides. I think Mosely was here to find out what you knew. It's lucky you had your mouth stitched shut."

Scalper looked confused. "He was here to kill me?"

"You were another loose end. He was probably carrying a dirty syringe with your name on it."

But then Daniel began to doubt his assumption. Fairbanks killed people who might grass him up, but he had only maimed Scalper. Severely maimed, but still. Had he cut open his face because he knew it would be stitched shut? Had that been his way of silencing Scalper without the need of killing him? If that were true, was this Fairbanks' way of showing mercy? The questions chilled him, but there was a cruel logic to it that fit his character. He didn't smile, but he wanted to. Daniel was starting to get a feel for who Fairbanks was.

"How long has this been going on?" Scalper asked.

He folded his arms and leaned back into his chair. "I'll tell you what I know. You deserve that much, but I came here to find out about Fairbanks so I need you to tell me everything you know first. And make sure that includes Mosely the snake."

Daniel traced the angry scar from Scalper's lip to under his right eyeball. It was weeping blood. "Do you think you can talk for that long?"

***

Leaving an exhausted Scalper to sleep, it was clear Fairbanks had infiltrated further into the Daytons than anybody had realised, like a tapeworm, growing and twisting inside its host.

Mosely had either been bought or threatened into working with him. Either explanation fit with a man who drugged women before sleeping with them. Daniel knew who to visit next, but he was close enough to the Children's Ward to quickly see his daughter.

As he approached, he saw the ward sister through the open door to Eisha's room. She was taking readings from the monitor and scribbling on a clipboard. He entered quietly. It was only when she heard the click of the closing door that she realised she wasn't alone. She dropped her pen in fright. He picked it up, placing it in his top pocket.

The ward sister pushed out her ample chest. "I'm carrying a panic button, Mr Dayton."

"I take it you've found Eisha's records?"

She reached into her hair and pulled out a second pen that held it in a bun on the top of her head. Her grey hair tumbled in locks around her face. She shook her head so it fell behind her shoulders.

Daniel was momentarily distracted.

"Yes, we have," she said. "Who told you?"

"No-one, but if you hadn't, you'd have already pushed your silly button. As if that would have made a difference."

"You're a bully, Mr Dayton. A mistake was made. I have corrected it and your daughter is back in safe hands."

"Whose hands? Yours or Hilltop's?"

The ward sister pretended to read through her notes on the clipboard. She made a few additions and checked the monitor again. Seemingly satisfied, she attempted to leave, but Daniel blocked her way. "Where is he?"

"Dr Hilltop is a very busy man and I am not his keeper."

"The last time we spoke, I got the impression you lacked confidence in the good doctor, but because you're a professional, you tried to protect him. You're doing the same thing now, but he only needs protecting if the accusations against him are false."

"This is my career, Mr Dayton. Some might say my life. You have no right to come in here and try to destroy it."

"Yes, I do," he said, pointing at his daughter. "She gives me that right."

Stepping around the ward sister, he went to Eisha's bedside. She was paler than before, her lips drained of blood. Even the hair she delighted in brushing every night lacked lustre. His daughter was slipping away and try as he might, there wasn't a thing he could do to stop it.

"She's turning into a waxwork," Daniel said.

The ward sister joined him, placing a comforting hand on his forearm. Daniel flinched at her touch and she quickly withdrew it. "I won't lie Mr Dayton, the longer she's in a coma, the worse it will get. I can assure you we're doing everything we can. Dr Hilltop has been very attentive."

"If he was so attentive," Daniel asked, "where was he the other night?"

She looked through the window in the door and then down at her shoes. "He was sick."

"But he's back? And he gave you the records?"

"Yes."

"He's been in to see her?"

"There's nothing on the charts."

He threw his hands in the air. "Fucking hell, woman. Do I have to drag it out of you each time? He's putting my daughter in danger. He doesn't deserve your loyalty. Just fucking talk. What aren't you telling me?"

She opened her mouth, but clamped it shut without making a sound.

"I won't tell anyone," Daniel assured her.

Daniel looked at his watch, not just to check the time, but to show the ward sister it was an issue.

"I didn't find those records. Dr Hilltop made an appearance and I took them before he had a chance to squirrel them away."

"Did he say why he was keeping them secret?"

She shook her head. "But he handed them over pretty quick. He knew he was in the wrong."

"What did the records say?"

"What I expected them to. Your daughter was admitted with a trauma to the back of her head causing unconsciousness. No liquid in her nose or ears. Pupils unresponsive. No other injury, internal or external. Effectively, your daughter is asleep. We have to wait until she wakes up."

"There's nothing you can do?"

"We monitor her. Give her fluids and we'll treat her if complications arise, but it's up to her."

He'd been stupid to think Scalper was Fairbanks' only surviving victim. His daughter was too. Dougherty was killed because he was a loose end that posed a threat. Scalper was damaged beyond reasonable repair. Daniel doubted he was in any danger, but what about his daughter? Was she a loose end that needed tying up?

"I need to talk to Hilltop," he said.

"He's gone. He said he was leaving for the day. He didn't say where."

"I don't believe this. I really don't. Is he sick again?"

The ward sister tucked her clipboard under her arm. "There's something going on here that I don't fully understand, but I will in time. Dr Hilltop monitored Eisha very closely when she first came in. At the expense of other patients, I might add. According to the records, that attention waned over time. When I saw him earlier, he wasn't ill. He looked as healthy as a horse. I even saw him playing with some of the children."

"What are you saying?" Daniel asked. He walked to the door, but the ward sister stopped him with a forceful hand on his chest. This time she didn't remove it.

"I'm saying the way he acted around Eisha has been very odd and I'm starting to suspect you and your family have something to do with that. I researched you on the internet. The Dayton name is as commonplace as porn and I don't approve of either."

He wondered how long it would take her to get suspicious. It was testament to how much she cared about her hospital that she'd started an investigation. He admired that, but she had to know his reputation was more than just words on a screen.

Her eyes bored into his. He took her hand and held it. "If you know who I am, you know I wouldn't think twice about crushing every bone in your fingers."

She didn't pull away. "If I find you or your family have endangered my patients in anyway, I'll drive over you in my car. And Mr Dayton? I'll reverse several times."

Movement caught his eye through the window. Lily was on the ward, talking to a nurse. She looked tired, which wasn't a shock given all she'd been though recently. Like the Sister, the Daytons were impacting on Lily's life and as usual, that influence was negative.

He turned to the ward sister. "I need you to get Hilltop's address."

"It's impossible. His computer is password protected and human resources won't give that information out."

He placed his hand on her shoulder. "Okay. I don't have time to argue. I have to go. It's up to you now. Make sure you look after her. My friend visits regularly. I'm also going to get a couple of guys to keep an eye out. Keep her safe."

The ward sister frowned. "Who are you protecting her from?"

Lily was still talking to the nurse, but he saw her edging away. "Is there another way out of here?"

"What's going on?"

"It's complicated. Another way out?"

Daniel followed the Sister's directions, slipping through a side exit and bounding down a set of stairs. He couldn't face Lily right now. He didn't know how to begin the conversation they needed to have. There was too much going on. He couldn't concentrate. His head was cluttered and whenever he thought of Lily, he unravelled.

He focused on the job at hand. He was satisfied Eisha was safe for the time being. The ward sister would do her job twice as efficiently as Hilltop, but their conversation raised questions the doctor would have to face soon. Why was he hiding information? Why did he keep disappearing? What was his role in the game?

But Hilltop was second on his list. Daniel wanted to find Fairbanks first and to do that, he had to go back to the beginning.

CHAPTER TWENTY

Daniel was a boy the last time he visited Mosely's home. Staring at his crumpled homework, his father had taken pity on him and suggested he witness his first cocaine deal instead. It was worth millions to the Daytons. The powder was weighed out using scales from Mosely's kitchen while Daniel watched on, eating a packet of cheese and onion crisps.

His home was in a suburb of Sunderland called Saltgrove Village. Its population consisted mainly of wealthy retirees and the white collar, middle class. They hid their detached houses behind privet hedges, marking a clear delineation between their home and the street. Entry was by invitation only.

Older now, he sat behind the wheel of his van and surveyed Mosely's property. It was set back from the road by a short, leafy driveway. There was a small overgrown garden, thick with brambles. Sun loungers lay on their side, blown over in the wind and never righted. He couldn't see the house, but judging by the garden, the place was deserted and had been for a while.

He froze as a figure paused by his window and gave him a small wave. It was a stubby legged postman with thick glasses, clutching a wad of envelopes to his chest. He mimed winding down a window and Daniel reluctantly complied.

"Morning, sir. Can I help you?" the postman asked, showing a gap in his front teeth as he smiled.

Daniel breathed deeply. "I'm fine. Thanks."

"If you're lost, I can give you directions?"

"I'm not lost."

The postman cast an appraising look over the van. "We don't get many strangers around here. Are you working in the area?"

"Visiting a friend."

"Okey-doke, sir. Well, I'll be in the street for a while. I'll keep an eye on you in case you need help."

The threat was clear and he sauntered along Mosely's driveway, whistling. Returning moments later, he waved and proceeded to a house two doors down, glancing over his shoulder after every second step. Daniel wound up his window, grinding his teeth. He'd wanted to be sure he wasn't walking into a trap like his brother, but any chance of undercover surveillance was gone. The longer he stayed, the more likely it was that the postman would return.

Waiting until the coast was clear, he bolted up the driveway. He found cover behind the trunk of a tree, viewing the house at last. The door was a glossy black with brass fittings and sandstone columns either side. The windows were large and rectangular, but the blinds were closed. From the outside, it looked like any other suburban home. There was no way of knowing what lurked inside.

He remembered patio doors around the back; the easiest way to gain entry into any home. Keeping low, he jogged the outskirts of the garden, skidding on the algae sludge of Mosely's decking. A quick glance through the glass told him the kitchen was empty. He reached up and tried the handle, hoping like hell the door was unlocked.

"Bollocks," he whispered.

It was an old Amico lock with a protruding keyhole. Daniel took a small hammer and chisel from his jacket and waited for the sound of busy traffic. Five minutes passed before a bin lorry rumbled by and he hit the chisel through the lock. The barrel fell onto the kitchen tiles with a clatter. Quickly, he slid the door open and stepped inside.

He replaced his tools in a pocket and smiled.

The house was silent and Daniel was grateful he hadn't tripped the alarm. Either it wasn't set when Mosely left or he was still here.

The kitchen was clean and stylish with teak coloured cabinets and a six ring cooker. He heard the hum of the fridge motor, proving the electricity was connected. He moved through the hallway. Framed, black and white etchings of naked women lay against the wall and a roll of bubble wrap lay close by. Mosely's expansive sitting room had thick, purple carpet, but there was little else. No television, no coffee table, no seating.

A sound came from upstairs. Daniel froze, waiting. When nothing more came, he inched up the staircase, breathing softly and quietly.

The door to the main bedroom was open. Again, there was no furniture, only a thick carpet and a pile of packed suitcases and bags halfway filled. Mosely was preparing to flee. No matter what he'd said to Scalper, it confirmed his guilt. He'd betrayed the Daytons and Daniel smiled. He was on the right track.

Closing his eyes, he tried to detect where he heard the sound come from. Radiators ticked as they cooled. Somewhere a window rattled. Had Daniel imagined someone moving around? He stepped further into the room. There was nothing there, except the suitcases and an antique wardrobe made from oak, deep enough to hide a man. The doors were shut, but not completely. The sliver of a gap allowed air in and out.

He yanked open the wardrobe with one hand, his other raised in a fist. Left over metal hangers rattled in agitation. It was empty. He was on his own after all. "Where the fuck are you?" he said to himself.

A floorboard creaked behind him. "I'm here." And a man rushed toward him.

CHAPTER TWENTY-ONE

The man was as wide as Daniel and almost as tall, wearing a camouflage jacket and army boots. His tangled beard hid the lower part of his face while wild, black hair obscured the rest. Daniel barely had time to register small black eyes glinting under the mass of hair before being forced into a fight.

His assailant hefted a meaty fist and swung it down to Daniel's face. He stepped from the blow, but couldn't avoid a second that struck his solar plexus. He gasped, the air pummelled out of him. He moved to the side, trying to catch his breath as another fist headed for the side of his head.

Stepping into the attack, Daniel shoved his left shoulder under the man's chin, forcing him off balance. He grabbed at his long hair and heaved his head backwards while reaching between the man's legs. He snatched his testicles, twisting viciously, left then right. Crying out, the man launched both hands into Daniel's chest and wrenched himself free.

Daniel advanced, not wanting to give his opponent any advantage, but didn't see the rabbit punch coming as it connected with his ribs. Even amidst the shuffling and the grunting of the fight, he heard the crack of bone. Daniel staggered, his elbow clamped to his injured side. His opponent followed, the shine of polished teeth beaming through his beard as he smiled.

Feinting to the left, Daniel grabbed him by the neck and brought him in for a head butt that broke his nose. The man lurched, tears in his eyes, blood streaming around his mouth. Daniel kicked him in the stomach with the heel of his foot. He bounced against the wardrobe and fell onto Daniel's right hook. There was a crunch as knuckle met jawbone. An arc of blood splashed on the wall, together with a tooth that deflected and accidentally hit Daniel in the eye. The man dropped with the thump of a felled tree.

Daniel leaned against the wall, breathing hard. He rubbed his teary eye where the tooth had struck, but didn't dare touch his ribs. They were too painful. He tasted blood in his mouth and spat at the man on the floor. "What's your name?" he asked.

The man stirred, but didn't open his eyes.

"I'll kick your balls off. Tell me your name?" he repeated.

Looking up from the floor, the man's eyes were glassy, but focused, flicking from Daniel to the open door and back. It wasn't hard to read his intentions.

"All I want is your name."

He sat up, stroking his jawline. "Reaver."

"What are you doing here?"

"Packing up Mosely's things. All his stuff is going into storage."

"If he's on the run, why don't you just burn everything?"

Reaver pinched his beard. "Greed, I guess. No-one turns on their friends without greed coming into it somewhere. Maybe it's so he feels comfortable wherever he ends up."

Legs straight. Feet splayed. Regular breaths. Even tone. Reaver was telling the truth, but Daniel wasn't certain. His hair obscured his face and made the signs difficult to interpret. He was also sending twice as many as most people did, as if he knew what Daniel was doing and was consciously muddying the waters.

"What did Mosely do for you?"

"Are you going to kill him?"

Daniel considered the question. "Would it make a difference if I did?"

"Find him and he's yours," Reaver answered, looking to the door. "If Fairbanks is letting Mosely go, then he must be done with him."

Daniel stamped heavily on Reaver's knee. He howled, grabbing it, pressing his palms into the joint to stop the pain from spreading anywhere else. "What did you do that for?"

Circling around him, Daniel searched for somewhere else to strike. Reaver tried to keep him in sight as he walked around and around. "Where is Fairbanks?" he asked.

"He doesn't tell us everything. Just what he needs us to know."

Picking up a suitcase, he hurled it across the room. The corner hit the side of Reaver's head and he toppled, eyes rolling. Daniel gave him a moment to regain his senses before dropping another suitcase on him.

"I don't know where he is," Reaver shouted.

There was another suitcase in the corner, but his ribs were screaming. There had to be a better way to get Reaver to submit. It had been a long time since he'd bitten off a man's ear, he thought and reached forward, teeth clacking together. Reaver scuttled away, pulling himself along the floor.

"Where is Fairbanks?" Daniel asked, slowly stalking him around the room.

"What do you want from me?"

"Tell me what you know."

"I told you, I don't know where he is." Reaver got to his knees and scrambled to the door. Daniel leapt in front him, blocking his way and swept his arms away with a foot. Reaver fell forward, his already broken nose hitting the floor. His shriek was muffled in the luxurious carpet.

Daniel dragged him onto his back, noting the greasy red stain he'd left behind. Reaver shook his head. "No more."

Smiling, Daniel watched the blood bubbles burst from his nose while he waited for Reaver to capitulate.

"There are three more men in a caravan park. South Shields," he said finally.

"They're the rest of your gang?"

Reaver nodded and Daniel stared into his ruined face. "You see, that wasn't so hard, was it?"

He stepped back, as if preparing to strike a football, and knocked Reaver out with a kick to the head.

Leaving the house, Daniel walked down the driveway to open the gates. The postman stood waiting, his eyes widening at the sight of the blood on Daniel's clothing.

"Please help me," Daniel said. "There's been an accident. I need my phone from the back of the van."

The postman reached it before him, hopping from one stubby leg to another while he waited. Daniel checked the street as he pulled his keys from his pocket. The only things moving along the pavement were fallen leaves caught in a breeze.

"We better call the police too," the postman said with an excited grin.

Daniel punched him in the face and he tumbled into the gutter. "Fucking neighbourhood watch twats."

Opening the van doors, he threw him inside and jumped into the driver's seat. He drove up the driveway and parked as close to Mosely's front door as he could. Rummaging through his glove compartment, he searched through business cards and receipt books, memories of his time in Hounswood and found an old lighter. He checked it worked before going inside.

Back in the bedroom, Daniel tied Reaver's hands behind his back and, scooping him up under the arms, he dragged him downstairs. It was hard work and the bones of his broken ribs nipped painfully together. He opened the front door and checked for more nosey neighbours. There was no-one in sight. With the last of his strength, he threw Reaver in with the dazed postman and locked the van.

Mosely's home had eleven rooms from front rooms to bathrooms. Daniel went through them all, checking for clues to Mosely's disappearance. He didn't expect to find anything and contented himself with ensuring all the windows were locked shut.

He hadn't found Mosely and he hadn't found Fairbanks, but he was pleased with the work he'd done on Reaver. He had another lead, another avenue to pursue. He'd keep knocking down walls and eventually, he'd get where he was going. A plan to extract Fairbanks' men from their caravan was already formulating in his mind.

In Mosely's kitchen, he turned on the knobs of the gas cooker and went upstairs. He was tired and aching after his fight, but Daniel believed in scorched earth and he wanted to do this right. The neighbourhood watch would love it. He stacked the suitcases containing Mosely's clothes in the centre of the room, hissing against the pain in his ribs. He paused for breath. Sweat ran down the contours of his back. One suitcase remained, standing on its own in the corner.

Pulling on the handle, it moved an inch and he was forced to stop. The case was heavy. He dragged it part way and was about to abandon it when he wondered about its contents. If the other cases contained clothes, what made this one so cumbersome?

The suitcase was a hard shell Samsonite, sealed shut by a sturdy padlock. He took out his lock picking kit and placed the chisel under the shackle. With three swift blows, the padlock broke and he twisted it loose. He lifted the lid and stared inside. He tutted then stood, looking about the room, as if an explanation might be written on the walls. They were as blank as he imagined his own expression to be.

His eyes returned to the suitcase. "Son of a bitch," he whispered.

Fairbanks didn't leave loose ends. Daniel knew that, Reaver had convinced him otherwise. It was unnerving and he felt a part of his self-belief shift like sand under his feet. He couldn't remember falling for a lie so completely and yet the evidence was here before him. Actually, there were lots of bits of evidence before him. Mosely hadn't escaped. He'd been dismembered and locked away in a suitcase.

His head lay on top of bloody thighs, which had been severed at the hip and above the knee. He couldn't see the calves and feet, but assumed they were in there somewhere. His arms had been cut off at the shoulder and inverted either side of his torso so his hands grabbed at his bloody neck. Still in his precious suit, Mosely was reduced to an ugly mess of body parts and judging by the ragged wounds, they had used something with a serrated edge.

Daniel closed his eyes, knowing he couldn't leave without searching the body. Getting comfortable, he reached into the secret pocket of Mosely's suit where the dealer hid his drugs. If there was a mobile phone with a contact number, that's where he'd find it. It was another chance to get closer to Fairbanks and Daniel couldn't help but feel excited.

The flesh was cold and wet. He avoided touching it as much as he could. Slipping his fingers along the blood soaked lining of the jacket, he found the pocket with his fingertips. There was nothing. He pushed deeper, his tongue sticking out the corner of his mouth until found something that shouldn't be there. Pinching it between his thumb and forefinger, he pulled it free.

It was an envelope, stained with crimson blood, but with writing clearly legible on the front. 'To Scalper'.

He opened it and saw an address and phone number for a woman called Jackie. It was Scalper's friend. The one Mosely had promised to find. He had done right by Scalper after all.

Daniel closed the lid. Balancing his lighter on the surface, he rethought his plan. People were complicated, he thought. Who would have thought a rat, a skunk and a bastard like Mosely would be capable of such an act of kindness? Perhaps he really did feel guilty. But maybe it wasn't kindness. Maybe it was one last act of redemption before he slipped away and the full extent of his treachery was revealed. Daniel would never know, but if Mosely had Jackie's contact details, she must have survived. Scalper would be pleased.

He tapped the lighter against the shell of the suitcase and it occurred to him how similar it was to a closed casket. Striking the lighter, an orange flame quivered and danced, decorating the room with a warm glow, as if he had lit a candle in church. What had started as an act of petty revenge would be a funeral pyre. No-one deserved to be remembered as a pile of body parts. It was an attempt at kindness, though he wasn't about to hang around and say a few words.

Rushing downstairs, he was met by a cloud of rising gas. He coughed and pulled his coat over his nose and mouth, stumbling over the last few steps. His eyes stung and he grew nauseous. The front door was straight ahead when Daniel staggered to a halt. If Reaver had lied about Mosely, had he lied about the three men in South Shields? Had all this been for nothing? How could he get him to tell the truth?

Opening the door and gulping down fresh air, Daniel decided to go to Five Oaks and a little room his father had in the wine cellar.

CHAPTER TWENTY-TWO

Evening drew in, stealing the sunlight from her kitchen. Liz flicked the switch on the wall and closed her eyes against the sudden fluorescence, turning it off again. Opening and closing cupboard doors, she found her last packet of painkillers. She dropped two tablets into her hand and swallowed them with the dregs of this morning's wine. The hangover couldn't slow her down. She was only halfway through.

Liz watched the countdown on her oven, feeling its heat warm her bare legs. She'd showered, re-applied her make-up and got dressed. Her reflection in the polished work surfaces told her she'd chosen her attire well. Black pants and bra with open toe high heels. She opened another bottle of wine while she waited for breakfast to cook.

Her iPhone rang as the cork popped.

"Hi Liz. It's me." Monica's voice sounded shaky, as if she had just stopped crying or was just about to start. Liz put the phone on speaker and turned her back to fetch a clean glass.

"I didn't know who else to call. I can't get through to anyone," she continued.

The queasiness of the first sip of wine too soon after a big session was something she was getting used to. She let her stomach settle and had a second sip, her eyes glancing at the red light on her phone.

"Liz? Are you there? I can hear you moving around."

Where the fuck was that cafetiere? Once again Liz searched through her cupboards. It had been a moving in present from Scott. She dropped to her knees, reaching to the back of a cupboard and there it was, sitting on top of the salad spinner Daniel had bought her. Placing it on the kitchen counter, she removed it from the unopened box.

"Please talk to me. I'm sorry," she heard Monica say.

Liz looked at the phone and smiled, pushing the box to one side. Slowly placing her hands either side, she leaned into it and counted to three. "Oh, babe, I forgot you were there. I'm not ignoring you. I'm just really, really busy. How are you, honey? Is everything okay?"

Monica was definitely crying now. Her breaths came as wet gasps. Checking the countdown on her oven, there were two minutes before her croissants were baked to perfection.

"I'm sorry about our argument. I said some terrible things. I shouldn't have. I'm sorry," Monica said.

She imagined Monica wiping her snotty nose with a tissue. Liz hoped she'd wipe it red raw. "Oh, babe. I haven't given it a second thought. We're still best friends, aren't we? Why don't you tell me what's wrong? I really am in a hurry."

While Monica gathered herself, Liz switched on the kettle and laid out cups and saucers.

"I haven't seen anyone for days. Five Oaks is deserted. It's just me. We used to have all these guards around, but they've disappeared. I've tried calling Ed and Scott. They're not picking up. I was wondering if you knew what was going on?"

"Sorry, babe. I don't know anything about it."

"Have you heard from Ed?"

Liz spooned some coffee into the cafetiere. "Why would he call me?"

"I don't know. I'm worried something bad has happened."

"There were times I wouldn't see him for weeks. He'll show up. He always does." The buzzer sounded on the oven and Liz pulled out all the drawers, looking for a glove. "In the meantime, you have to calm down, okay? It's not good for the baby. Ed wouldn't like it. When I had Scott and Daniel, he wouldn't let me lift a finger."

"You haven't told him about me being pregnant, have you? Is that why he's avoiding me?"

Liz tried not to laugh. If she'd told Ed about the kid, Monica would be getting patched up in hospital by now. "Of course, I haven't told him. That's your job. You have to tell him. You're going to do that, aren't you, babe?"

There was a pause before Monica answered. "Yes. I promise."

"Good," Liz said, sliding the golden brown croissants onto a plate. "I have to go, okay? Speak soon."

"Liz, is there anything you're not telling me?"

Pressing call end, Liz arranged the croissants and the cafetiere filled with rich coffee onto a silver breakfast tray. She remembered her purse sitting on the table in the sitting room and had an idea. She emptied its contents on the kitchen counter. There was one condom left and she placed it on the tray next to the cups and saucers.

She tousled her blonde hair and went to the bedroom where she was hit with the smell of last night's alcohol and the grubby sex that followed. The room was decorated in pastels from the light green walls to the light blue carpet. The window faced out over the cityscape of Gateshead and in the morning, she would often lie and watch the morning shift arrive at Tesco.

Liz leaned seductively against the door frame. "Ed? Are you awake?"

A muffled snore came from her queen sized bed. Stirring at the sound of her voice, he stuck his arse out from under the duvet and fell back asleep.

His breakfast cooled on the tray. Steam rose from the coffee, forming a question mark. Pulling back the covers and revealing his naked form, Liz perched on the side of the bed, the tray resting on her knees. "What the fuck is that?"

She shot to her feet, examining the mattress. "For God's sake," she said.

Pushing the tray onto her bedside table, the picture of her family in Marbella fell to the floor. She left it there as she touched the dampness on her legs. "Wake up, Ed."

When she got no response, she shook him by the shoulder. "Ed, wake up. You pissed the fucking bed."

He rolled onto this back and opened his eyes. "What is it?"

"You've pissed in my bed. Get up. Get in the shower."

She helped him onto unsteady feet. He swayed, holding his head. "Give me a minute, will you?" He stared around the room until his gaze found her semi-naked form stripping the sheets. She guessed where his thoughts were heading.

"Will you please get a shower, Ed? You stink and you're covered in piss."

He held up hands in surrender and padded out of the door in search of the bathroom. Liz threw the pillows to the other side of the room and dragged the duvet to the floor. The under sheets were bunched into a ball and hurled into a corner. At the end of it all, Liz was left with a bed frame and a stained mattress.

Just as she had with the bed, she stripped off her underwear and high heels and put on her pink cashmere pyjamas, the ones she wore most nights. She would need another shower, but for now, they were warm and comforting. The condom was tucked away in a drawer.

Leaving the room, she stopped when she found Ed's phone lying on the floor. It didn't take much to guess his pin number. She entered one, two, three and four and the phone came to life. Not for the first time, she wondered how he'd survived this long. Scrolling through the history, she saw several missed calls, mostly from Monica, but some from Noodles and one from Daniel, who had yet to contact her since his return. It was tempting to listen to the voicemail messages, but Ed would see she'd been in his phone. She took it with her to the sitting room.

Today wasn't about gaining information. It was about implanting it.

Liz was curled up in a chair when Ed walked in, cradling her third glass of wine and staring out over Newcastle. Fog rolled in over the river, swallowing it, hiding it from her view.

She turned to him, catching the disappointment in his face when he saw she was dressed. He was in the clothes he wore when he banged on her apartment door early this morning. Despite it all, she had to admit he looked good. "There's more wine in the fridge if you want any."

He pulled a disgusted face. "I've already drank too much."

"Don't I know it," she said looking away. "You'll be paying for a new mattress."

"Listen, I should be getting back."

"To Monica?"

"Yes to Monica and to the business falling down around my head. It used to be important to you too."

"Your empire was never important to me. We were important to me. My family was important."

"That's why I have to get back." Ed sat next to her, his elbows on his knees as he stared at the floor. "I told you what Noodles said. He has insiders on the force. Scott's been nicked for murder. He's going to jail. We were set up by Fairbanks."

Liz waved him away with one hand. "He's not going to jail. We have people to take care of that sort of stuff. He'll be fine."

"I haven't told you everything."

"Well, I have something to tell you." She took a long drink of her wine. Ed waited, his eyes expectant. Liz leaned forward. Were those tears she could see? She put her glass to one side and hid a shudder of disgust. It would take more than a shower to feel clean after this day. "What if I told you I was going to adopt a child? I miss having children around. I miss being a mother."

"What about Scott and Daniel?"

"What about them? They're grown men and they've grown up to be very different from what I wanted them to be."

"Not this again." Ed got up and paced the room. "They live in a violent world. I had to train them to be hard."

"They're more than hard and you know it." Liz felt old anxieties rising in her throat like bile. She swallowed them down and met Ed's imploring gaze. "You owe me."

He glanced over his shoulder at the bedroom door. "For last night? Is that what it was about?"

"You're weak, Ed. You're forgetting who you are. The man I knew would never have cheated on his wife. This Fairbanks thing has got you messed up, but what's worse is you're forgetting who I am and I'm not asking for your permission."

Ed's iPhone rang from the folds of Liz's pyjamas. She handed it over. His eyes narrowed in suspicion before he answered.

"I'm in the middle of something. What is it?" he asked.

"Ah, Mr Dayton, I have you at last."

He placed his hand over the phone. "It's Noodles."

"Is it about Scott? I want to listen."

Ed put the phone on speaker. "Talk," he said, sitting next to Liz.

"As you know, your son and his men were arrested last night at the scene of the murder of one Marcus Dougherty. The good news is I have managed to arrange for the release of his men."

"But not Scott?"

"Your protectors in the Northumbrian Police force won't allow you to act without impunity anymore. They are withdrawing their help for non-payment of services. You're fortunate I got the result I did."

Liz pressed her fingers against her lips. "They can't lock up my boy."

"Liz? Is that you?" Noodles asked with a titter. "At least I know exactly what you were in the middle of, Mr Dayton. Your ex-wife's shapely thighs."

"Who the fuck do you think you're talking to?" Ed's face was crimson. If he could have reached down the phone and throttled him, Liz suspected they'd be talking to a dead lawyer right now. She relaxed, smiling over the rim of her wine glass. That was the man she needed.

"Mr Dayton, let me tell you what I know. Scott was involved in a one-sided gunfight that ended in the death of Mr Dougherty. Early ballistic reports show the only guns to be fired were those belonging to Scott and his men. However, a digital recording of semi-automatic gunfire was found at the scene. It will be my contention that Scott was responding to the belief he was under attack. They attempted to escape through an exit where-upon the unfortunate victim Mr Dougherty was presented to them as a secondary threat. They opened fire and killed him in self-defence."

Ed glanced at Liz. "So we're in the clear?"

"You are far from being in the clear, Mr Dayton. I have to explain why Scott entered the warehouse in the first place. An unlocked door is not an invitation in the eyes of the law. I have to explain why they were carrying unlicensed firearms and using CR gas smoke bombs. And even if I magically manage to explain all of this away, there are still two bodies to account for."

"Two bodies?"

"A man called Bobcat was also found dead at the scene. I will try to attribute this death to the mysterious second party, which we both know is Fairbanks, but which the rest of the world, including the police, have no proof even exists. What will be shown however are the bullets from Scott's gun and those of his men were the direct cause of Mr Dougherty's death."

"Won't Fairbanks' fingerprints be all over the warehouse?"

"What if they were?" asked Noodles. "DC Spencer confirmed he has no prior record. There'd be no match in the database. Mr Fairbanks has orchestrated a crime so convoluted, the investigating team won't believe it. Much easier for them to take the easy answer, especially when that answer is the legendary Scott Dayton."

"What are you going to do, Ed?" Her ex looked at her blank-faced. Her hand itched to slap him. "You can't let them take my boy away."

"It's a very complicated case, which will stretch on for months," Noodles said. "Only an extremely gifted barrister could argue Scott's defence."

Ed looked down at the phone, his jaw set firm. "What are you saying?"

Noodles gave a sharp intake of breath. "I will be increasing my fees from here on in."

"You back stabbing son of a bitch. I'll have you killed."

"I doubt it," he said, snickering again. "Your son would be jailed for certain without my help and please remember, I know where the bodies are buried. Literally."

"You can't do this."

"I think it only fair. Over the years, I've grown quite tired of your petulance and insults. Everyone can see you're not the leader you were. I warned you again and again. You simply don't have the power you once had."

Ed placed his phone on mute. "What should I do?" he whispered.

Liz saw him crumbling before her. He was white. His eyes were tearing up again. What had happened to him? She needed him to be strong and take care of this Fairbanks nonsense, but he was failing at every pass. Where was the man she once admired?

Placing a tender hand on his, she looked into his watery eyes. "Give him his money. I've lost Daniel. I couldn't bear to lose Scott as well."

"Then what?"

"Forget about what I said earlier. I want you to go home and hug your wife. Talk to her. Ask her how she is. She'll remind you of the strength family brings."

Ed nodded and unmuted the phone. They heard Noodles humming to himself. "Okay, scumbag. Take your extra pound of flesh, but you're over, you hear? Over."

She sensed Noodles smiling. "As are you, Mr Dayton. As are you."

Noodles ended the call before Ed had the chance to hurl more insults. He thrust the phone into his pocket and brooded. Liz knew better than to interject and gave him time to fume. He stood, walked to the front door, only to walk back into the room, his palms turned upward.

"Go home, Ed," she said. "There's nothing more for you to do here."

She didn't wait for him to answer and gave him the cold shoulder. The front door opened and slammed shut. A pressure built behind her eyes and she squeezed them shut. The countdown on her state of the art oven flashed in her mind. Time was running out on her dreams of a new family. Ordinarily, she didn't concern herself with Ed and his businesses as long as her money arrived every month, but Fairbanks was a bigger problem than she'd first surmised. They'd weather the storm. They always did, but in the meantime, she could use the chaos to feather her own nest.

Ed was under her spell again. Monica was as needy as ever. She'd put them together to watch them fall apart and Liz would be there to pick up the pieces.

It was what a good mother did.

CHAPTER TWENTY-THREE

Monica pursed her lips, applying coral lipstick. Her foundation was pale and her eyeliner dark. Her eyes and lips would be the first things people saw. She adjusted her black halter neck top and admired her cleavage. Those would be the second things. With a pair of skinny fit jeans and a spritz of Victoria Beckham's latest perfume, Monica was finally ready.

Downing a shot of Grey Goose vodka, she speed dialled on her phone. "Hey, babe. Just putting the finishing touches to my outfit. Have you called the taxi yet?"

She checked through her purse while she waited for an answer. It contained over two hundred pounds, her house keys and a condom.

"Monica? Is that you?" Sophie had been her closest friend at school. She'd been a small, mousey haired girl when they were kids, but judging by her profile on Facebook, she'd grown into a beautiful and determined looking woman. Monica had found her a few weeks ago and they'd been catching up via the message service. When Sophie passed on her phone number, Monica couldn't resist giving her a call.

"Of course, it's me. Are you all set for a night on the town?"

"I'm so sorry. I completely forgot."

She sat on the edge of the bed and cradled the phone to her ear. "But you're still coming out, aren't you? You said it would be nice to catch up properly."

"I know, I know, but we didn't really firm anything up and Jeremy's come down with a cold. With Ian working away, I –"

"Is Jeremy your kid?"

There was a pause from Sophie. "Yes. I told you that."

"And your husband can't look after him? Can you get a babysitter?"

"I'm sorry, Monica."

She reached for the half empty bottle of vodka and sipped from the neck. "My husband works away a lot too."

"I thought you said his businesses were based in Newcastle."

Ed hadn't called back. He wasn't an attentive husband, but he had been markedly distant these past few weeks. Everyone had. There was an oppressive atmosphere at Five Oaks. Everyone seemed scared, as if her house was home to a ghoul that wandered the rooms after dark. It weighed upon her and she was desperate to lighten the load.

"Look, don't worry about it," Monica said.

"We'll do it another night. I promise."

"No, I mean, I can come to your house. We can have a girly night in. Talk about boys, like the old days."

"No," Sophie said. "No, I don't think so."

"It'll be fun. I have money for pizza or a Chinese if you prefer. I'll bring the booze."

"Sounds like you've had enough already."

"Fuck you then," she said as she threw the phone to the other side of the room. If Sophie wasn't available, Monica would throw a party of her own.

Taking the vodka, Monica wandered through the rooms of Five Oaks. The only sound came from her footsteps and the occasional clatter as she fell against the walls. She looked behind doors and around corners. The house was bereft.

She found herself at the gym and stood in the doorway. There were two treadmills, two exercise bikes and two cross-trainers.

Monica had asked Ed to build it so they could train and keep in shape together. They'd once had sex here, watching their reflection in a wall made entirely of mirrors. Now there was her and a red eyed image reflected back to her a dozen times over. It was the most company she'd had in weeks.

Ed had been a surprise. Their love affair was passionate and filled with grand gestures; impromptu trips to the Seychelles in private jets, Michelin starred restaurants. They had even sat next to a member of the royal family at Ascot to watch the Coronation Stakes. Through it all, she knew such passion couldn't last. Monica thought their relationship would fizzle out as quickly as it ignited. She had been right, but what made it more painful, was the daring hope she could be wrong.

Ed apologised profusely the first time he forgot an anniversary. He seemed less concerned the second time. It was no excuse for taking another lover, she thought, but it was a damn good reason.

She turned her back on her reflection and stumbled along the corridor to their bedroom. Catching her foot, she tripped and landed hard. Her first thought was for the vodka. The bottle slipped from her grasp, rolling along the floor. The clear liquid leaked from the open top, soaking into the carpet she'd chosen because it was the most expensive in the shop. She watched the last drops eke away and climbed precariously to her feet, holding onto the wall for balance.

What the hell was she doing? She was pregnant and she was drinking. A fall like that could have damaged its skull or something. She might turn it into a retard. Then Ed really would be pissed. Monica stifled a giggle, as if there was someone around to read her thoughts. If he didn't want kids, he definitely wouldn't want one with L-plates.

Easing along the corridor, she remembered a bottle of wine she'd hidden under her bed and picked up her pace.

Whatever happened, she'd have to tell him. The old bitch Liz was right. Not about the lovers she'd taken, but about the baby; the baby that was absolutely his and not anyone else's. She'd grown surer of it as the night drew on.

***

Ed sat in his idling BMW as the gates to Five Oaks closed behind him. He couldn't shake the notion his house had been corrupted. Whether it was by Fairbanks' creeping influence or the betrayal of men he once trusted, Five Oaks didn't feel like home, but his fear had faded enough to follow Liz's advice. He'd talk to Monica and maybe she could help.

Waiting by the front door was another BMW. It was burgundy with rust on its wheel arches and dints in the bonnet. Ed eased his seventy-five thousand pound car into his usual parking space and got out. Gravel crunched under his feet, but it wasn't loud enough to wake the rust bucket's sleeping occupant.

He wrapped his knuckles on the window.

Bronson jumped, blinking the tiredness from his eyes. "Just catching forty winks, boss. Sorry."

"How long have you been here?"

"Got my release papers half an hour ago. I was up half the night talking to some DI Dick. Credit where credit's due. They might be on shit pay, but when it comes to getting a confession, they put the hours in."

Ed picked a fleck of paint off the roof of Bronson's car. "This your motor?"

"My Ferrari's in the garage." Bronson smiled and his cheek twitched. Ed doubted he'd even sat in a Ferrari, much less owned one.

He stared around the empty grounds. There were no lights, no guards, only long shadows cast by the moon. An urban fox cried out from the darkness. "Where is everyone else?"

Bronson shook his head. "Sorry, boss. I couldn't persuade anyone to come with me. They were all pretty tired. I think they just went home."

"But they'll be here tomorrow?"

Bronson refused to meet his eye. Ed was the sinking ship and they were the rats. Noodles' prophesy was coming true. He was being taken apart, bit by bit and only the loyal would remain.

He tapped the roof of Bronson's car. "Why don't you take off for the night, mate?"

"No. I better stay. Just in case."

"Just in case, my arse. The minute I step inside, you'll be asleep again. Fairbanks could write on your face with permanent marker and you wouldn't wake up."

"Are you sure? Will you be okay here on your own? I'll be back first thing in the morning."

"Do you think I'm some sort of pansy?" Ed said, smiling. He handed over the ignition fob to his BMW. "Take my car. You'll be lucky if this heap of shit makes it to the end of the driveway."

The twitch in Bronson's cheek stopped momentarily. "Your car?"

"It's yours, mate and it's long overdue," he said, walking to the front door. "Now fuck off. That's an order."

It was cold inside Five Oaks, as if the heating had been switched off. He climbed the inner staircase, hoping to find Monica in their bedroom. Making time for her seemed like such a small thing considering everything else. Small, but important. Perhaps that's why Liz was so insistent he spoke with her. This could be the end of Ed Dayton, but at least he'd have his wife by his side.

After Liz left, meeting Monica was a rebirth of sorts. It lent new energy to the Dayton empire. He courted influential contacts among the rich and powerful. He recruited young blood to harvest the potential of the internet. And he encouraged his two boys in criminal enterprises that saw them flourish as men.

Monica fuelled his success and he followed the power blindly, putting greater distance between them. She was the cause of her own downfall without sharing any of the blame. He had left her behind and it was time to make amends.

With his hand on the bedroom door handle, Ed paused. He heard Monica on the other side, humming a tune he remembered from his childhood. It was a nursery rhyme, conjuring a memory of his mother that made him uncomfortable, though he couldn't say why. Gritting his teeth, he entered, but Monica didn't turn to greet him as he expected she would. She was absorbed by her image in the mirror, a cushion tucked under her top.

"What the hell are you doing?"

Drunk and startled, Monica span at the sound of Ed's voice. Teetering on high heel shoes, she fell to the ground with a giggle.

"Baby, you're back. I knew you'd come back."

He pulled her upright, turning his face away from the smell of the alcohol on her breath. He was still queasy from earlier in the day.

The cushion slipped from under her top. Ed watched it roll under the bed. "What are you doing?" he asked.

"Isn't it wonderful?"

Ed's jaw tightened. "Let me get you some water," he said.

She threw her arms around him, pressing wet kisses on his cheek. "I don't want any water. I want you."

Peeling Monica's grip from his neck, he sat her down on the bed. She flopped to her side and closed her eyes. Ed bit back a sigh. He wanted to talk. He wanted to mend the gulf between them, but Monica was in no fit state to understand. It would have to wait.

He picked the cushion from the floor and felt Monica's warmth on the fabric. Ed went to place it under his wife's head and stopped.

"Wait a minute," he said. "What do you mean, 'Isn't it wonderful?'"

Monica mumbled something. He shook her shoulder, rousing her before she slipped into a drunken sleep. "Monica? What do you mean?"

Slowly, she opened her eyes and looked surprised to see him there.

"You're back," she whispered.

Whatever patience Ed possessed, it was spent. "Monica, are you fucking pregnant?"

The question woke her with a start. Ed saw she was trying to remember if she'd let anything slip, but it was too late and he felt hot, stinging tears rolling down his cheeks. He hated the fact he was crying, but he hated the woman before him even more.

He raised his hand and slapped her across the face. "How could you do this to me?"

"I didn't do anything, Eddie. I promise."

"Don't you dare lie to me."

Ed grabbed her slim ankle and dragged her off the bed like a rag doll. He pulled her around the room, searching for something to beat her with. Monica cried and kicked, but she couldn't free herself from his grasp. At last, he found a tall porcelain lamp and tore it from the wall.

"Eddie, please. Don't. Why are you doing this?"

The lamp swung toward her and Monica closed her eyes against the blow.

CHAPTER TWENTY-FOUR

"**Y**ou're not going to say anything to anyone, are you?" Daniel asked.

The postman stood in his underwear, shivering in the cold air. "No, sir."

They were in an industrial estate by Newcastle Airport. Planes destined to cities all over the world flew overhead, their engines thundering, their taillights tracing arcs in the night sky. The estate was abandoned and the only witnesses to Daniel's crime were hundreds of feet in the air.

"And what else did I tell you?" he asked, getting back into his van.

The postman cleared his throat. "Neighbourhood watch are a bunch of twats."

By the time Daniel arrived at Five Oaks, his other prisoner had regained consciousness. He opened the door and Reaver stared at him, his eyes glazed and his cuts scabbing over. Daniel didn't know if he was responsible for chopping Mosely to pieces. There'd be no point in asking him without the proper tools and those were inside. He wasn't taking chances either way.

He found a rope he used for climbing trees and tied it tightly around Reaver's neck, leading him out of his van like a dog. They crunched their way along the driveway.

But Daniel couldn't resist testing himself one last time.

"Did you kill Mosely?" he asked, turning to him.

Reaver looked at him blankly. "No."

"I can't tell if you're lying to me or not."

"Don't worry about it."

Reaver looked bored. This isn't the first time he's heard this, Daniel thought. "So you're a liar, then? That's your thing?"

"It's the only thing I was ever good at. Fairbanks says it's my gift."

"But I can always tell if someone is lying. That's my gift."

They heard a scream from the house and they looked to an upstairs window. Reflections merged with shadows and obscured the view. It wasn't clear, but it looked like two people grappling.

Daniel tugged on Reaver's rope and they jogged through the doors of the house. There was no-one around. Raised voices, louder this time, came from his father's bedroom. Daniel quickly tethered Reaver, his hands still bound behind his back, to the bottom of the staircase.

"When I'm done with this," Daniel said," I'm coming back for you and I will get the truth."

Reaver shrugged and Daniel took the stairs two at a time. Following the noise, he threw the bedroom door wide open.

Monica was sprawled on the floor, her face red and blotchy, but there was no blood as far as he could tell. Her top was pulled up to her neck, exposing her stomach and a red bra. His father stood over her, pointing angrily. Pieces of a smashed porcelain were scattered across the room and their marital bed was broken in two.

Monica saw him from the corner of her eye. Scrambling on her hands and knees, she hid behind Daniel's legs, peering through them like bars of a cage. "He's going to kill me. He's going to do it. He told me."

His father shadowed her. "You know I can't kill you. I'm not a monster, but I can hurt you. Hurt you badly."

The tendons in his father's neck stretched taught, like piano wire wound too tightly. Froth gathered at the corners of his mouth and his eyes blazed at Daniel. "And what are you going to do about it, eh? She's a whore. I'm going to drop the bitch in the Tyne."

Daniel tried to stay calm, but his father was manic. He had seen him like this once before, on the day he defied the last request his father made of him. The image had returned to him night after night as he lay in bed at his new home in Scotland. No matter how far he ran, the picture of his father's insanity followed.

Ed's wide eyes searched to the floor, resting on a shard on porcelain. He swooped upon it and waved it toward Monica. "I'll cut it out of you. I'll cut the little bastard out."

"He's gone crazy," Monica said, scuttling backward.

Ed lunged at her. Daniel swatted his father with the back of his hand, spinning him on the spot. They wrestled and he grabbed his father's wrist. Daniel was stronger, but his father was a powerful man and his anger made him feral. Blood wept from Ed's hand where he gripped the porcelain too tightly.

Daniel bore down and with a quick twist, broke the bones in his father's wrist. Ed cried out, dropping his shard. He withdrew a couple of steps, saliva hanging from bloodless lips, nursing a hand that flapped uselessly. "You're against me too. You're just like her. You betrayed me. I loved you both and you turned on me like vipers."

Daniel turned to Monica for some sort of answer. He'd disobeyed his father and to a man like him, there was no greater offense, but he couldn't imagine what Monica might have done. And then he remembered. Scott and Monica by the lake. The embrace. The hurried escape. He bit the inside of his cheek. No wonder his father was hysterical, he thought.

She half lay, half sat on the floor, her large eyes streaked black with running mascara. "I thought it would be okay. It's just another baby. It's a brother or sister for Scott and Daniel."

"She's pregnant and it's not mine," Ed shouted at her.

"It is. It is, Eddie. It's yours. I would never betray you. I love you."

"You're a lying bitch." His father dropped his broken wrist and reached out with his good hand, clasping and unclasping his fingers as if he already had her by the throat.

Daniel pushed him away. "How do you know it's not yours?"

Ed smiled. It was cruel and knowing. "You ask her."

"Don't do this to me, Eddie."

"Ask her, Daniel. You'll see I'm right. If I'm wrong," he said, shrugging, "well, we'll patch things up and go about our days as if this never happened. But if I'm right, then maybe it's time to visit the room downstairs."

It was impossible for Daniel to imagine his brother and step-mother together like that. True he'd seen them by the lake, but he'd convinced himself it was a mistake, an honest misunder-standing. Turning around meant learning something he couldn't unlearn. His family was fucked up enough as it was.

"You won't do it, will you?" Ed asked. "You won't look because you know she's lying."

"I don't know anything."

"That's true," his father said, staggering toward him, "but we both know she betrayed me."

"The question is how do you know?"

His father stood in front of Daniel, drawing himself to his full height, which was eight inches smaller than his son. He was diminished in Daniel's eyes. He had commanded armies. He had destroyed enemies, but for all his talk of loyalty, he had betrayed his duty as a father a hundred times over. Looking at him now, it was as if all his sins had come home to roost in a single night.

"You hate me, don't you?" Ed asked. "You hate your own father. Well that's not something you need to worry about any-more. I can't believe I ever called you my son."

With a bowed head, his father wept. Tears ran down his cheeks and dripped off his chin. It was undignified, but Daniel hid his embarrassment. It was the least he could do for a man who had lost so much.

Behind him, Monica stood. He sensed her approaching and turned to warn her to stay where she was. He caught her eye and in an instant, he saw it all, confirming his father's fears. Shame. Guilt. Remorse. It was all there. She couldn't be as sure as Ed appeared to be, but she had her suspicions. Her doubt was evidence enough for Daniel. He looked away and she did too.

Ed started laughing. He had seen the moment between them. He wiped his face clean of tears and replaced them with a sneer. "I'm finished with both of you. Everywhere I turn, people are sharpening their knives, but it was the two of you who really stabbed me in the back. You broke my fucking heart."

Supporting his broken wrist, he shuffled to the door, stopping to take a final look at his wife. "I'm sterile. I've never been able to have kids. That's how I knew it wasn't mine."

Ed looked over his shoulder at Daniel.

"You and your brother are adopted mongrels from a dirty back street clinic. There's nothing of me in you."

Before anyone could stop him, Ed was out of the door. Daniel and Monica stared at each other in amazement when they heard a gunshot from the hallway.

CHAPTER TWENTY-FIVE

Daniel was out first and found his father leaning over the railing looking into the hallway below. He could see Reaver sitting awkwardly on the stairs. His hands were still bound, but the rope around his neck had been loosened. A young man ascended the stairs, a rifle pressed into his shoulder and the sights aimed at Daniel. He wore a Tweed jacket, dark moleskin trousers and riding boots, as if he had abandoned a deer hunt to stalk humans instead. His bulbous eyes never left Daniel's face.

Monica rushed out of the bedroom, but jolted to a halt when she saw the man with the rifle. She pressed into Daniel's side while Ed hung onto the railing for support.

"You shouldn't have brought Mr Reaver here. I'm not keen on hatching escape plans."

Daniel took a step forward. He'd found Fairbanks at last. "I guess we've under-estimated you again. How did you know he was here?"

"I'm guessing you're Daniel? The prodigal son?"

Daniel didn't know what prodigal meant and fixed him with a cold stare rather than answer. Fairbanks smiled in response.

"GPS," he said. "My men are tagged like animals. I don't like them going astray."

"What do you want?" Ed asked. His skin was grey and his legs were shaking.

"Ed, I want you to stay where you are. I'll explain what I'm doing to you, but you're in no fit state to move."

Daniel followed Fairbanks' gaze to where his father – his adoptive father – struggled to stay on his feet, pitching from side to side. He saw a patch of blood flowering in his father's stomach where the gunshot they'd heard had hit its target. Ed was upright, but it was only pride that kept him there.

There hadn't been time to process what Ed had told him. He was adopted. He was a mongrel. He didn't belong. Daniel shut the thought process down before it gained momentum. This was another life or death situation. There could be no distractions. If they lived through this, then he'd figure out what the fuck was going on afterward.

"It takes a long time to die from a stomach wound, but I won't keep you," Fairbanks said. "Daniel can call for an ambulance for you as soon as I leave."

Daniel cast his eyes away from his father, a gesture that Fairbanks noticed immediately. "You will call for an ambulance, won't you, Daniel? I need your father alive. For a little longer, anyway."

"Tell us why you're here and then fuck off," Daniel said.

Ed slipped to the floor. He groaned through clenched teeth before using his good hand to pull himself back to his feet. He swayed unsteadily, like he was standing on the deck of a sinking ship. "Answer my son," he said.

"I'm not your son, Ed."

Fairbanks watched them both for a long while. The great hall of Five Oaks was silent, except for Ed's laboured breathing. Finally, Fairbanks shrugged. "It's simple really. I want ten million pounds. As head of the Daytons, you are the only one who can issue that to me."

"You don't want to take over?" Ed asked.

Fairbanks blinked repeatedly. "I have a handful of men at my disposal. You have hundreds. Why would you even think that?"

"Because men like Ed believe everyone wants what he has," Daniel said. "It never occurred to him that this was nothing more than a hostage demand."

"And it occurred to you?"

Daniel shook his head. "I didn't know what you were up to. I just knew you weren't after the throne. Had he listened to your earlier demands, I imagine you would have taken the money and ran."

Fairbanks lowered his rifle an inch. "There would have been no need for all this unpleasantness."

"But he ignored you so you tightened the screws. It's a classic interrogation technique. You don't go in hard and then let your subject relax."

"It's my scorched earth policy. Give them nowhere to run."

Fairbanks was relaxing. He was enjoying himself. Daniel could see it in his eyes. Good, he thought. It wasn't a victory, but he only needed him to shelve his defences for a second. Then he could show the little freak what scorched earth really was.

Fairbanks dropped his rifle lower and climbed a step higher. "You're more intelligent than you're given credit for. I gather you don't work for the family firm, do you? I'm my own boss these days and now that Dougherty has been fired, so to speak, there's an opening on my team."

"He'll never work for you. He's a Dayton," Ed said.

Daniel tried to hide his anger. Even though Ed had cast him aside in the cruellest of ways, the greed of the man wouldn't relinquish its hold. No distractions, he reminded himself. He breathed deeply and smiled. "Actually, all ties to the Dayton family have just been severed. I might take you up on your offer after all."

He shuffled forward, closing down the distance between them. Fairbanks whipped the rifle butt into his shoulder and aimed at Monica. As she screamed, Daniel ran back to her side and leapt in front of her, his bulk easily hiding her from the bullet destined to kill her and her baby.

"Interesting," Fairbanks said, talking to Ed, but looking at Daniel. "No matter what your son says, no matter what's going on between you, you're correct, Ed. This man is a Dayton through and through."

"I decide my own destiny. Not you or him," Daniel said, jabbing his finger at his father.

"He thought by lowering my rifle, I was giving him a chance to grab me, but it was a test. You see, I'm still not sure about him. If he'd been serious about joining me and hating you, he would have let me shoot your wife. He's quite homicidal in that regard, but there is something keeping him here, possibly something he doesn't quite understand himself."

"Leave them alone," Ed said. His voice was weak, sounding like the slurred words of a drunk. "It's me you need. Not them. Let them be."

All three of them turned their eyes to Ed. He was standing on the wrong side of the wooden railing, his good hand holding him firm. Below was a deadly drop and while his feet were chocked on the floor, his legs were buckling. He was gasping for breath.

"Eddie, don't." Monica tried to rush to his aid, but Daniel wrapped an unyielding arm around her.

"Don't be a fool," Fairbanks said.

"Let them go. I'm the only one who can get you your money. You don't need them."

Fairbanks bit his lip. It was the first time Daniel had seen him express a genuine emotion. Stepping to one side, he pointed down the stairs.

"You two, get out."

Daniel led Monica down the staircase. He paused briefly when he came to Reaver sitting in a heap on a stair. "Worried your master is going to punish you for going astray?"

Reaver didn't meet his gaze. "No."

"I said, get out," Fairbanks shouted and Daniel led Monica to the door. She struggled in his grasp, digging her heels into the floor like a child. "We can't go, Daniel. Not like this."

She wouldn't leave and he wouldn't leave without her, but there was something else; something in what Fairbanks had said earlier. Deep down in a part of him he didn't understand, something was preventing him from abandoning his father. The door out of Five Oaks was open, but he knew he had to stay.

Fairbanks rubbed his fingers along the creases in his forehead. "Are you satisfied, Ed?"

"I'm pretty fucking far from satisfied."

Fairbanks sidled closer, taking a few cautious steps toward Ed, preparing to pull him back over the railing. "Look at it this way. In five minutes, this will all be over. You transfer the funds to my designated account and I'm gone. What's ten million pounds to you? I bet you could recoup that within six months."

"You think? Without my two sons? Without a wife or a family to support me?"

"At least, you'll be alive enough to try. I'll call an ambulance for you on the way to my next job."

"Don't do me any favours."

"At least I'd make the call. I don't think Daniel will bother."

"Me neither," Ed said, catching Daniel's eye as he lingered in the hallway. Daniel was the first to look away. "You brought me so low, Fairbanks. I was arrogant enough to think that it was impossible. Of all the sins I've committed, it's that one that's brought me here."

"I think you have a right to be arrogant," Fairbanks said. "Look at everything you've done."

Daniel opened one of the front doors, urging Monica through it, sensing his father was about to make a move. She tried to skirt by him and he shoved her in the chest. She staggered backward over the threshold. He swung the door shut and locked it to the sounds of her fists beating against the other side.

"If I had my time again, I might make other choices," Ed said.

"I'm here to give you that time." Fairbanks laid down his rifle and moved forward a step, fidgeting with his earring.

Glancing over his shoulder, Ed looked to the ground below and then to Daniel. He shrugged his shoulders and Daniel saw something wash out of him, as if he suddenly realised his life had taken the wrong course.

Ed's eyes screwed into pinpricks and he looked at Fairbanks. "I'll never give you that money. There'll be no cheques, no transfers. You'll never get a penny off me. Not as long as there are clouds in the sky."

Daniel saw what he was about to do and pounded up the stairs. His father watched him run. "I shouldn't have asked you to do it, son. I'm sorry."

Reaching out, Fairbanks' fingertips brushed Ed's as he let go. He tumbled through the air, arms across his chest, his clothes whipping by his side. Daniel stood on the stairs and watched him sail by.

It was over in a heartbeat. From the dive to the crack of his bones on flooring that had cost forty-seven pounds per square metre. His head splintered loudly and his torso split open with the impact, spilling his bloody innards in a graceless pool spreading outwards in a red ring.

Daniel blinked twice. The air was still. His father was dead and for a moment, he had forgotten how to breathe. Finally, he gasped, pressing his hand to the side of his face. He wanted to look around the hall, check if anything else in his world had changed, but he couldn't tear his eyes from the twitching corpse below.

The creak of the railing woke him and he saw Fairbanks staring at what remained of his father. Stunned into paralysis, he barely noticed Daniel bounding up the stairs until it was too late. Turning to face him, Fairbanks ducked quickly under his arm. He scooped up his rifle and took off down the corridor with Daniel in pursuit.

The door of a room slammed shut. Daniel reached it seconds later and found it was his old bedroom. He hadn't been inside for years. His father had bought him a flat not long after Eisha was born. To aid the bonding process between father and child, he'd said at the time. Daniel saw a red ring of blood in his mind's eye and shook his head clear of the image.

"You can't get out, Fairbanks," he said through the door, "and you can't climb down from my window. Believe me, I've tried."

Two shots erupted, bursting through the door and spraying Daniel in splinters of wood. Fairbanks was trapped inside, he thought, but he was trapped outside. He could wait him out, but Daniel wanted to be the first to make Fairbanks bleed. The sole purpose of his return to Newcastle was revenge. Behind the door was the man who hurt his daughter, hounded his father to his death and held his family to ransom.

Daniel wouldn't be denied and ran back down the staircase. Reaver was struggling against his restraints. Daniel untied the knot at the post and punched him in the stomach, knocking any further fight out of him. He dragged up the stairs by the rope around his neck.

Returning to his bedroom door, Daniel clamped a hand over Reaver's mouth. "I'm going to count to three, Fairbanks and then I'm coming in."

Daniel didn't count. He didn't even think. He kicked open the door and barrelled inside using Reaver as a shield. Fairbanks had upended his bed, crouching behind it for protection, his rifle pointed at the door. Reaver tried to twist free as a shot rang out.

He suddenly felt heavy in Daniel's arms. Fairbanks fired again, the bullet thudding into Reaver so hard Daniel was forced to brace against the impact. Reaver grunted and spluttered blood. Daniel didn't wait for a third shot. He threw Reaver's limp body at the bed, knocking Fairbanks off balance. Leaping over a tangle of bed sheets, Daniel wrenched the rifle from Fairbanks' hands and heaved him to his feet.

Holding him by the lapels of his ridiculous Tweed jacket, Daniel expected to feel a grim satisfaction. Instead, he was unnerved. The man before him was smart enough to know he was about to be tortured to death, but there wasn't a glimpse of fear in him. His glassy, bulbous eyes. The pink tinge to his cheeks. The half-smile on his lips. Fairbanks was amused and Daniel didn't know why.

"I'm going to take a wild guess," Fairbanks said. "You're an orphan too."

CHAPTER TWENTY-SIX

Daniel had never thought about this room in all the time he'd been away. Now that he was back, he saw it had been left as a shrine. Nothing had changed. The carpet was still ocean blue, though patches had faded in the sun, and the walls were still cream. Even the view from the window was familiar. As a child, he would often while away the hours staring at the grey lake and its island of evergreen shrubs. Scott had told him there were bodies buried out there and Daniel believed him. He had put two there himself.

The posters he'd chosen as a child remained pinned to the wall. Oasis, the Killers and Eminem were mounted on his friend's recommendations, but there was no CD player or iPod. Daniel didn't like music.

He pulled a chair into the centre of the room from the desk where he once sat struggling with his homework. Fairbanks sat down, adjusting his trousers to make himself more comfortable. Taking the rope from a motionless Reaver, Daniel tied his arms over the back.

"It was clever of you to use him as a shield," Fairbanks said. "Do you think I killed him?"

The body lay face down on the bed, blood soaking into the same blankets Daniel had gripped as he tried to sleep at night. If he wasn't dead, he thought, he soon would be.

"Reaver was an orphan like you," Fairbanks said. "We all were. Abandoned by our families. Left to roam the streets. It was dangerous out there, I can tell you, but being adopted by the Daytons? I bet they messed you up. You'd have been better off with us."

Daniel wanted to prolong Fairbanks' pain without killing him. He dismissed the idea of taking him down to the room in the cellar. There were too many cool toys and he didn't want to get carried away.

"How did you know I was adopted?"

"Just the things you were saying. Plus you have the look of a man seeking a home. You only ever see it in people without a family."

Daniel tested his knots. Happy that they were tight, he went to his desk looking for something he was sure would still be there. Opening the top drawer, he found a pen with multi-coloured nibs and a collection of erasers smelling vaguely of fruit. There was a maths textbook and a photocopied hand-out from a chemistry lesson he'd never attended. He brushed them all aside and found his Swiss Army knife, the one he carried with him every day of his school life.

"I wonder what would have happened if I'd been adopted," Fairbanks said. "Maybe I would have taken a truer path. Perhaps I'd have been a librarian. I've always liked books."

Extending the blade on his knife, he wiped it clean on his shirt. "I'm not much of a reader."

"My uncle read a lot. He was the one who taught me to fish. Every Saturday afternoon while my father drank himself insensible watching football, he'd take me to the local river and we'd fish for chub or bream." Fairbanks stared out of the window and looked at the lake. "I think that's the happiest I've ever been."

The glass in Fairbanks' earring caught the light and drew Daniel toward it. He pressed the tip of his knife into his ear and

Fairbanks stiffened. "If you cut off my ear, can I ask you to place it in the top pocket of my jacket afterward please? That earring is very precious to me."

"Relax," Daniel said, moving behind him. "We're not doing that today."

The material of Fairbank's jacket was heavy and it took time to cut through it. He cursed himself for not removing it first. Taking the knife, he slowly sliced through the sleeves so they hung in tatters from his arms. Then he started on the shirt.

"Dougherty told me about the earring. You must have really loved that dog."

"Dogs," Fairbanks said.

He paused in the middle of the second sleeve. "What?"

"When I first met Dougherty, he tried to drown me in a bag with a Jack Russell. The poor thing was terrified, but it was biting and scratching me. I had no choice but to strangle it. I didn't want to. I love dogs."

"You made it into an earring?"

Laughing, Fairbanks shook his head. "The process involves turning the ashes into a glass-like substance. It's expensive. I was ten at the time. I didn't have the money. When I was a little older, I cut off a Labrador's head and used that instead. This is a reminder."

Daniel removed the last of the material around Fairbanks' arms, exposing his bony elbows. "Jesus, and they say I'm sick."

"So how do you feel knowing you're not the man they said you were? Somewhat adrift, I shouldn't wonder. Maybe relieved. It's like having your identity wiped clean, isn't it? How could you possibly know who you are when it's all been a lie?"

"Be quiet," Daniel said.

The knots were tight. The elbows were secure against the chair and wouldn't move, even when Fairbanks bucked and writhed against the pain. He tried to focus. Monica must have raised the alarm by now. His father's men, what remained of them, could charge into Five Oaks at any time. He didn't want that. He needed this time with Fairbanks. Finish it and avenge your daughter, his heart told him. It's the only way to exorcise the demons threatening to swallow you whole.

Daniel stood in front of Fairbanks, his arms folded over his thick chest.

"Are we starting?" Fairbanks asked.

The vein in Fairbanks' neck pulsed rapidly, but otherwise he appeared relaxed. He fixed his eyes on Daniel and didn't blink.

"I always tell my men to give up all they know when they're in situations like this. It would come out eventually. At least, they might save themselves some pain. I never tell them everything anyway so I'm quite safe, but it's different with me. I have all the answers. I'd still like to save myself some pain, though."

The tool Daniel needed was in the utility room, not in the wine cellar. His father had various tools for various jobs around the house. He never used them, of course. He paid someone to do the maintenance work at Five Oaks, but occasionally he'd use some of them for situations like this.

"What I'm saying, Daniel, is that you can ask me what you want. To be honest, I don't know what I'm going to do next. Your father was the key to getting my money. Killing himself was the best way to protect it. It was quite a clever, noble thing to do. Your father –"

Fairbanks stopped himself. His eyes went blank and he cocked his head to one side. "Should I keep calling him your father? Because he wasn't, was he? Should I call him Ed?"

The blood crept up Daniel's neck and into his jaw muscles. If he got angry, it would be over too soon. He calmed himself and managed a smile. "I'm going to ask you a question, then I'm going to torture you, then I'm going to ask you again."

"What if I answer you the first time?"

Daniel shook his head.

"I see. This isn't just about getting me to talk, is it? So why are you doing it? To avenge a man who wasn't your father? Someone you clearly hated? I don't understand."

A sigh escaped Fairbanks' lips. It wasn't one of fear, Daniel realised, but of exasperation. He watched as Fairbanks searched inwardly for an answer. He wasn't afraid of the oncoming pain. He was frustrated because he didn't know why it was being inflicted.

"Are you venting your anger?" Fairbanks asked. "I think so, but it's more than that. The guilt of being an orphan? The pain of being rejected?"

Daniel double checked his bindings and left, hurrying down the stairs. He paused briefly to look at the ruination of his father before continuing to the utility room. Searching the shelves, he pulled away boxes and old jars filled with nails. They bounced and broke on the floor. He found screwdrivers, pick handles and a brand new claw hammer with the price tag still attached. They fell away until the refuse on the floor was almost a foot deep. And then he found what he was looking for and held it up to the light.

A four inch, two hundred and forty Watt belt sander.

He ran his fingers over the sand paper. It was new and rough. Sanding off the skin on Fairbanks' elbows would cause a lot of blood spray and he regretted not having a change of clothes. Once he'd got down to bone, he'd travel the sander over the fleshy parts of his arm to his shoulder blades. The room would be a right off, but it needed redecorating anyhow.

Whistling as he climbed the stairs, he wondered what colour he'd get when he mixed the blue of his old carpet with the red of Fairbanks' blood. It would be like being back at school, he thought with a smile.

But standing in the doorway of his bedroom, the smile dropped from his face. The sander slipped from his fingers. "What the fuck?"

The room was empty. Fairbanks was gone and so was Reaver. The rope used to hold Fairbanks was in a neat coil on the floor, like a resting snake. The bed was back in its rightful place, the sheets folded neatly on top. The chair was pushed back under the desk. There was no avoiding the blood stains, but they were minimal in comparison to what he had planned. He turned on the spot over and over, expecting them to magically appear. When they didn't, he ran a hand through his hair, pulling at it in anger until a clump came away in his fingers. The pain focused his attention and he scanned the room for clues.

A blood trail in the carpet led out of the room. Just as Reaver had tricked him over Mosely's whereabouts, he had fooled Daniel into thinking he was dead, but Fairbanks had known. He fired the shot, after all. No wonder he had been so calm. A superficial wounding, painful, but not life threatening and Reaver the liar instinctively knew to play along. They waited for Daniel's stupidity to lend them their means of escape.

He ran to the window and saw them climbing into his van. Fairbanks helped an injured Reaver into the passenger seat and jogged to the driver's door, the sleeves of his shirt and jacket in ribbons. He looked up to the window, his eyebrows arching in surprise when he saw Daniel staring down at him. He waved and got into the van.

Daniel bolted from the room, almost tumbling down the stairs in his haste. Flinging the front doors open, he was in time to see his van speeding down the driveway. He shielded his face with an arm as gravel sprayed like buckshot from the back tyres.

His iPhone trilled. It was a phone number he didn't recognise and Daniel answered distractedly.

"What was the question?"

His heart beat quickly. "Fairbanks?"

"Don't ask me how I got your number. Somethings I won't share, but I was being honest when I told you I'd answer your questions."

"How did you escape?"

"I shot Reaver in the shoulder. Same place, both times. Easy enough to recover from with medical attention. He freed me when you left the room. Not bad for a dead man."

Daniel looked over his father's man-made lake. Bodies under the surface. Bodies on the island. What had been his intentions in building something like that? To create a beauty spot or a graveyard?

"You beat us again," he said.

"'Us?' Are you an 'us'? Take it from a fellow orphan, Daniel. You need to decide if you're a Dayton or someone else. You can't be both. It'll rip you apart."

"Why are you calling?" he asked, kicking gravel at a shitty, burgundy BMW.

"Firstly, I'll be firebombing your van when I'm done, but I also want to know what your question was. When you stood in front of me with your arms crossed? What was your question?"

Daniel watched a fox appear from the laurel bush he had hidden under as a boy. It was a tatty thing with matted hair, but with green eyes constantly on alert for danger and a nose twitching for the scent of prey. It was gathering information, deciding what it needed to survive. The fox faced him, lifting its nose in the air. They watched each other through the darkness of the night before it took a dump on the driveway and trotted out of sight.

"I'm not going to feed you information you can turn against me, Fairbanks," he said.

The voice on the other side of the line chuckled. "You're beginning to understand who I am. Good for you."

"I'll say this. There are no questions. I have nothing for you," Daniel said. "You put my daughter in a coma. I want to hurt you for it."

He heard whispering, but couldn't make out the words.

"Was your question – why did I put your daughter in a coma?"

Daniel breathed slowly and stayed silent.

"If you don't have a question for me then let me ask you one," Fairbanks said. "You were out of the picture, right? Living God knows where, doing God knows what, but very definitely not working for your father."

The gravel crunched loudly as Daniel paced along the driveway, waiting for Fairbanks to continue.

"My question is this – why would I want you back?"

"Because you ..." Daniel stopped walking and looked down at his boots. There were scuff marks down one side and blood spatter from somewhere else. They were the boots of another man. Not his. Not the man he had intended to become.

Fairbanks laughed. "Who would benefit from your return? Me or your adopted family?"

Fairbanks cut the connection and Daniel stared open mouthed at his phone. He had been moving in the wrong direction, using those boots to stomp through his opposition. Fairbanks was right. Why would he want Daniel hunting him? He had assumed Fairbanks was behind his daughter's attack only because it seemed obvious, but nothing was that clear. What if his father had been lying? What if it been him all along? He had almost admitted as much when Daniel confronted him in his office. Putting Eisha in a coma wasn't Fairbanks' style, but there could be no greater motivation for Daniel if he was needed as a weapon.

He heard a crack from the phone's casing and eased his grip. Threatened and desperate, had his father hurt his own granddaughter to involve Daniel in a war?

CHAPTER TWENTY-SEVEN

The grey house on Rosebush Avenue looked empty. Curtains were missing from the windows and junk mail choked the letterbox. The front lawn was over grown. Piles of litter lay trapped and sun bleached under the privet hedge. Despite that, it was a busy street with plenty of vehicles. Daniel parked his stolen transit van among them without arousing suspicion.

He rubbed his tired face and closed his eyes. Sleep seemed like a memory. He'd spent the night leaning against the railing his father had jumped from and replaying his conversation with Fairbanks. His father had questioned Eisha's role in this and Daniel had been wrong to dismiss him, like he'd been wrong about a lot of things. When the sun rose, turning the great hall from black to orange, Bronson arrived, rushing to his father's side as he entered. Daniel plodded down the staircase, startling him as he turned. "He jumped," he said and left to chase the only concrete lead he had.

On the other side of Rosebush Avenue was the entrance to Thornly Caravan and Leisure Parade. The site was surrounded by panelled fencing painted green and gold. Beyond it was grassy pasture land for touring caravans and tents. A group of boys no older than sixteen staggered out of the site carrying plastic bags filled with bottles of cider. They wore tracksuit bottoms, but had removed their tops in the midday sun. Their skin was pink with sunburn. Shouting and laughing, mothers and fathers crossed the street to avoid them.

"I remember when you were a kid like that," Scalper said from the passenger seat.

He looked healthier out of the hospital, though his recovery would continue to be a marathon battle. Scalper winced as he moved and it occurred to Daniel he was holding himself together by sheer force of will.

"I had more class than that, Scalp."

"'Course, you did. Remember when you tried to get into the Glitterball? Oh, you kicked off, alright. I had to call your Dad to pick you up. He tanned your hide right in front of everyone."

Daniel shifted uncomfortably, as if he could still feel the beating he took. "He was a real sweetheart about it."

Scalper slid his body around to face him. "He did it for your own good. Might not have seemed like it at the time, but that's the burden of being a parent. You have to be a bad guy every now and again."

Daniel opened the glove compartment and shut it again, not sure what he was looking for. "Do you think he could harm a child? A young child?"

A look of alarm passed over Scalper's face. "A kid? Your Dad?"

"I'm not saying for no reason. I mean if it, I don't know, furthered his goals or something."

Winding down the window, Scalper closed his eyes against a warm breeze. "I'm going to miss your Dad. I don't like you talking about him like that."

"But do you think it's possible?"

Scalper didn't answer. The breeze carried the smoke of someone's barbeque and it reminded Daniel of his family holidays in Marbella. Every evening, his father would cook dinner on a barbeque made from an old oil drum. It was the only second hand item he ever owned. His mother would have fish while the rest of them ate their weight in red meat.

The memory didn't make him hungry. It made him ill and he was glad to put it out of his mind. "Do you remember the plan?"

Scalper nodded. "Are you sure this Reaver guy was telling the truth?"

"It's a lot harder to lie when you're getting the shit kicked out of you." Daniel rubbed his ribs, easing the pain that lingered there. He turned to Scalper. "You're the only one who can help, but I don't want you to do it if you think you can't manage it."

Scalper grimaced as he grabbed his walking stick. "I'll put that down to nerves, boy. I've never backed out of a fight in my life. It's the reason I've got to use this fucking thing in the first place and now it's time for payback."

He opened the door and carefully placed his feet on the pavement, wobbling slightly as he got his balance. Daniel reached into his pocket and pulled out the envelope he'd retrieved from Mosely's body. With one hand on his walking stick, Scalper ripped it open with his free hand and teeth. He looked up at Daniel when he finished reading.

"We can check on her later," Daniel said.

Scalper smiled and nodded. "I guess he wasn't a complete twat after all."

He crushed the letter into his back pocket and hobbled into the caravan park while Daniel followed in the van. The site was busy. Adults reclined in stripy deckchairs, their eyes closed against the sun, listening to radios. Children ran after cheap, yellow footballs or chased each other with water pistols. In the centre of the park was the barbeque he'd smelled earlier. A young man with a goatee was in the process of impressing a gaggle of young women by cremating chicken and giving them salmonella.

Moving down a row of white caravans, Scalper took a deep breath and started screaming, waving his walking stick around like a broad sword, smashing caravan windows and braying on doors. The crowd stopped what they were doing and watched in horror.

"I know you're here. Come out and face me like men."

The children were ushered inside by frantic parents. Doors slammed shut. Tents were zipped closed. The man at the barbeque ran for the nearest exit, leaving the women to fend for themselves. Christ, they'd have to be quick, thought Daniel. All around the park mobile phones were connecting to the emergency services.

He watched the windows of the caravans and waited.

"Come and finish the job, you bastards. Fairbanks isn't here to protect you now."

The curtains of a secluded caravan twitched. Daniel saw it. Scalper saw it too and staggered forward.

"Come on, you bastards. Did you think I wouldn't find you?" He swung the crook of his walking stick into the caravan. Several dints appeared in quick succession.

Three men rushed outside. One of them punched Scalper in the face. He used his waking stick to defend himself, but Scalper was knocked to the ground. The other two grabbed him and dragged him inside the caravan. The door slammed shut and the caravan park was silent in seconds.

Daniel gunned the engine, skidding to a halt outside their door. Jumping from the van, he burst inside to find Scalper lying on the floor, cradling a broken nose. His skin was grey and slick with sweat, and there was a tremor in his left hand Daniel hadn't noticed before.

Scalper gave him a weak smile, but he read the urgency in his eyes.

Launching at the three men, the caravan rocked on its axle as Daniel rained down heavy fists from above. Two men were rendered unconscious immediately, but the last man remained standing. He swayed on his feet and beckoned Daniel toward him. Daniel ran forward, raising his elbow high, intending to bring it down on the bridge of his opponent's nose. The man swung a defensive right hook, connecting heavily with Daniel's already damaged ribs and he dropped to the floor, flaying against kicks aimed at his face. Scalper was on his feet and threw himself at the man. Too weak to fight, his weight was enough to bring them down in a heap. Arms and legs thrashed wildly as three grown men grappled within the tiny confines of a caravan floor. Daniel broke free and dragged Scalper to the kitchen.

Daniel searched frantically for a weapon. The other man lumbered closer, wiping his bloody face with the back of his hand. Daniel ducked under a blow to the head, finding a carving knife in a drawer with his free hand. He held it in front of him. The man stopped mid-fight, his eyes fearful. Daniel used the distraction to kick him between the legs. He lifted an inch off the floor and fell back with a groan.

Daniel pocketed the knife and went to Scalper's side. The police had probably been alerted by now. Their time was almost gone.

"Scalper? Can you hear me?"

A ghost of a smile passed over his face.

"I need to get you to a hospital. I'm going to carry you to the van. Just hold on, mate."

Daniel swung him onto his shoulder, ignoring the pain in his ribs. He nudged open the caravan door and checked the police weren't waiting outside. It was all clear and Daniel bolted. He strapped Scalper into the passenger seat and went to the rear of the van. He opened the doors and returned to the caravan. One by one, Daniel dumped the three men inside the van, tying them to hooks secured to the interior walls. He locked the doors shut, closed the caravan and jumped into the driver's seat.

"We did it, buddy," Scalper said through painful gasps.

Daniel glanced at him from the corner of his eye as he pulled away. The damage done by his first beating was compounded by the second. He was alive, but only just. The plan had been to use Scalper to draw them out and he had readily agreed. He'd known the risks, but Daniel hadn't known Scalper was lying about his recovery. He should never have left the hospital.

"Are we taking them to Five Oaks for interrogation?" Scalper asked.

"You're going to hospital."

Scalper rubbed the scar around his mouth with a shaking hand. "That wasn't the plan."

"Fuck the plan. You almost died for the Daytons once. It's not going to happen a second time."

At the exit of the park, they were blocked by a vehicle trying to enter. Heedless of the attention he drew, Daniel blasted his horn in frustration. The driver of the other car sat rigid with surprise. Daniel sounded the horn again, giving the driver a hard look through the glare of his windscreen. The driver casually rolled down his window and stuck his head out, his bulbous eyes creased with amusement.

"Fucking Jesus, it's Fairbanks." Daniel jumped from the van to see a rifle levelled through Fairbanks' window. A shot rang in his ears and he fell to the ground. Fairbanks reversed and Daniel watched him speed down Rosebush Avenue. Looking to his van, he saw a bullet hole in the centre of cracked glass. Scalper's head lay to one side, blood pumping from a wound in his throat. It coated the interior of the van in a red hue.

The engine was still running. Daniel jumped inside and drove away to the sound of distant police sirens. This was fucked up. He was too fucking stupid to pull off a stunt like this. Hadn't his Dad always told him? He was the hammer, not the hand who drove it. He took orders. He was too dumb to give them.

He kept to the back streets, trying to ignore how the sun shone through the glaze of Scalper's blood on the window. Not good enough, he hissed over and over. You're not good enough. Scalper died because of you. Your daughter is in a coma because of you.

He found a building site where a transit van could be left without question. There were a handful of contractors in the scaffolding. They worked steadily and didn't notice Daniel's arrival.

He didn't feel like it, but he had to work fast.

Taking a cloth from the glove compartment, he wiped down the interior of the van. He rubbed down the outside of the driver's door and did the same with the passenger side.

He hoped Scalper's beloved mother would forgive him for abandoning the son she loved so much.

Daniel pulled the kitchen knife from his pocket. He wanted to question the three men in the back of the van, but it would take too long. If he didn't question them, his pursuit of Fairbanks would be over. He couldn't allow them to go free, but he didn't have the time to kill them.

Taking the envelope from Scalper's dead body, he put it in his pocket, aware it was stained with the blood of two men. He didn't know why he was taking it, but it seemed important somehow. Perhaps he wanted it as a souvenir or a reminder of how deadly the hunt for Fairbanks had become.

He wiped his fingerprints from the handle of the knife and threw it into a patch of wild grass. The driver's door was open. He reached inside and smashed the centre of the steering wheel with his elbow. The van horn blared and continued to sound as Daniel ran for cover. When all eyes were drawn to the wailing van, Daniel sprinted from the building site to the relative safety of the streets.

When the contractors alerted the police, Fairbanks' men would be taken into custody. Men like that always had records. With any luck, Daniel would never hear from them again.

Fairbanks had used the police in a trap to capture his brother. At long last, Daniel had repaid the favour.

The thin trail of breadcrumbs to Fairbanks was gone. The men in the caravan were his last chance and they had been sacrificed to save his own skin. To make matters worse, Scalper had died for nothing. Daniel was no closer to the people who had hurt Eisha than he was when he arrived.

The only difference now was that following his conversation with Scalper, he was beginning to suspect the Daytons were somehow involved.

CHAPTER TWENTY-EIGHT

His minestrone soup had gone cold. Swirling it around his bowl, he'd watched the steam curl into the ceiling until all that was left was a watery mess he had no appetite for. He handed it back to Colon, a skinny twenty-year-old who waited anxiously by his side.

"Not hungry, boss?" Colon asked.

"You can have it."

Colon, so-called for his preferred method of smuggling heroin across the English Channel, slurped from the bowl. Prisoners weren't allowed cutlery in their cells. Even a spoon could be turned into a deadly weapon. Harold Spicer, a lifer and hard con, watched in disgust as bullet-like peas and strips of pasta dripped from Colon's stubbly chin.

Sighing, he lay down on his creaky bed and tucked his hands behind his head. His cell was six foot by eight. He'd been moved around a lot from Belmarsh to Wakefield. This time it was HM Frankland, but the cells remained the same. They were suffocating with a bunkbed, sink, toilet and a twenty-two hour lockdown. On the pockmarked walls were signed messages from previous occupants. The one to his right read, "Even Jonny Cash never came here. Smally 2010."

Spicer was whippet lean with sparse blonde hair and pale green eyes. He wore a black tracksuit, which he insisted Colon ironed everyday whether it was clean or not. "Anything I should know about on the wing?"

"No, boss."

He looked up at Colon's stunted reply. His skin was the colour of wet pastry. The tremors in his hand were a dead giveaway. It wasn't soup Colon was after.

"Okay. Thanks for bringing my lunch. Tell Queenie I want to see him when you get your bird."

Spicer had barely finished speaking before Colon was out of the door, tucking the empty bowl under his T-shirt to avoid detection from the guards. Queenie was Spicer's right-hand man. He doled out the bird. It was too risky to have it in his own cell. Bird, or bird's eye, was prison slang for a tiny drop of smack. He used it to control a private army of druggies, who would do anything for a fix. It's what made him King of the Wing and afforded him his small pleasures. Why did things have to change, he wondered?

Queenie stepped into his cell, making the room feel smaller. His heavy muscle had turned to fat and his skin was busy with the blue ink of prison tattoos, including a badly drawn tiara wrapped around his pink, bald head.

"Has Dayton started his shift yet?" Spicer asked.

"Should have started five minutes ago. I was on my way to see you when Colon came in."

"Did you pay him?"

Queenie nodded and Spicer got to his feet, stretching his arms skyward. "You're in charge of the shanks. When we're done, it's up to you to get rid of them. I can't afford to have any more time added to my sentence."

"What about my sentence?"

Smoothing down the blankets of his bed, Spicer spoke over his shoulder. "You're a brutal rapist and sex offender, Queenie. You don't deserve to be released." He turned to see the sloppy grin on Queenie's face. "Are you sure Dayton's alone?"

"Apparently, he insists on it."

"The fucker's been on my wing less than five minutes and he's throwing his weight around already. Come on. Let's go teach him a lesson."

Queenie scratched at his crotch and followed him out.

The library was two cells knocked through into one. The walls were lined with shelves and filled with books donated by charities and Christian groups. Unlike the rest of Frankland, it was warm and free of damp. It was an open room, but secluded and given that it was generally run by model prisoners, the guards rarely visited. For Spicer's purposes, it was perfect. For Queenie's too.

Colon was already high as a kite, pacing his cell and blabbering about cross Channel ferries. Spicer stationed another of his junkies, a fat man called Graham, outside the library as a lookout. The place was empty, except for Dayton who sat at a green baize table with his head in his hands. He didn't look up when they entered.

"Penny for your thoughts?" Spicer asked.

Scott jumped, wiping his cheeks with the back of his hand. His eyes were red and puffy. He glanced over Spicer, but braced himself when he saw Queenie and the look in his eyes.

"We don't stock gay porn so what do you want?" he asked.

Picking a book from the shelf, Spicer pretended to read the inner cover. "I'd like to say I've come to improve my mind, but actually it's yours that's in need of some education. How long have you been here?"

"Long enough to get the measure of you."

"I don't think you have. It takes years to earn enough brownie points to run the library. You haven't even been sentenced and yet, here you are."

He expected Dayton to react to the threat in his voice, but he remained seated, staring vacantly at his hands. Spicer looked at Queenie, who shrugged in response. He tossed the book onto the floor and selected another. "I guess your hard man reputation doesn't count for much in here. You're just a Daddy's boy really."

Scott raised his head slowly, his hands balling into fists. The look in his eyes was enough to force Spicer back a step. Queenie stepped forward, but he was just as wary.

"I heard about your father," Spicer said. "Committed suicide, didn't he? Threw himself to his death?"

He dropped his book on Scott's table.

"Splat," Scott said quietly, pulling it closer. On the cover was a picture of the crucifixion with the title 'The Sacrifice of Our Lord'. He knocked it to the floor and mumbled to himself.

"What was that?" Spicer asked.

Scott cleared his throat. "Just take what you want and go."

Taking off his tracksuit top, Spicer wrapped it around his thin waist. He nodded at Queenie, who tugged free his tracksuit bottoms, exposing his grey, dirty underwear and the growing bulge underneath.

Spicer averted his eyes. "I'm sorry about this, Scott. I thought you'd come here to be the big I am, but you don't have it in you anymore, do you?"

"Don't worry. I'm going to put something in you instead. Everything will be okay," Queenie said.

"Actually, Queenie here as just been diagnosed with HIV so nothing's going to be okay for you ever again," Spicer said.

Queenie pouted and blew Scott a kiss. When Scott snarled back, Spicer saw a glimpse of the man he used to be.

"Come anyway near me and I'll kill you both," Scott said.

"I don't think so. Grief is a terrible thing. Makes a man weak, but I have to send a message out to the rest of the wing."

The shank appeared from nowhere and into Spicer's hand. It was the signal to move and Queenie rushed behind Scott, who looked up to see a sharpened toothbrush slice the air inches from his face. He attempted to stand, but Queenie wrapped his thick arm around his neck, choking the air out of him, driving him face down on the table.

He fought, but he was no match for Queenie's depravity. Spicer leaned in so close he could feel Dayton's panicked breath on his face. His eyes were wide and fearful. At last, thought Spicer, he was getting the reaction he hoped for.

"You're not going to like this, Scott. There's probably going to be a lot of blood, but I want you to remember this is all your fault. Just like your Daddy's death."

Scott bucked against Queenie, finding space to rise from the table, but Queenie slammed an elbow into his lower back and he crumpled.

"That's it, bitch," he said. "Fight me. Make me hard."

Spicer smiled. "If you'd been a free man, maybe you'd have stopped your father from jumping. I guess we'll never know."

He gave Queenie the nod and stepped outside. He hated watching the next bit, but as he joined Graham outside, a prison guard approached along the gangway. Spicer threw his shank back into the library where it slid under a shelf.

"Hello, Officer Montague," he said loudly.

Immediately suspicious, the guard picked up his pace. He was one of the younger, newer recruits. Still green, his eyes were bright with enthusiasm. "I didn't peg you as a book lover, Spicer."

"You know me. Always looking to improve."

The rattle of scraping furniture came from the library and Montague craned his neck around the open door. Shit, thought Spicer.

"Against the wall. Against the wall," the guard shouted, pushing him in the chest. Spicer reluctantly complied while Graham made to scamper away. Montague dragged him back to a standing position. "Don't move."

"Hey, we came to borrow books, that's all."

Montague spoke rapidly into a comms unit mounted on his shoulder. "Request assistance. D wing library. Repeat. Request assistance. Code orange."

He waded into the library, snatching his pepper spray from his belt. Spicer didn't need to watch. He knew what happened next. Startled from his attack, Queenie would surrender. He'd be ordered to face the wall and he'd be cuffed. What happened thereafter depended on the guard. By rights, his detainee should be marched to solitary, charged and dispatched to another prison where he'd serve out his current sentence and any time added. But it all depended on the guard and rapists were the lowest of the low.

Four burly guards stampeded down the gangway. He heard Queenie scream inside the library. They squeezed through the doorway and returned moments later, carrying a semi-conscious Queenie in their arms. His eyes were bloodshot. Tears and snot streamed down his face. He gasped for breath. As he was bundled passed Spicer, he looked to him for help, but Spicer was examining his fingernails.

Montague stepped out of the library, his back a little straighter than when he entered. Spicer smiled at him. "I didn't think you had the balls," he said as the guard reattached the pepper spray to his belt.

"Did you have anything to do with this?"

"Me and my friend Graham were simply out taking some air. Still got his cherry, I hope."

"If I'd been any later, this would be a very different assault charge, Spicer and I would have made sure some of it stuck to you."

Scott loomed in the doorway, holding onto it for support.

"Are you okay, Dayton?" Montague asked. "Do you need to see a doctor?"

He shook his head. His face was paler than usual. The only colour to it was the bruising around his left eye. He was shaking and there was a rip in his tracksuit bottoms.

"How did your date go?" Spicer asked. Scott ignored him and he pulled a sympathetic face. "Never mind. There's always next time."

Scott leaned in to Montague. "Can I go back to my cell now, Officer?"

"No. I came here to get you. There's a visitor waiting."

He looked surprised and Spicer bit down on his tongue. There was a shank under the bookcase and lesson time wasn't over yet. Dayton didn't have to be hurt in the library. Spicer was happy to do him in his cell. He was sure Graham would take care of it for a little extra bird.

Scott avoided his hateful stare as he was led away by the guard. Spicer spat on the floor. "There's always next time, Dayton," he shouted. "There's always a tomorrow."

CHAPTER TWENTY-NINE

HM Frankland was a prison in County Durham housing high security Category A and B prisoners. These men had committed the worst crimes imaginable. If they ever escaped, they were considered a danger to the public, but an exodus seemed unlikely. The prison was surrounded by thirty-foot walls topped with razor wire. Then came electrified chain link fences topped with more razor wire. Getting out was almost impossible, but breaking in was manageable.

Fairbanks adjusted his paisley tie and handed over his identification documents to a prison guard at the front entrance. He waited while the guard ran the necessary security checks, playing with the strap of his shoulder bag.

The guard had a cropped beard struggling over a double chin. He looked up from his computer screen. "It says you're here on behalf of Reeceman and Co. for a Mr Scott Dayton?"

"That's right," Fairbanks said, nodding. "My boss is Walter Reeceman, but we call him Noodles."

The guard returned his identification with a short smile. "Why do they call him that?"

Fairbanks' jaw dropped. He didn't know. It wasn't in his research. He thought quickly. "He likes Chinese food?"

Apparently, the guard didn't care and handed over a security pass without further comment. Fairbanks pinned it to his pressed white shirt and followed a second guard through a grey corridor, attempting not to jump every time a door slammed shut.

They reached a checkpoint where a third guard took over from the second. He looked young, but was at least thirty pounds overweight. He gestured for Fairbanks' documentation, scrupulously examining every detail. He then searched his bag, pulling out stolen headed notepaper reading Reeceman and Co, Barristers at Law. "Could you stand on the red line please, sir?" he asked.

Fairbanks complied.

The guard ran his hands along Fairbanks' outstretched arms and down his legs. By the time he finished, the guard was perspiring and dropped back into his seat with a grunt. "Through that door there, sir," he said and continued with a half-eaten ham sandwich on his desk.

The metal door with a small mesh window squeaked as Fairbanks pulled it open. He stepped inside and shivered, though he didn't know if it was from the fall in temperature or his feeling of claustrophobia. The floor was concrete and painted grey, decorated with the scuff marks of countless shoes. The walls were a washed out yellow and daubed with graffiti. It smelled of stale aftershave and body odour. A red blinking light alerted him to the security camera keeping a silent vigil. Fairbanks lowered his head.

Sitting behind a table bolted to the floor, he loosened his tie and waited for the door on the other side of the room to open.

It wasn't long before Scott Dayton was shown inside. The young guard he knew as Montague gave him a wink and left them to it. Scott looked ruffled. His glacial eyes scanned the room and settled on Fairbanks, who met his gaze with his own blank stare.

Fairbanks was puzzled to see he'd been crying.

"I was told my brief wanted a word with me," Scott said.

"That's what I told them to say." He pointed to the other side of the desk. "Would you like to sit down?"

Scott shifted his weight from one foot to the other, but stayed where he was. "Who are you?"

"Before we begin, I want you to know no-one is sorrier at the news of your father's death than me."

Scott took a sharp breath inward, as if he'd been immersed in icy water. His lower lip trembled for a fraction of a second before he regained control.

"It does leave us with a problem, however," Fairbanks continued. "This little war we're embroiled in will only continue unless you help me. The Daytons need someone to lead them, Scott and you can't do that behind bars."

Scott glanced at the security camera and then back to Fairbanks, who shook his head. "There are guards either side of these two doors and that camera will record everything. You attack me and you'll never see daylight again."

"According to Noodles, I'm facing life anyway. What difference does breaking your neck make?"

Fairbanks opened his bag and brought out a sheaf of legal documentation. "These are your way out. I file these and you're free as a bird."

"Bullshit."

"I never planned to kill you, Scott. You would have become a martyr to the Dayton cause. Better for me that you ended up in prison alone and impotent, but things change. Now I need you on the outside."

Scott pulled up a chair and sat down. Close up, he was more dishevelled than Fairbanks first noted. The hair on his chin was so blonde it couldn't be seen at a distance, but Scott was clearly unshaven. His hair was unwashed and he smelled of the same disinfectant and body odour as the rest of the prison.

"You're Fairbanks? You look more like a paperboy to me."

Fairbanks pushed the documentation toward Scott, who grabbed his hand and crushed it in his own. The bones clicked painfully together and he squeezed his eyes shut.

"I can't believe you're the snivelling arse-wipe that's been causing us all this bother," Scott said.

"How is prison?" he asked between gasps. "Dangerous?"

Scott released his grip and Fairbanks snatched back his hand. He saw the white marks of Scott's fingers on his skin. It looked like he'd been burned by frostbite. He leaned away from Scott's reach. "I can't understand why you're not coping better with prison life. Yes, you're upset over your father's demise, but look at you. You're a mess."

Scott folded his arms. As he did, Fairbanks saw the sweat stains in his armpits. "Some people thrive on being alone. Others take strength from their families. Without it, they wither and die. Which one do you think you are?"

"Let's turn off the cameras and find out."

Fairbanks drummed his fingers on the table. "I met your brother the other day. Daniel?"

"I know who he is."

"Out of the both of you, I thought you might be more amenable. I don't think Daniel likes being told what to do."

"Neither do I."

"I understand, but Daniel has his liberty. You don't. All I want is money. Plain and simple. Of course, I could leave you here and persuade Daniel to take over the Daytons. You know I can be very persuasive. I think he'd give me every penny just to spite you."

"He'd never do it. He hates being a Dayton. There's no way he'd take over."

A knock came at the door behind Scott. "Two more minutes, Mr Fairbanks," Montague said.

"Your freedom in return for a bank transfer. Or I can give Daniel something he wants and maybe he'll give me the money. He seemed very interested in knowing who hurt his daughter."

Scott looked at the legal papers in front of him, skimming them before pushing them away. "What is all this?"

"Actually, they're bullshit, like you said. Part of my cover for getting in here. You were refused bail because you're a danger to public safety. No amount of whinnying from your lawyer will change that, but I've paid a substantial amount of money to some powerful people. You will be released this afternoon."

"So what? I get out. They put me back in after the trial."

"I have the secret bank account details of the Police Commissioner and several members of the executive board. They show erroneous payments going back years. Not just from you, but from the Maguires and Curley's Crew. Not to mention the investment of my own. Your case will be dismissed in light of the corruption of public officials."

Scott looked toward the door he had appeared from and shivered. There was something behind it he feared, thought Fairbanks. Perhaps he had met a bigger bully than himself, though Fairbanks had trouble envisaging such a spectre. Perhaps it was incarceration itself, that same feeling of claustrophobia Fairbanks felt entering this room. Whatever it was, there was a weakness to Scott that made him happy.

"I want to be absolutely clear with you," he said. "If you renege on this deal, I will send you back here. I'll find out what's scaring you and I'll triple it. You won't die. I won't allow it. You'll spend every day of your sentence longing for my very kind offer. Understand?"

Scott nodded, a greedy smile on his face.

"Are you sure? I'm asking you to betray your family. To deny your father's dying wish? Are you ready for that? It's the price of your freedom."

Fairbanks watched him closely while he waited for an answer. His red eyes filled with tears, like the rising of the tide, but with a blink, they were gone. Scott's jaw set firm. His nostrils flared and if Fairbanks didn't feel cold before, he did now.

Fairbanks hid his smile. He'd make the phone call when he left the prison grounds. It was almost pay day. He'd chosen the correct brother.

Scott slowly unfolded his arms and laid his hands on the table. "How much can I give you?" he asked.

CHAPTER THIRTY

Having read the cover article of the Evening Chronicle, the ward sister's usual night time routine was ruined. She tried to cook dinner, but burned the beans and singed the toast. Her soap operas were on, but she couldn't concentrate. Switching off the TV, she went to her 'treat' cupboard. She sat in the dark, listening to the sound of traffic outside her downstairs flat and crunched through her jammy dodgers. The ward sister finished the pack and decided to call a friend.

The following morning, she stood under a steaming shower and washed the tiredness from her body. Every day she looked at her left breast and the crescent moon scar left by the surgeon. Ductal carcinoma. Removed to prevent it turning into cancer and corrupting the rest of her body. At least they'd caught it early.

Sacrificing her usual bacon sandwich, she went to work early and marched into Eisha Dayton's room. "Who would assault such a beautiful, young girl?"

Daniel was staring into the quiet face of his daughter when the ward sister arrived. He turned to her and she saw black rings under his eyes. He hadn't shaved and there was a dark smudge of bristle on his jaw. "I was thinking the same thing," he said.

"Can you give me any further details regarding the attack on your daughter?"

"I was working away when it happened. I don't know anything."

The ward sister consulted the clipboard nestled to her bosom and wrote 'Absent Parents' in her notes. She waved it in front of Daniel, making sure he saw it.

"You don't know anything about the incident?" she asked again, her eyebrows arched.

He cracked his knuckles and shook his head, but she persevered. "The misappropriation of Eisha's records threw me a little and I haven't been able to give you my full attention, but I thought a lot about you last night, Mr Dayton and there's something very wrong."

"What are you talking about?" he said, shifting in his chair.

She perched on the side of the bed, stroking the blanket covering Eisha's thin leg. "I was sorry to hear about your father in the Evening Chronicle."

He cast his eyes to the ground. "Tragic," he said.

"'Local Businessman in Suicide Shock,' but what I found shocking was the coincidence of it all. One Dayton commits suicide. Another in a coma and one more running around my ward like a madman."

"What's your point?"

"The point is I don't like it. I met my friend here last night. He works in the morgue. He said your father was shot in the stomach, but it was never mentioned in the report. Judging by the look on your face, I'd say you already knew that."

He stood and his shadow fell across her. She slipped her hand inside a pocket containing a syringe filled with five cubic centimetres of sedative, enough to stop a horse. She wished she had more.

"I'm sorry, Sister. I've had a difficult few days."

"I warned you, Mr Dayton. If your family endangered the lives of my patients, there'd be consequences and yet here you all are. Spreading like a cancer."

"And cancer needs to be cut out?"

"Every time. The only reason I haven't informed the police is because of this poor girl here. I think she's been caught up in something and I think you're to blame."

Daniel looked at his daughter, running his finger along the creases of the blanket. The ward sister left the syringe where it was and yanked the paperwork free from her clipboard. "And as for that fucking Hilltop, I'm going to swing for him the next time I see him."

She crumpled up the paper and threw it in the medical waste bin.

"What are you doing?" he asked.

"That was a requisition form for more cleaning supplies. I just wanted you to know what I think of you."

"It seems like you might have had a change of opinion regarding Hilltop too."

"I remembered how he forbade any of the staff to examine Eisha. He said, it was enough that she was examined when she was admitted."

Daniel frowned. "Is that normal?"

"No, not really," she said, chewing the inside of her cheek, "but he's a doctor and like I've said, he was being very attentive."

The ward sister had the eerie sensation that Daniel was studying her. His eyes were everywhere and nowhere at once and while she froze under his searchlight gaze, he appeared to relax.

"You went against his orders, didn't you?" he said with a knowing look.

"Speaking to my friend wasn't the only thing I did last night. When no-one was around, I looked at your daughter's wounds. There was nothing there. Eisha wasn't assaulted. There wasn't a cut or contusion anywhere."

"Of course, she was assaulted. Why else would she be in a coma?"

He reached out and placed his hands on her shoulders. She braced herself for an attack, wishing her hand was closer to the syringe. He stood there, motionless, his brown eyes wide and lost.

"What's wrong with my daughter, Sister?" he asked.

"I was hoping you could tell me. What is it you do, Mr Dayton?"

"I'm a tree surgeon," he said, dropping back down into his seat.

"But what do you really do?"

Daniel sighed and cracked his knuckles again. The ward sister waited.

"I wasn't involved in what happened to Eisha, if that's what you mean," he said. "I came back to punish the man who hurt her. And now you're telling me she hasn't been hurt. You're telling me she's in a coma and there's nothing we can do."

Sitting on Eisha's bed, the ward sister was wary of getting too close. Whatever had happened to Daniel Dayton over the past few days or the past few years even, had scarred him. He was the product of his environment. She hated to think what that environment had been.

"What happened to you?" she asked.

Daniel rubbed his eyes. "I don't know anymore. I was a father who ran out on his daughter. I was a son until I wasn't. I come from a dangerous world; a cancerous world. I could tell you what you want to know, but you'd feel compelled to act, Sister. It would be better if you let me handle things on my own."

"You don't have to do it on your own."

"There's no-one I can trust." He tucked his chin into his large chest and stared at the floor.

"Is that it?" she asked.

He looked up, but his mouth was clamped shut. She walked to the medical waste bin and dropped the sedative inside. "You're too big to be feeling sorry for yourself, Mr Dayton. Do you think I got to run this ward because I cried every time those stupid doctors talked down to me or criticised my work?"

"What are you saying?"

"I'm saying – grow up."

The ward sister smiled and produced a notepad from her pocket. "And I didn't say there was nothing we could do."

CHAPTER THIRTY-ONE

Scott walked free from Frankland prison in a suit left for him by Fairbanks. It was black and shiny with worn patches at the elbows of the jacket. It fit, but only just. His personal effects were returned, amounting to a handful of change and half a pack of spearmint gum.

There was no-one to greet him and although, he'd been granted a phone call to arrange transportation, he hadn't used it. The afternoon sun was strong and his jacket was soon slung over his shoulder as he walked two miles to the village of Brasside. He intended on taking a bus to Newcastle. It was his first time on public transport and he was nervous. Growing up, there was always a car and a driver to take him wherever he wanted to go. The tattered paper timetable confounded him. Unable to decipher it, he decided to wait.

He sat in the plastic bus stop and wiped his brow. His view of oncoming traffic was blocked where someone had put a lighter to the plastic window and burned it opaque. He tapped his foot. What he didn't do was think about where he'd been and what he was about to do next.

"What time is the thirty-two, mate?"

Scott squinted against the sunshine and saw a bald man in his thirties wearing a tracksuit similar to the one he'd been wearing when he was almost raped. He swallowed. "I don't know."

"The timetable is over there. Can't you read?" The man entered the bus stop, kicking Scott's long legs on his way to examine the schedule. "Watch where you put your feet, mate."

The fluttering sensation in his chest was unfamiliar to him. It increased whenever he glanced at the other man.

"Can you spare me some money to get the bus, mate?" the bald man asked.

"I don't have enough."

"How much is it to Newcastle?"

Scott wiped his brow again. "I don't know."

The bald man stood over him, his hands down the front of his tracksuit bottoms, rearranging his junk. "How do you know you don't have enough then? Come on. Let's see how much you've got."

Scott was hungry by the time the bus arrived, but that wasn't his only problem. The door opened with a hiss. He climbed on board and was hit by the smell of diesel riding on a wave of heat. The driver stared at him over his hook nose. He waited expectantly as Scott stood with his hands in his pockets.

"Where are we going to?" the driver finally asked.

"Newcastle."

"It's a big place. Whereabouts?"

Scott looked down the aisle, hoping someone might rescue him, but he was greeted by empty seats and the pages of the local newspaper scattered on the floor. "The city centre please," he said, "but I don't have any money. I lost it."

The driver rolled his eyes and shifted the bus into gear. "'Course, you did, mate. That's what they all say. Just got out of Frankland, did you? Sit down and don't cause any trouble. Okay?"

As Scott found a seat, the bus pulled away from the curb. He closed his eyes, feeling the reverberations of the engine and listening to the driver's lecture on smackheads and charity cases.

Alighting near Eldon Square, he ignored the driver's offer to join a prayer meeting and found the nearest phone box. Reversing the charges, he made a call.

He'd grown up on the streets of Newcastle. They were home to him, but today they were filled with aliens. Gastro pubs with outside seating bustled with loud mouthed men in pin striped suits. Goths with stained black hair read Morrissey lyrics on The Green while teenage mothers with orange tans pushed their latest baby around in the latest designer pushchair.

Since the arrest, his family and all other known associates eschewed any contact. They weren't about to risk being dragged down with him. He had done the same when a childhood friend of his had been done for arson. Scott had never felt so alone and even back on familiar territory, he couldn't shake the feeling he was one man in a sea of strangers.

Turning down Grainger Street, he found Carlo's, a quiet coffee house where he knew the owner. He entered through a red door and climbed a flight of stairs to reach a dark room filled with the aroma of roasting coffee beans. Hanging from the ceiling were dried flowers Carlo had received for services rendered. The majority of them were from his female customers, but his main business was providing neutral ground for clandestine meetings for which he was paid in cold, hard cash. The tables were small and only sat two. There was no music, but the sizzle of the coffee machines disguised the whispered conversations held there.

Scott waited with an untouched espresso, his jacket back on his shoulders. He didn't want anyone to see the sweat stains on his shirt.

He stood from his seat when Monica walked in, accidentally spilling his coffee. She wore a canvas coat so big she could have worn it twice. A member of staff wiped down his table as she came over and two new cups were produced by the time she sat down.

Even in this dim light, he saw there were lines around her eyes and mouth. She pushed her coffee away and pulled down the sleeves of her coat, covering her hands. A bead of sweat trickled down his spine.

"I didn't expect to see you again," she said.

"Would you feel better if I was still in prison?"

She looked away and he felt a stab of guilt. While he waited for her to respond, they watched a young waiter deliver a cappuccino into a shadowy corner to return empty handed and shaking.

"How did you get out?" Monica asked.

"Does it matter?"

Monica pushed out her chair and made to leave.

"Wait. I'm sorry. You know I'm not good at this," he said.

She hovered, running her hands through her spiky hair. Scott tried to remain calm. He knew what he wanted to say, but couldn't find the words. It was typical of his life. He just had to hope Monica was feeling sympathetic.

She sat back down, breathing heavily through her nose. "I'm sorry about your Dad."

"Are people talking?" he asked, peering into his inky coffee.

"About what?" Monica adjusted the sleeves on her coat again. "If you're talking about us having sex –"

"Making love," Scott corrected before Monica continued with a grimace. "If you're talking about us fucking all over Five Oaks, then no. Nobody knows."

Scott straightened in his chair. He took a sip of his coffee. It was cold and bitter in his mouth. "I thought we fell in love."

"We slept together."

"But I told you how I felt by the lake," he said. "I've never said those words to anyone before."

"Not even your wife?"

"Especially not her."

He scratched at his temple and fought a rising panic. He wasn't accustomed to these emotions. They were overwhelming. He had no idea what that might herald for his future, but sensing he was about to lose the only woman he had ever loved, Scott was willing to try harder.

"I married Lily because it was the right thing to do. It looked good on paper and she never asked for much, but I fell in love with you even though it was wrong." He shook his head, feeling the heat in his face. "Does that make any sense? I just want you to know how I feel."

Monica smiled at him, her eyes brightening. She reached over the table and took his hand. He let her do it, glad for the smallest of contact with her, but he didn't return her smile. There was something wolfish about Monica's face that made him uneasy.

"I have something to tell you," she said. "You're going to be a father."

It was as if he had suddenly been hollowed out. His breath, his ability to move, his sense of direction. They were all gone, replaced with a serious bout of vertigo, but the room was motionless. It was Scott who was spinning.

"But...?" Scott asked, not wanting to be blunt.

She patted him on the hand. "It's yours. Trust me."

"Mine?" He smiled into space and although they were in a darkened room, he felt sure the world saw how happy he was. Why were they drinking coffee? It should be champagne, he thought. It should be a celebration. At Five Oaks with family. He looked at Monica and lost himself in her big, round eyes. Five Oaks with *my* family and a new start for all of us.

"Mine?" he asked again.

Monica nodded, letting go of his hand and steepling her fingers together. "Now I know we can't be together. You're obviously bothered about people talking about us, but I don't have a job or friends or a place to stay."

Scott's face clouded over. "What do you mean?"

"I can't raise a baby on my own without money, Scott. If you could maybe give me an allowance or something, I could have your child."

"I have money. You know that. I've inherited my father's empire. You'll be set for life."

"I need enough for a new house with a garden for the baby when it grows up. A car. Money for a nanny. It all adds up. What if I wanted to go on holiday? How am I going to afford that?"

She had no idea what he'd endured since his arrest, but this moment was by far his worst. Dreams raised and crushed over and over in a split, dizzying second. He might not feel like himself, but his father hadn't raised a fool. He was raised to be sharper than most. Sharp enough to draw blood, in fact.

"We'll have to go private for the birth," he said. "Say, why don't we pay Dr Hilltop to be our private physician? Just until the baby's born."

Monica clapped her hands. "And for a few months afterward. To make sure I'm okay after the birth."

"I can't believe I'm going to be a father," he said, grinning.

Monica placed her hand on his. "And I think you'll be a wonderful, generous father, Scott. I really do."

He snatched her hand, holding it firmly, but not so hard as to hurt her. He loved this woman after all. "You can have it all, Monica. Wealth, power, luxury, but nothing comes for free."

"What do you want in return? We can't have sex again. Your Dad's dead. It's too freaky even for us."

Scott's cold heart pumped again, dowsing the flames of his wild emotions with liquid ice. It was an easy sensation, recognisable and comforting. It didn't make him happy because the old Scott didn't know what that meant. It made him feel numb and he preferred that.

Tomorrow, when this was all over, he'd find that bald man by the bus stop and take him out onto the moors. He wasn't sure what he'd do then. Maybe choke him to death on small change, he mused. He'd work the details out later, but Harold Spicer was definitely in for a raping. He wondered if Spicer's mother was still alive. He could arrange for the event to be taped and sent to her for Christmas.

"Scott? Are you listening to me?"

He tuned back in and saw Monica staring at him, a crease in her perfect brow. At that moment, he loved her more than ever and though she might not love him now, she would in time.

Stretching out the fingers of his hand, Scott slowly closed them into a fist. "Well, if I can't have your body, I'll take your life instead."

CHAPTER THIRTY-TWO

The ward sister showed Daniel into a small office and quickly closed the door behind them. The room was filled with metal filing cabinets and cork noticeboards covered with memos and pamphlets. There were files in beige boxes and in the corner, a mainframe computer. With its grey walls and grey carpet, it reminded Daniel of a prison cell.

The ward sister rubbed her nose against the dust motes in the air. "I hate coming in here. It's all admin. I got into nursing to help people."

Switching on the computer, she placed her notebook by the keyboard. Daniel stood dumbly by as she made her way through various screens until she reached a login page.

"The way Hilltop locked us out of Eisha's records was beyond unprofessional. It was reckless."

"I notice you're calling him Hilltop, not doctor. Do I need to worry?"

"Everyone thinks I'm just a busybody, but I see things, Mr Dayton. I pride myself on it. Without conscientious people like me, this hospital would collapse. The way he fussed over Eisha like a mother hen. I'm sorry, but there are other patients who needed his help. He's not going to risk another child's life so he can take a day off." She turned in her chair to face him. "This is me putting an end to whatever relationship he has with the Daytons. Are you okay with that?"

The floor creaked as Daniel shifted his weight. He'd said nothing of Hilltop's role in his father's organisation nor how he ended up there. For a woman as intelligent as the ward sister, the connection was obvious and there was no need to go into the details now. He was simply pleased she'd switched alliances. If things played out the way he anticipated they would, it was a move she may come to regret. Because everyone regretted getting involved with a Dayton.

"Is this how you access patients' records?" he asked.

The Sister tapped her notebook. "If you have the right password."

"You stole it?"

She turned back to the computer and her fingers pecked at the keyboard. The screen changed several times until she entered Eisha's name and patient number, and stopped to examine her records. Her eyes grew wide and she placed a shaking hand on her lips.

"What is it?" Daniel asked.

"Nothing."

"Don't lie to me, Sister. What is it?"

"Do you know what benzodiazepine is?"

He shot her the kind of look that left scorch marks, but the ward sister didn't see it. She was fixated on the screen. "Hilltop has been combining it with zolpidem to keep your daughter in a tranquilised state."

"A fucking tranquilised state? What do you mean?"

"Calm down, Mr Dayton."

Daniel lashed out at a pile of paperwork stacked neatly on the filing cabinet. The papers parachuted to the ground. "I don't understand. Is that medicine? What is it?"

The Sister looked at the paper littered around her feet. "It will take a full day to collate that back together, Mr Dayton."

He paced the room, leaving footprints on the scattered paper, trying to ignore the Sister's withering glare. He had travelled back to Newcastle for answers. It hadn't occurred to him how much it would hurt when he found them.

"The whole thing was a lie designed to lure me back," he said, remembering his enemy's counsel. "It was my father. He was the only one who wanted me to return. He wanted to use me as a weapon against Fairbanks."

The ward sister hurled her notebook at him. It slapped his face and dropped to the floor. "I was right. This is all about your family, isn't it?"

He stopped pacing. "It always is."

"Eisha is in a coma: an induced coma caused by the medication Hilltop was giving her. The records given to the nurses make no mention of it. Obviously. As far as we were concerned, she was on saline and nutrient bags. That's all."

"Hilltop made it look like she was in a coma when there was nothing actually wrong with her?"

She studied the screen, her fingers tapping angrily on the keyboard.

"This is terrible. Just terrible."

"Answer me," Daniel shouted.

The Sister turned in her chair and fixed him with a stern, matriarchal stare.

"Let's not have any more temper tantrums, Mr Dayton. I've just discovered my precious ward is a place of child abuse. If you take a deep breath and give me a moment, I would like to know if my life's work has been built on sand."

Her face was a naked mixture of anger and grief stopping him in his tracks. She returned to the screen and he looked at the mess he'd made of her paperwork. Stooping to the floor, he fumbled it together and made slow work of putting it in alphabetical order. By the time he realised it probably wasn't arranged in alphabetical order to begin with, it formed a neat pile on top of the filing cabinet.

The ward sister finished reading Eisha's records and pinched the bridge of her nose. "This file is in his private directory. It isn't linked to the system. Why would he keep a record of his crime? We were bound to find it eventually."

He placed a gentle hand on her shoulder. "Is my daughter okay?"

"She's fine," she said, patting his hand, "apart from being mistreated by a doctor who will shortly be going to jail."

"Is there anything in there about who brought Eisha in? Hilltop wasn't behind this. Someone made him do it."

"Someone you know?"

She attempted to scrutinise his expression, but he was impervious. The less she knew, the safer she would be, he thought. He owed her that much.

The ward sister finally relented and turned back to the computer. "There's nothing in there."

"Does it have Hilltop's address?"

The Sister hesitated. "Are you taking him to the police?"

It was a stupid question and she knew it. Still she wrote down Hilltop's address on a piece of paper and gave it to Daniel. He noticed her hand shake as she let go, her eyes never leaving its surface.

"He's done a terrible thing, hasn't he?" she asked him.

Daniel nodded, folding the paper in two before placing it in his back pocket. "You said yourself, he's a child abuser. He may have been keeping an eye on her, but he still falsely imprisoned a child, whether she was in a hospital or not."

"But the law states –"

"I know what the law states, Sister, but the law lets people down. How can you expect people to move on when punishment is limited to feeding and clothing someone for the rest of their lives? Hilltop deserves something more."

The ward sister fought back a sob. "You've stained me, Mr Dayton. Before I met you, all I wanted was to do my job and now I've become an accomplice in something that sickens me to my soul."

Daniel ran his hands down his face. "It happens to everyone eventually."

The ward sister dried her eyes and switched off the computer, sending the room into muted darkness. When she looked at him, her face was hard. "The next time I see you, Mr Dayton, it will be to collect your daughter from my ward. I don't want to see either of you again. Understand?"

"Can you get my daughter out of her coma?"

"Don't worry about that. Worry about what I'm telling you. Your daughter will wake up in the next twenty-four hours. I'll cover this up as best I can, but remember what I said. The next time I see you will be the last."

Daniel nodded his consent. "I don't want my daughter caught up in this. I don't want her to know the truth. Not yet, anyway."

"What are you going to do about Hilltop?"

He couldn't answer the question. Not because he didn't know, but because it would place the ward sister in further trouble. Hilltop was as guilty as a man could be, but he was acting under orders. Daniel needed to know whose orders he had followed.

They walked out of the room together. The ward sister didn't say goodbye. She turned her back and walked away.

"Sister?"

She stopped, but didn't face him. There was something about the stiffness in her shoulders that dried his mouth.

"If you ever need anything, we're … the Daytons, I mean … we can help. With things."

Disappointment radiated from her. She picked up her pace and disappeared around a corner. He listened to the squeak of her shoes fade into silence.

If the measure of his origins was how far he could corrupt innocent people, then Daniel was a Dayton to his core. Just like the father who hurt his family to win a war. Just like everyone who bore the Dayton name. It was in him as sure as he had blood in his veins.

He wasn't going to let that corruption seep into his daughter. Eisha would be back in his arms in twenty-four hours and it would be over at last. He could take her to a new home, perhaps taking Lily too and they could start a life with Newcastle and the Daytons far behind them.

But there was blood to be shed first.

CHAPTER THIRTY-THREE

D r Hilltop eased himself on to the garden bench and dusted dry soil from his work trousers. He lived alone in a three storey Edwardian house in the suburbs of Sunderland. The area was quiet and the neighbours kept themselves to themselves, save for occasionally troubling him to sign a petition against council changes effecting their comfortable lives. Since his wife died last year, it was up to him to smile gamely and listen to their complaints.

Retirement age was looming. He remained active, playing golf twice a week, but his greatest joy was his garden. It was long and narrow with a green lawn he fed on a monthly basis and borders stocked with mature, herbaceous plants. It had been neglected lately due to other demands on his time. He blamed the Daytons for that, but his nightmare would be over soon and he could get back to his simple pleasures.

His last job today was the biggest. Although the weeds had been cleared, he still had to chop down the cherry tree at the bottom of his garden. He had planted it as a sapling when his son Brandon was born and like his son, the tree had fully matured. He remembered sitting under it on the day Brandon had received his university results. He hated the idea of destroying something that held so many memories, but it was a job he had been putting off for years. It was too big and cast too many shadows. He would replace it with a play house. Perhaps Brandon might introduce him to his grandchild then, who was now four years old.

"You can't keep doing this," Brandon had said, "and I can't watch you do it. Think about Mam. Think about the stress you're putting her under. You'll kill her one of these days."

What would Brandon have done? It was a question he asked himself over and over, but his son was no gambler. He had witnessed how close his father had repeatedly brought them to ruination. Losing serious money to Ed Dayton was a dangerous hobby and debts always had to be paid. At first it had been false prescriptions and tending to knife and gunshot wounds. When Daniel Dayton foolishly got his girlfriend pregnant, it was Hilltop who delivered the baby and falsified the documentation. Afterwards, he became the Dayton's personal physician and his fate was sealed.

But when he was approached to look after Eisha, it had all gone too far. It didn't matter that he acted under duress and he pleaded not to be involved. He had done something his son would never countenance.

As he studied the cherry tree, calculating which branch to remove first, guilt gnawed at his conscience. He could have gone to the police and told them everything. Redemption didn't always follow confession, but at least his family would have been safe. Or would they? If the Daytons could buy themselves a doctor, he was sure they could buy themselves a policeman or two.

He didn't know much about their organisation, but he'd heard things at the roulette table. There was a back room in a pub called The Royal Oak. He had checked in his coat and ordered an orange juice while he took his lucky seat at the table. The crumbling walls were decorated in neon signs for Budweiser and Pepsi. The carpet stuck to his feet if he lingered too long, but it didn't matter. Neither he nor his fellow degenerates were there for the atmosphere.

He nodded at the man sitting by his side. No-one here offered their names, but he recognised his oily ponytail and the stench of his aftershave. Hilltop hadn't seen him for a while, but the lure of the tables was too strong to resist. After he'd sold Brandon's new car to cover a debt, his shame sent him to Gambler's Anonymous, but he only attended for two months. It had felt like an eternity.

The man pushed a pile of chips onto red. "Bet the house, my man. Bet the house." His voice was thick with alcohol and he wore the sloppy grin of a drunk.

"Too rich for my blood," Hilltop said, placing a single blue chip on the first twelve, though experience told him his conservatism wouldn't last.

"I know what I'm talking about." The man went to tap the side of his nose and missed. "The Daytons? The people who own this place? They're going down. They won't last another week."

The next day, he called in sick, expecting someone to look for him. It was the first holiday he'd taken since Eisha was admitted. He was exhausted, but couldn't rest. He sat in the hallway on a chair he'd dragged from the kitchen and waited for a knock on his door that never came.

Day turned into night and he paid a secret visit to Eisha. If the rumours were true, then he couldn't allow this little girl to pay for his mistakes. Hilltop lowered the dosage on the medication and started a private record of her treatment. He'd use it as evidence in his defence, though he doubted it would protect his medical license. His best hope was to show that despite his crimes, he was still a professional.

When news of Ed Dayton's death reached him, he knew he had been saved. He was free to be the doctor he had trained to be all those years ago, but he had to be careful. The ward sister was like a terrier when things looked wrong. Eisha needed to be weaned off the drugs, but he'd have to do it secretly.

For now, his most important task was to avoid Daniel Dayton, whose presence at the hospital was both a surprise and a worry. He remembered him from Eisha's birth. Even as a young man,

Daniel had scared him. It wasn't just his temper that was unnerving. Training as a doctor, Hilltop had dissected many cadavers, but Daniel was the only person he knew who could cut a man open simply by looking at him. Hilltop's guilt was written on his face and Daniel would recognise it instantly.

The muscles in his body stiffened. He'd have to keep moving or he'd never get off this garden bench. It was time for action.

He replenished the petrol in his chainsaw. Checking the chain was tight around the guide bar, he primed the pump. Hilltop pulled the starter and it started first time. He smiled to himself. His luck was changing for the better already.

Hilltop sawed through the lower branches, peppering himself in sweet smelling wood shavings. He wondered what his grandchild looked like. Did he have Brandon's strong nose? His shaggy hair? He hoped to see a little of his wife in there too, as he did when he saw hurt in Brandon's eyes.

He didn't hear the squeak of his garden gate as it opened behind him and although Daniel's approaching footsteps were heavy, the sound of the chainsaw drowned them out. Hilltop was oblivious until it was too late.

CHAPTER THIRTY-FOUR

Standing on one leg, Bronson discreetly polished his shoe on the back of his trousers. He had spent the morning buffing them to a high shine, but after Scott ordered him to make a sweep of the garden, they were dirty again. He smoothed down his suit and sipped his lager, attempting to relax. This wasn't the time to embarrass himself.

Five Oaks was filled with the clink of champagne flutes and music from a string quartet in the corner. No-one had told them they were seated on the site where Ed had crashed to his death. His body was still at the mortuary so Scott had organised a memorial. The hall housed top ranking criminals from all over the country. Mo Curley and Mr and Mrs Maguire huddled in a group of their own. The Glasgow contingent was represented by Smally and his Uncle Pete Joley. They had brought their mistresses in place of their wives and Bronson wondered if they were here to pay their respects or for the party. There were a few members of the Elephant boys, a large criminal fraternity from South London and several men and women from Liverpool.

Where other teenagers had grown up worshiping footballers or film stars, Bronson admired the people in this room. Like him, they had come from nothing, but by optimising their talent for violence, they had become living legends. One day, he hoped to himself. One day.

Smally caught Bronson staring at him. He whispered into his mistresses' ear and she giggled, looking over her shoulder. Slapping her on the arse, Smally excused himself and approached.

"It's a pleasure to meet you, Mr Washington," Bronson said, offering his hand. "Can I help you with anything?"

Smally looked down at Bronson's out stretched hand while stuffing his own into his pocket. "Where are the toilets?" he asked.

Bronson pointed to a door and watched him waddle away.

"Don't mind him, Charlie. He's a prick." Liz was at his side. She wore a shimmering silk dress with a matching scarf. He tried to ignore the way her clothes clung to her figure. She twirled an empty champagne flute by the stem.

"Can I get you another, Mrs Dayton?" he asked.

"I'm capable of getting my own booze and how many times do I have to tell you? It's Liz."

Bronson smiled awkwardly. Smally left the toilets, dusting away the tell-tale signs of cocaine from his nose and headed in their direction. He grinned at Liz, his fat cheeks wobbling as he leered at her body. "And how's the beautiful widow?" he asked. "Not too sad, I hope. There's plenty of ways I can cheer you up."

She pushed her glass under his chins and forced him to look her in the eye. "Do they call you Smally because you're short or because you have a tiny dick?"

Bronson snickered, trying to hide his laughter and a red faced Smally shot him a hard stare. "I think I will shake your hand now," he said, grabbing Bronson's. "I didn't wash after taking a shit, but that won't bother you, will it?"

Smally gave him a wink before returning to his date, who was already flirting with his uncle.

"When did drug dealers and pimps have such an inflated sense of their own worth?" Liz asked. "People like that have no respect. This is Ed's funeral, for God's sake."

Suddenly, she was crying and Bronson pulled her into an embrace. She was taller than him and he was aware how close his face was to her breasts. He smelled her floral perfume. Her body trembled in grief and her arm snaked around his broad back to hold him closer. He moved away, handing her a handkerchief.

Ma Dayton stepped in between them, appearing in a puff of cigarette smoke.

"Apparently, our Scott is going to make an announcement."

As she spoke, the music stopped and the eyes of the guests looked Up at the second floor where the office door opened. Scott and Monica walked out, arm in arm. He was dressed in a slim fitting dinner suit while Monica wore a sparkling gown of white that floated around her ankles. They descended the stairs, smiling and waving at the guests.

The atmosphere in the room changed. The mouths of the guests hung open. They were statues, like the marble ones Ed used to decorate the hall.

Scott stopped halfway down the stairs and placed a gentle kiss on Monica's cheek.

"What are they bloody playing at?" Ma Dayton asked.

Liz tapped her finger against her glass while Ma Dayton puffed on her cigarette. They were acting like royalty, Bronson thought. Worse than that, they were acting like a couple. It was beyond disrespectful. It was an insult to a man who had yet to be buried.

Leaning into him for support, Liz's eyes were transfixed on the drama playing out on the stairs.

Scott raised his hands, as if he were halting applause, though the room was bewildered into silence. He smiled and turned to Monica, who cleared her throat.

"Thank you for joining us on this sad occasion. I'm sure Ed would have been touched by your attendance."

"As you know, these have been difficult times for the Daytons," Scott said, "but we will rise above it. I can assure all our friends and business partners, our troubles are over. My father was a great man and will be missed by us all, but I'm in charge now. I have brokered a deal between ourselves and the crew that have supposedly been targeting us. By this time tomorrow, the Daytons will be back in power."

There was a ripple of applause, but it was less than heartfelt. Looking at the guests, Bronson saw disappointment, anger and jealousy. Some guests looked perturbed and others were uncomfortable, but they were all trying to work out how this affected their bottom line.

"What is he playing at?" asked Ma Dayton. She looked at Liz, but neither she nor Bronson had an answer.

Scott waved the clapping crowd quiet again. "And there's more good news. This is a new beginning for all of us. As a celebration of that, I want to announce that Monica and I are getting married."

There was a sharp intake of breath from the whole room.

"You can't," shouted Liz.

"And we're having a baby," Scott continued. "As you can see, I am every bit of the man my father used to be. I have his power, his wealth and his wife. I don't want your condolences and I don't need your blessing. But I will have your respect."

"It's a disgrace," Ma Dayton said, pushing through the crowd. "It's incest. You're disgusting. The pair of you. My son died not ten feet from where you're standing."

Monica clasped her hands together, a smile frozen on her face. "I'm so glad you could be here."

"Shut up, Nanna," Scott said, "and stop smoking in my fucking house."

Spitting her cigarette to the floor, Ma Dayton waved her fists. "If my Ed were alive today, he'd tear you two to pieces. How dare you trash his good name? There was always something wrong with you, Scott. And you," she shouted, steering her attention to Monica. "You're nothing but a money grabbing hussy."

All eyes were on Ma Dayton, except for Bronson's. His were on Daniel as he entered the hall carrying a plastic bag. He walked calmly through the crowd and found a space at its centre. Bronson's instinct was to rush forward, to stop Daniel doing whatever it was he'd come here to do, but his feet were like lead.

And if Daniel was here to kill his brother, Bronson wasn't sure he wanted to stop him anyway.

"It was Scott. It was Scott," Liz repeated in a whisper.

Ma Dayton lit another cigarette. "Is this how you grieve, lad? Is this how you repay your father for his sacrifices? Mark my words. The devil will come for you one day."

Daniel launched the bag into the air. Scott and Monica saw it first, ducking as it sailed above their heads, landing behind them on the stairs. Ma Dayton stopped shouting to watch the bag bounce down the stairs, trundling by the happy couples' legs before it spilled its contents on the floor. A bloody head rolled free, resting at Ma Dayton's feet. The milky, lifeless eyes of Dr Hilltop looked at the crowd, his face contorted in a final scream.

CHAPTER THIRTY-FIVE

The crowd ran for the exits. There were cries and screams. People fell under one another's shoes, unheeded and trampled on by the desperate. Bronson elbowed his way through, leading Liz by the hand. She stumbled, toppling off her high heels. He swept her up before she sank and carried her to the main doors. "Get out of here," he said. "Don't come back."

Liz ran down the steps, fumbling in her handbag for her car keys. Bronson fought to get back into the hall. It was harder going against the tide. Using his shoulders, he barged his way in.

Ma Dayton stood screaming, her arms pressed to her side, attempting to make herself a smaller target. Outside, car engines fired into life. Launching into the churning crowd, Bronson grappled his way forward, pulling Ma Dayton to safety. He held her tightly as he looked at the main doors. They were blocked by people clambering over one another. He saw Smally inching his bulk to freedom. There was no sign of his date.

He dragged Ma Dayton toward the throng, kicking and punching anyone in his way. Mr and Mrs Maguire scrambled ahead of him. He reached out and used Mr Maguire's shirt collar to yank him backwards and onto the floor. Mrs Maguire was too focused on her own escape to notice. Bronson used her as a battering ram and broke through the jam at the door. They all fell forward until they were free and tasted fresh air.

Bronson and Ma Dayton hurried down the outside steps. Liz was trapped in a bottle neck of cars and he marched the elderly woman to the passenger side of her car.

"Can you take her home?" he asked, opening the door.

Ma Dayton was white with shock. She didn't even have a cigarette in her mouth. He threw her into the car and slammed the door behind her, running back into the hall.

The guests were gone. Scott and Monica were frozen on the staircase. Daniel prowled the hall, his eyes fixed on theirs, his muscles bunched and primed for attack. He looked rabid and Bronson knew whatever happened next, he couldn't take Daniel down on his own. Out of the corner of his eye, he saw No Neck approaching softly. A cowering Noodles used a statue for cover.

The head of Dr Hilltop lay where it fell, the flesh of his neck wound dry and grey.

Monica ran her hands through her hair, her eyes wide and manic. "What have you done?"

Daniel stopped pacing the floor and looked at her. "Why don't you ask your fiancé?"

"What's he talking about?" asked Bronson.

All eyes were on Scott. His conviviality had left with the fleeing crowd. His face was as still as ice, a cruel sneer on his lips. He pulled on his tie, leaving it to hang loose over a crisp white shirt.

"Poor Dr Hilltop. So close to retirement," he said.

Scott stepped down the staircase, standing in front of his brother. He shrugged off his jacket and let it slip to the floor. It fell over Hilltop's dismembered head and hid its anguish from view. Tugging out his gold cufflinks, he threw them to one side and rolled up his sleeves. Daniel raised his fists and Bronson swallowed hard. No Neck stepped back.

"For the record, I was against you coming back at all," Scott said. They circled each other, two Titans ready to clash. "But there's nothing like a good, old fashioned tragedy to bring a family together."

"Did you do it?" Daniel asked, lowering his guard.

"It's what Dad wanted and what Dad wanted, I made sure he got."

"And they call me the idiot? There was one thing he wanted above all else, but I wouldn't give it to him."

Scott paused, a quizzical look on his face and waited for an explanation.

"I never told you why I left, did I?" Daniel said.

Bronson's heart clenched like a fist in his chest. What the hell was going on?

Daniel met everyone's gaze. His fury crackled off him like static, but there was a sadness in the lines around his eyes. No, not sadness, thought Bronson. Resignation, as if the secret he'd hoped to keep was being forced into the open.

"I know why," Scott said, opening his arms to the room. "We all know why. You're a coward and cowards have no place calling themselves a Dayton."

He took a step forward, crushing a champagne glass under his foot.

Daniel allowed him to get as close as he dared and pointed a finger at his brother. "I left because Dad wanted you dead. He wanted me to kill you and take over the family when he was gone."

Scott's eyes tightened and what little blood was in his face drained away. "You're lying."

Daniel shook his head. "We had it all. The money. The infamy. Why would I walk away from that? It was because of you. He made you as indifferent to human suffering as the fucking moon. I've done my fair share of evil, but he went too far with you. You were his atom bomb, something that couldn't be stopped once it exploded."

"And you were his favourite?"

"No. I don't know. I don't care. He saw something else in me," Daniel said. "Someone who could manipulate people in ways he never could with us."

The blood in Bronson's ears thudded loudly. He was dizzy. He glanced at the spot where he'd found Ed's destroyed body, his organs spilling onto the floor, steam rising as they cooled in the air. He remembered his sorrow and desolation. His world spun out of control and it was happening again right where it had happened before. The ground was shaking beneath him. Lifting his fingers to his cheek, it twitched and went still.

Scott took another step closer to Daniel and gave a hollow laugh. "Now I understand why you're spinning these lies. Dad's dead and you want to step into his shoes, is that it? I'm not good enough."

Daniel looked away and Bronson saw he'd made a mistake. Scott swung an almighty fist. There was a sound like someone striking a timpani drum and Daniel was lifted off his feet. Bronson and No Neck rushed forward and pinned Daniel where he fell.

"I know he loved you more," Scott said. "It didn't matter you were thicker than shit as long as you had your gift. I was glad when you left. Finally, I'd have him all to himself. I could prove myself."

"Our whole lives were leading up to that point, Scott. Like we were graduating from gladiator school. He only wanted the strongest. If I managed to kill you, he'd made the right decision. If you killed me, then he'd been wrong and you were the right man for the job. He'd sacrifice a son simply to ensure his empire survived. I had to disappear, don't you see? He would never have left us alone. One of us had to go."

Jesus Christ, thought Bronson. He's telling the truth. About all of it. Releasing his hold, he sat back on his heels and searched Daniel's face. No Neck held firm, looking at him in panic, but Bronson didn't care. He was watching the destruction of a world he believed in. The family he served, the men he loved, were nothing but animals.

Daniel lay on the floor, looking up at his brother. "You brought me here, Scott. You're going to pay for what you did to my daughter."

"Who's going to make me do that? You?" Scott asked through a sneer before turning to Bronson. "Get him upstairs."

The twitch in his cheek jerked rapidly, returning to its irregular beat while its owner remained stationery. "What did he do to Eisha?"

"Did you hear what I said?" Scott shouted. "Get the scumbag upstairs."

Daniel's lips trembled. His eyes welled up. He squeezed them shut and a tear rolled down his cheek. "He forced Hilltop to put his own niece in a coma."

A cry of shock escaped Monica's pursed lips. Noodles leaned against the wall for support. Even No Neck was stunned. Bronson got to his feet, wiping his hands on his trousers. "You killed the doctor? And now you're here to take revenge on your brother?" he asked Daniel, but he didn't answer.

Bronson picked up Hilltop's head by the ears and levelled it at Scott. "This is because of you."

Scott slapped Hilltop across the face and Bronson lost his grip. The head bounced along the floor, stopping at an abandoned cello. Searching the room, Scott tried to catch an eye, but no-one looked at him.

"It was my fault," Daniel said. "I shouldn't have left Eisha with you. I assumed she'd be safe with family."

Balancing on one leg, Scott polished his shoe on the back of his trousers. "Well, you know what they say about assumptions," he said, inspecting the shine before stamping hard on Daniel's upturned face. There was a crack of bone and Daniel's head rolled to one side, blood leaking down his face, his tearful eyes finally closed.

CHAPTER THIRTY-SIX

Daniel woke to the sound of arguing voices. His jaw ached and he searched his swollen mouth with his tongue for missing teeth. They were all there, but he could taste the strong flavour of blood. His nose throbbed and his face felt thick with bruising. He'd been thrown onto the sofa. Trying to get comfortable, he discovered his hands were bound behind his back.

He was in his father's office. Bronson and No Neck were nose to nose, spittle flying between them as they shouted at each other. Noodles paced the floor, his fingers clicking together. Monica was missing, but Daniel wasn't surprised. Fratricide was men's work.

He drew in a low, steady breath and found Scott behind their father's old desk, one hand slowly rubbing his lips, watching him wake through narrow eyes.

"Enough," shouted Scott.

A hush fell over the room and Noodles stepped forward. "I think we would all like to bid a fond farewell to Mr Ed Dayton, who was both a leader and a friend. I'm sure Scott, as the new head of the family, will steer us through current troubles and onto greater heights. Anything less wouldn't be the Dayton way."

Scott grimaced. "Thank you for your sincere words, Noodles. Now will everyone stop kissing Dad's fucking arse? This is my time. We have business to discuss."

Smacking his lips, Scott reached into his desk drawer to produce a bottle of Glenfiddich, like their father had done at the start of every meeting. When he placed it on the desk, it was empty and he knocked it to the floor, muttering under his breath.

"You mentioned something about solving our Fairbanks problem," Noodles prompted.

"Shouldn't we talk about…?" Bronson let the question hang in the air, but everyone knew what he was referring to. Their eyes glanced in Daniel's direction and he smiled back at them.

"What is it you want to talk about, Bronson?" Scott asked.

"It's just there was a lot of shit said down in the hall."

"Are you saying you believe Daniel over me?"

Bronson looked down at his shoes.

"Go on," said Scott.

"It's just that –"

"Just, what? Do you think I'm the kind of man who would harm his niece?"

"Go easy on him, Scott," Daniel said. "You're fucking your stepmother. Who knows what kind of man you are? I think Bronson has a right to ask."

He relaxed into the sofa. Scott's face went white with rage. It was a look he had grown accustomed to over the years. It usually heralded a death and Daniel hoped it might be his.

Instead, Scott turned his attention to Bronson. "Why does your cheek twitch so much?"

Bronson lifted his hand to his face as if Scott had hit him. Noodles and No Neck pretended to stare out of the crosshair porthole. Daniel strained against his bonds.

"You know why," Bronson said, turning away.

"I'm not done with you yet, you twitchy motherfucker. I want you to tell us all why you're a freak."

"What's this about?" Daniel asked.

"We're having a laugh, that's all. Like when you told me my own father wanted me dead. Come on, Bronson. Tell us the story. We could do with a giggle, couldn't we?"

Bronson's cheek danced frenetically, pleased to be the centre of attention. If his twitch was happy, Bronson was not. His face was crimson and he shuffled on his feet. Daniel imagined he was waiting for a hole to open up and swallow him.

Instead, Bronson raised his head, tucked his shoulders back and walked up to Scott, showing him his cheek. "I got this in a fight with a bully. He shoved a pencil in my face and caused nerve damage. Have you had a good look, Scott?"

"When you talk to me, you address me as Mr Dayton."

Shaking his head, Bronson walked away and dropped into the sofa next to Daniel, who shot him an admiring glance. Bronson crossed his legs and clasped his hands in his lap. "Let's get back to business, shall we? How have you solved our problem? And I also want to know how you got out of Frankland. You weren't in there long enough to dig a tunnel, so who gave you the keys?"

The atmosphere in the room grew oppressive. It was the first time Daniel had seen Scott unsure. He stood from the desk and leaned on it, pressing his knuckles into the surface. He looked like a silverback gorilla attempting to re-establish his authority. And he'd probably do it if Daniel didn't stop him first.

"I was there when Dad killed himself," he said. "Fairbanks doesn't want to take over the Daytons. He wants a ransom. Pure and simple. Scott's agreed to give him the money. It's the only way he could have been released from prison."

"Is that the deal you were talking about?" Bronson asked. "You bought your way out?"

"Fairbanks got the charges against me dropped. He had no choice but to go to the next in line. Being the eldest, that's me."

Daniel didn't know what was holding his hands together, but it was biting into his wrists as he twisted against it. "Dad gave his life to protect that money. He wasn't going to hand it over. My brother will though."

Scott slammed his fist into the desk and everybody jumped. "Yes, I'm going to pay him. You don't know what it was like in there. I'm going to pay him and he's going to go away."

"How do you know?" asked Daniel.

"It's about money. It's always been about money. Once Fairbanks has it, he has no other reason to stay."

Bronson stood from the sofa and approached Scott behind his desk. Daniel wondered if he would ever have been so brazen had his father still been alive. Scott stared at the desk, his knuckles whitening.

"I don't like it," Bronson said.

Scott refused to acknowledge his presence.

Bronson cleared his throat. "I don't like giving in. Your Dad didn't and I don't think you should either. Think of your reputation. Think of your father's legacy."

Scott raised his hand and slapped Bronson across his twitching cheek. The sound echoed around an otherwise quiet room. "No-one gives a fuck what you think. I'm running the show. You do as I say."

Bronson stood firm and Scott appraised him coolly. "You're like a dog, Bronson. Like a Labrador and it doesn't matter how often you beat a Labrador, it will always come back. The only thing they know is how to obey. Don't you ever talk to me like that again. You better make your mind up. You're either loyal to my father or to me. Now fuck off before I knock that twitch to the other side of your face."

Bronson did as he was told, pausing by Daniel. "I gave him a chance. It's up to you now." He shrugged and patted Daniel on the shoulder. Something slid down his back, falling near his fingertips. Bronson kept his eyes to the floor and stationed himself by the window.

Scott watched him with a snarl on his face and then turned to the lawyer. "How do I get my hands on that money, Noodles?"

"The coroner has issued an interim death certificate due to the ongoing inquest into your father's death. It means your father's legitimate assets have been transferred to an executorship account which I control."

Daniel didn't understand what Noodles was talking about. Nobody did, but it smelled like trouble for Scott.

"He's given you all our money?" Scott asked.

"I control it, but I can't spend it. After I have excised my duties and paid the outstanding tax, the assets will be transferred to a bank account no-one has access to for a period of six months."

Daniel laughed out loud. "Guess you won't be buying your way out of this one."

Scott ignored him. "Why would he do that?"

"It's a standard clause when businesses are inherited rather than bought. It's known as proof of competency. The children of many a wealthy family have squandered their parent's legacies rather than prospered by them. Essentially, you will have to show you are capable of running the business before it is entirely yours. It is an old tradition, but one we will have to abide by for the time being."

Scott paced the room. "We can't get money out of the legal businesses?"

Noodles shook his head. "Not for another six months. Your father always thought of them as his retirement fund. That is where the majority of the money resides."

"What about the other businesses? The main ones."

"Those are fluid accounts. Money goes in and out. I have those details. They are yours to do with as you will. Well, yours and Daniel's."

"What do you mean mine and Daniel's? Didn't my father say who was in charge?"

"Not exactly. Nothing was ever committed to paper. It would count as evidence."

Daniel leaned forward. His fingers were numb, no doubt purple and bloated with blood. They felt around a metal oblong with a textured surface. There was a small round button at the top. Pressing it, something whipped out of the oblong. He smiled when he recognised what it was.

"Dad never saw it as a problem," Daniel said. "He expected one of us to be dead by now. I told you I was telling the truth. If it makes you feel better, I want nothing to do with it. All I want is my daughter."

"Without naming a successor, there will always be talk about who the true boss is. Everyone knows I'm buying my way out of trouble instead of fighting. Shit, I'm in love with my dead Dad's wife. My reputation is fucked before I even start."

Daniel shrugged his shoulders and stared at the floor. His fingers fumbled with the knife Bronson gave him. He dropped it repeatedly. Any moment, Scott would figure out the answer to his problem and knowing Scott, he'd make it messier than it had to be.

"I can't let you leave this room." Looking up, he saw Scott holding an Automag V, a light weight semi-automatic pistol. Shit it, he thought.

"You and I will always be in competition. There'll always be a fight between us," Scott said. He aimed the pistol as Daniel worked frantically with the knife.

"The thing is, I have one more secret to tell you. It's about Dad."

"Don't care." His finger was on the trigger.

"Are you sure? It will blow your mind."

"The only person whose mind is going to be blown is yours, brother. Along with the rest of your fucking head."

"Don't do it," Bronson said, taking a step forward.

Scott glanced in his direction, a cold smile creeping across his face. "Why don't you sit next to your buddy?" He waved impatiently with the gun and Bronson joined Daniel on the sofa. "At least that way, if I miss, I might hit you."

The doors to the office slammed shut. They jumped at the noise and stared around the room. It was missing a lawyer. Noodles had bolted.

"He never could stand the sight of blood," Scott said. He aimed his gun at No Neck, who stood like a rabbit frozen in the glare of an Automag V. "You're not thinking of running off, are you?"

"No, sir, Mr Dayton. Not me."

"Good. Take a seat next to those two."

He hesitated, glancing at the door. Bronson turned, patting the arm of the sofa. "Come on, mate. We don't bite."

Trailing his feet, he reluctantly settled his bulk next to Bronson, who had to squeeze along to make more space.

Scott studied them over the barrel of his gun. "There's a way out of this. I kill you all. I pay off Fairbanks and no-one will ever know except Noodles and as we just saw, he's too spineless to do anything about it. Everything goes back to normal with my reputation intact."

No Neck jumped from the sofa, as if it was white hot. "Don't kill me. I can help you. I can help you get rid of the bodies."

"What a hero," Bronson said under his breath.

Daniel smiled. He had almost cut through his bindings.

"Yeah? Well maybe I let him live, Bronson and you're the one that goes to the bottom of the Tyne?"

"I'd sooner be face to face with a fucking halibut than take orders from a psycho. Working for the Daytons used to mean something."

"Do you want to know my other secret now?" Daniel asked.

Scott rolled his eyes and turned the gun on him. "And what's that?"

No Neck saw his chance and ran for the exit. Scott fired, but missed, hitting the door. Daniel leapt from the sofa, his hands loose, but his legs were weak. He stumbled, falling face down, his nose exploding with a fresh bout of pain. A shot rang out. He didn't feel anything and he knew instantly Bronson had taken the bullet. He was next and scrambled on the floor. There was the sound of fast footsteps. And the sound of a snap, leather slapping leather.

Something fell on him, something heavy. A body. It was Bronson, his weight pinning him down, preventing his escape. He wriggled, flipping onto his back. With a groan, he lifted him to one side and rolled to freedom.

Standing, but only barely, Daniel rubbed his throbbing face and looked about the room. "Jesus, what did you do?"

Bronson wasn't dead. He was propped against the sofa, holding Scott's gun by the barrel. His hands were shaking and his breath came in short, quick gulps. Daniel followed the direction of his gaze to where Scott lay on the floor. He looked back to Bronson. A bullet had grazed his arm. His clothing was torn and smouldering, but he wasn't bleeding. He'd been lucky, thought Daniel. Luckier than his brother.

"He missed me by a millimetre. I grabbed the gun and whipped him with it. I couldn't kill him, Daniel. Doesn't matter what he did. I'm sorry," Bronson said.

The gun clattered to the floor and Bronson cleaned his hand on his trousers in a slow, rhythmic circle that threatened to wear a hole in the material. His mouth was open. Pale skin. Chattering teeth. He was in shock, but Daniel doubted it had anything to do with narrowly avoiding death.

They stood in silence, watching Scott's chest moving in and out.

"We can't leave him," Daniel said. "If he wakes up, he'll kill you and –"

"I know. You want revenge for what he did to your daughter."

Picking up the Automag, Daniel checked there were enough bullets to do the job. It was still warm. "I'll do it."

Bronson held out his hand. "Give it to me. Your brother was a bad man, but he was still your brother. I'll take him somewhere and do it there. No-one will find him."

"He wasn't the man you thought he was, Bronson. I showed you that."

"None of you are. I looked up to him. Shit, I wanted to be him, but no matter what I did, I was always on the outside." Bronson took the gun from Daniel and slid it into the back of his trousers. "He deserves to be killed by someone who cares."

"I still need my revenge."

Bronson wiped his mouth with the back of his hand. "There's more to life, Daniel, but don't worry. Where he's going, he'll get his punishment."

His brother's death would be painless. Bronson would make sure of it. If he woke up, he'd be knocked out again before the bullet entered his brain. Double tap. Gangland-style. Hilltop had suffered a worse fate and he'd been a pawn in a much bigger game. It didn't seem fair, but then what death was?

He could ask himself if it had all been worth it. A dead father who wasn't his father. A brother who had died hating him. A life's work destroyed. And then he thought of Eisha and of Lily. There was a life waiting for all three of them. His life's work was only beginning.

As Bronson kneeled next to Scott's body with his head bowed, Daniel searched through the drawers of his father's desk. There were blank notebooks, old biro pens and a stray bullet from an unknown gun. He found what he wanted in the lowest drawer and threw his father's beloved family photo at Scott. It landed on his chest and jerked Bronson back to reality.

"Bury him with that," Daniel said, walking out of the room. "The Daytons are over."

CHAPTER THIRTY-SEVEN

Daniel stood in Lily's kitchen, squeezed between a kitchen table and a refrigerator humming loudly. The linoleum from the floor was rolled up and leaning in a corner, exposing rough, paint flecked floorboards. Boxes labelled 'photos' and 'towels' were stacked against the wall. It was her new home in Bensham, Gateshead, next door to a pizza shop that had recently burned down.

Lily had her back to him as she made coffee, cursing as she struggled to unscrew the top off a bottle of milk. He reached over her shoulder and took the bottle from her. Twisting it, the ridges grated against his skin. "Jesus. That's stuck fast. Sorry."

He handed it back and Lily dropped it in the bin.

"I take it you don't want sugar either?" she asked.

They sat at the kitchen table covered with a checked tablecloth. An empty vase stuffed with newspaper stood in the centre. They wrapped their hands around steaming mugs of black coffee.

"I knew this day would come," Lily said.

He smelled her perfume. It was light and fresh, in direct contrast to the damp he detected as soon as he entered. There was mould in the air. Somewhere a black fungus was growing.

Daniel moved the vase and reached out for her. She took his hand, but he sensed her reluctance.

"How did he die?" she asked.

His heart hammered in his chest and he swallowed down bile that burned the back of his throat. "I told you."

She caught his eye and he was too afraid to look away in case she caught him out in his lie. "You told me a man called Fairbanks killed him. That it was one of your stupid turf wars."

"That's right," he said, controlling his breathing.

He remembered tearing up the expensive carpet in the office. Together, Bronson and he wrapped up an unconscious Scott to muddy any evidence trail and carried him downstairs to a waiting car, bumping his head on the stairs as they went.

"But what happened?" Lily asked.

They'd dropped him into the boot and Daniel closed it quickly before he came to his senses.

"How are you going to do it?" he'd asked Bronson.

He'd shrugged and climbed into his car. "I've got a tyre iron in here."

"Wouldn't you prefer to use his gun? Might make it easier."

Bronson started the engine. "I'd prefer not to do it at all."

Slamming his door shut, Bronson sped down the gravel driveway. Daniel watched him leave and then collected the head of Dr Hilltop, pitching it into the lake.

Lily wrung his hand and he rubbed her knuckles with a fingertip. "There was a fight."

"And that's how you got the bruises on your face?"

He nodded. "Fairbanks had a gun. I couldn't stop him. He –"

Lily's face creased in pain. "I'm sorry," she said. "This can't be easy for you."

"It's not me I'm worried about." Daniel straightened in his chair. "I know you still care about him. I think it's best if I spare you the details. Try and remember him the way he was."

She looked away, her eyes travelling over the grease marks on her kitchen wall. He knew it would all come out eventually, but he wanted to save her from the worst for as long as he could.

How would she react when she learned her ex-husband had harmed Eisha? What would she say when she discovered Daniel had killed him for it? It was an unbearable thought and one he pushed to the back of his mind.

"I wish I could see him," Lily said. "Tell him I didn't hate him for leaving and landing me in this dump. It was part of his nature. He was distant. I don't think he'd have been happy with anyone, really."

The hum of the refrigerator grated on Daniel's nerves, putting him on edge. He was sure it would blow at any moment and shower them in ice. The room was claustrophobic. The smell of damp was cloying. He had to get out. He had to get away. His guilt was choking him.

"How many people have died because of this Fairbanks man?"

"Too many."

"Is it over now?"

He'd call Noodles later to arrange for the ransom money. Scott's plan to pay Fairbanks was as good as any. At least Daniel didn't have to worry about losing face. He and Bronson would get the money together and bring it back to Five Oaks. It would be safe there until Fairbanks contacted them.

"I'd do anything to keep you safe, Lily," he said. "You don't have to worry about Fairbanks."

Lily finished the dregs of her coffee, carefully placing the mug on the table. "I better get back to unpacking."

She reached for the vase and pulled out the newspaper. Smoothing it out, Lily slowly folded it into a square and tucked it in her pocket. Daniel caught sight of the date in the corner. It was over three months old.

"I thought you'd moved in recently," he said.

Shaking her head, the curls of her hair hid her face. "There never seems to be enough time to unpack. I had to bring Eisha with me and she didn't like it at first. She started acting up and then she was in hospital. I'll get around to it eventually. I sometimes think if I unpack, I'll have to accept I really live here."

"Maybe you won't have to unpack. Have you ever been to Scotland?" he asked.

"Isn't that where you ran away to?"

He winced at her wording, but described his cottage and the rolling hills that surrounded it. He told her about his business, his honest income and his plans for the future. He told her how he hoped Eisha would settle down quickly and make friends. Maybe he'd try to make a few friends himself.

When he finished, he was flush with excitement. He hadn't realised how much he missed his home until he'd described it to someone else.

"It sounds lovely, Daniel," she said.

Lily placed their mugs in the sink. Daniel stood behind her. He reached out, but stopped himself at the last second. If he touched her that way, the way he wanted to, it would be much more than words. He would make it real and it scared him. He feared her rejection, but he feared hurting her more.

Lily leaned on the sink for support. "I was hoping you would stay here. With me."

"I was hoping you'd leave."

He couldn't stay. The Daytons would crush him as they crushed everyone who tried to control them. He would be subsumed like a mouse in the stomach of a cat and his daughter would be next.

"Don't make your mind up yet," he said. "Come with me to the hospital. See your niece. Eisha will be awake by now."

Lily turned to face him. Her jaw was set and there were angry lines around her mouth. "How do you know she's awake? The last time I spoke to a nurse, she said there was no telling when she'd wake up. You haven't had any phone calls so how do you know?"

He shrugged and stared at the floor.

Lily jabbed him in the chest. "Stop trying to protect me and talk to me like an adult instead."

The weight of Daniel's head seemed impossible to lift.

Picking up his mug, she threw it against the refrigerator. Ceramic shards burst like a firework and the refrigerator stopping humming. "Answer me for once, Daniel. How do you know? Who attacked her? What happened to Scott? What do you want with me?"

Before he knew what he was doing, his lips were on hers and they kissed, desperate to find something in their embrace they couldn't express in words, but the moment passed quickly. Lily pushed him away, ignoring the pleading in his eyes. "There are too many lies in the Dayton world. I don't want the same life with you that I had with Scott."

"I would never lie to you," he said, remembering the story he invented regarding Scott's death. "Come with me to Scotland. We can start again. As a family."

"No."

"Why not?"

"When Scott left me, I saw what I was missing. A normal life with normal friends."

"That's what I'm offering you."

"Without secrets, Daniel. You measure out truth like you hand out sweets to a child. I thought you might have changed. I hoped it with all my heart, but you're a Dayton and you always will be."

"I'm trying to change. I'm trying to be free of this life. Believe me, I know how dangerous secrets can be."

Daniel heard a whining in his voice he didn't recognise as his own.

Lily's emerald eyes blazed. Her mouth was straight, but there was doubt in her face. She was waiting for reassurance and he couldn't give her any. There was none to give. She was right.

He gritted his teeth. "I'll be around for a few more days," he said. "You know how to reach me."

Lily nodded, holding back her tears.

"If you need anything…"

He left the sentence unfinished. Closing the door, he lingered on the step gulping fresh air. There was a click behind him and he knew Lily was on the other side, turning the lock. He forced his heart to harden, but he couldn't stop loving her while he could taste her on his lips. With nothing more to say and nothing he could do, he turned up the collar on his coat and walked away, knowing he would never return.

CHAPTER THIRTY-EIGHT

"**D**ad?"

Eisha's eyes fluttered open. Her voice was weak, but there was a crumpled smile on her face. Daniel had left Lily's home and went directly to the hospital where he'd waited by his daughter's bedside. The nurses had offered him countless cups of tea and coffee, which he'd dismissed, though the ward sister had kept her distance. He was content to sit and watch his daughter, and imagine the future they'd soon be living together.

"Is it really you, Daddy?"

He embraced her. "Yes, it's me, baby."

She trembled beneath him. The warmth of her arms around his neck went straight to his heart. It was almost too much to take. He buried her face in kisses.

"Where am I?" she asked.

He sat down, but held fast to her hand. "You're in hospital."

Eisha looked scared, scrutinising the medical equipment in her room. "Is there something wrong with me?"

"You just had a long sleep, that's all."

She relaxed and smiled at him, rubbing her eyes. He hadn't seen them in so long, he'd forgotten they were the same shade of hazel as his own.

"I still feel sleepy," she said.

"What's the last thing you remember?" Daniel asked.

She scrunched up her face as she tried to answer. Daniel waited patiently, but Eisha shook her head. "I can't remember. I'm sorry."

"It's okay." He was glad in a way. There'd be time to tell her everything later when they'd both had time to adjust. Luckily, for him at least, it wasn't going to be today.

"It's all mushy in my head. Is that what's wrong with me?"

"It's just the medicine they gave you when you were asleep. Dad's head is mushy all the time and I'm okay, aren't I?"

She watched him carefully, her eyebrows raised. She looked worried again.

"What is it?" he asked.

"You were away for ages. Much longer than I liked."

"I know, but things have changed. We can be together again."

Eisha's face brightened. "Good. I missed you. I don't mind falling asleep and waking up in hospital if it means you're going to stay."

Daniel shifted uncomfortably.

"Do you remember what I said when you went away?" she asked.

He frowned. "What do you mean?"

"When you were in the car and you left me in the rain?"

The memory rushed at him and he was sliding down a sink-hole. The hospital was gone and he was back in his car. Daniel remembered. He remembered leaving her very well. She had spoken to him, but her words were drowned in the drumming of the rain.

"I told you," he said, trying to keep his voice from breaking, "my head's mushy all the time. I can't remember. What did you say?"

Eisha placed her hand on top of his. It was so light, he hardly felt it.

"I said, 'I'm angry.'"

He sat up slowly in his chair, watching her watching him. Angry? Because he left? Or because of something else? She had always been a wilful child, but never angry. Then again, he was often working. Perhaps he had missed the worst of her tantrums, leaving them to be dealt with by Lily. She'd mentioned Eisha had been acting up. Was it all part of the same thing?

"Why were you angry, honey?" he asked.

Eisha gave him a comforting smile. "I just am. All the time."

The ward sister appeared at the door. Her stern face lit up when she saw Eisha awake and well. "Hello there, pumpkin. How are you feeling?"

"My Dad has come back," Eisha answered, pointing at him.

The Sister consulted the monitors, scribbling numbers in her notebook. It was the same one she'd used to access Hilltop's records that ultimately cost him his life. "He's like a lost penny, isn't he? Though not quite as valuable."

Daniel coughed into his hand. "We were just talking about how Eisha doesn't know how she got here."

Glancing up from her notes, the ward sister met his gaze and her face grew stern again. "Do you?"

Hilltop had told him everything. Scott had drugged his daughter and presented her to the doctor for safe keeping. The exact details didn't bother him. He had found the men responsible and they had been punished accordingly. That was all he cared about.

He patted his daughter's knee. "How would I know?"

His iPhone sounded a message and he retrieved it from his pocket. It read '5pm. Bring a picnic to Jesmond Dene.' Fairbanks had called the meet. By tomorrow evening, this would all be over, he thought and sighed his relief.

Placing the phone back in his pocket, he noticed the ward sister watching him, her eyes glinting.

"I'll leave you two to catch up. Family time is so important," she said before leaving.

For the next hour, he sat at Eisha's bed and talked as father and daughter. Eisha told him about school, her new dress and Auntie Lily. He talked about the weather, Scotland and Auntie Lily. Occasionally, Eisha frowned and Daniel asked if she was okay. She smiled or nodded and told him she was fine.

And all the while, Daniel was trying to forget what his daughter had said about being angry.

She began to tire, snapping her eyes open every time her lids drooped, but it was a losing battle. Daniel tucked the blanket around her and kissed her forehead.

"I don't want to go to sleep again, Dad," she said.

"It's okay, pet. It'll only be for a little bit. Not like last time."

"Will you be here when I wake up?"

Daniel was about to answer, but Eisha was already asleep. He sneaked out of her room, casting a backward glance when the ward sister approached. "Can I have a word, Mr Dayton?"

Daniel followed her into the waiting room. It was empty again. Did anyone ever come to see these sick kids, he wondered?

"Eisha is doing well," the ward sister said. Her voice was flat, as if the last few days had robbed her of sleep. "She's ready to go home."

Daniel held up his hands, but she immediately shooed them away. "No, Mr Dayton, we had an agreement."

"I know and I'm sorry, but I can't take her. She needs someone to look after her and I can't be there."

"Why?"

Daniel grazed his cheek with the palm of his hand and swallowed hard. "I'm busy."

The ward sister ground her heel into the floor. "Busy? Are you her father or not?"

"Sister, I appreciate all you've done, but it's not safe to take Eisha home at the moment. One more day. Surely you can't discharge her the moment she wakes?"

"You will not use this hospital as a surrogate family, Daniel. You need to take some responsibility."

He looked at the Disney characters on the wall. Whoever had drawn them was good, but not that good. The characters weren't quite right. The smile on Donald Duck's face made him look sad. Cinderella's eyes were crossed. They were poor imitations of what they were supposed to be and everybody knew it.

The ward sister cleared her throat. "Dr Hilltop hasn't been to work and there is no answer at his home. Do you know anything about that?"

Daniel took a deep breath and let it out slowly. "No."

She held his gaze and then frowned, checking the watch pinned to her uniform. "I can feel your presence dirtying everything I hold dear. I want you out."

"I'll go, but Eisha has to stay. I'll send someone to pick her up. Okay?"

Her disgust was written all over her face. Daniel flushed, admonished by her judgement. Another broken promise, he thought. The ward sister had done so much to help him. It was because of her his daughter was back in his life.

"This is no way to thank you, but –"

She didn't stay to hear the rest of his apology. Returning to the nurses' station, the ward sister busied herself with pointless paperwork, striving not to look in his direction.

He hated leaving Eisha so soon after getting her back, but she was in the best of care. No matter what she felt about him, the ward sister was a professional. Daniel left the hospital and texted Lily about Eisha. He couldn't bring himself to speak to her in person yet.

Leaving the hospital, Daniel called Bronson and gave him his instructions.

CHAPTER THIRTY-NINE

The offices of Reeceman and Co were above a branch of Laurie's Estate Agents in Walker. Its heavy door was clean, but unmaintained. Black paint flaked away to reveal a red undercoat. Electrical wires hung loose from the doorway where the doorbell had been. By the brass handle was a handwritten note taped to the door with one word on it – 'Closed'.

Daniel had watched the entrance for over an hour while waiting for Bronson to arrive. No-one came or went. He wasn't surprised. The Daytons were Noodles' only clients, but the note on his door worried him. His patience was stretched thinly enough. He emerged from his hiding spot by the bins of a bakery called Bagel of the North and tried the door. It was open.

Climbing a narrow staircase to the second floor, Daniel winced every time a step creaked. He found a glass door marked Office, but no receptionist. Packing boxes were stacked against the wall.

"Daniel? Is that you?"

He entered and saw Noodles by the window, his hands clasped behind his back. He wore another ill-fitting suit and a smile that showed his yellow teeth. The room was lit by two dirty windows and a bare bulb hanging from the ceiling. Dented metal filing cabinets lay open and empty. There were more packing boxes standing on Noodles' desk.

"Going somewhere?" Daniel asked.

"Yes. Far away from here."

"And when were you going to tell me?"

"I wasn't going to tell you. I worked for your father, not you. I entertained the idea of working for your brother. There is still money to be made from the Dayton name, but having narrowly escaped with my life, I realised my time here had come to a close."

The carpet of the office was threadbare. Daniel's footsteps reverberated as he closed the gap between them, but Noodles was faster than he anticipated, retreating quickly behind his desk. The barrier was more psychological than physical. There was no need to breach it yet.

Daniel stepped back. "I'm not here to hurt you and I have no problem with you leaving, but I need access to my money."

Noodles' fingers clicked together like the mandibles of an ant. "What money?"

"The money that's held in trust. Dad's dead. Scott's dead. That money belongs to me."

Noodles smiled and made a show of patting his pockets. "I'm afraid I don't have it on me."

Daniel looked about the room, trying to appear casual as he searched for a potential weapon. "What's in the boxes?"

Noodles lifted a box from his desk with a groan. The weight was too much and it slipped from his grasp. As it hit the floor, the box burst open, shedding countless sheets of paper covered in spidery black writing. He tutted and braced his hands on the small of his back. Daniel could tell he was playing for time. He just didn't know why.

"This is my insurance. I have catalogued every transaction, every deal, every crime the Daytons ever committed since they came to power. Should anything happen to me, they are destined for the hands of some very powerful and law abiding men."

"You have everything in there? Including details of my adoption?"

Noodles' eyebrows arched in amazement and he slowly started clapping. "You finally worked it out. Good for you. Those types of secrets can kill a family, don't you think?"

"Do you?" he asked again.

Daniel forgot about Fairbanks and his money. This was his chance to get some answers about his real parents. It might help him understand why he was so isolated or maybe why his daughter was so angry.

He kept his eyes trained on the paper slewed across the floor as if it were the Holy Grail.

"No, I don't have any record of that, Daniel. I knew it was something I could never use. Your father had you and your brother so brainwashed into believing you were Daytons, I was sure you would kill me for even hinting it might be otherwise."

"You don't know anything?"

"I only have a name. Ranta Mustonen. Finnish, I believe, but working with the Network in Glasgow. I didn't see the need to delve any deeper. Frankly, I didn't care. Now if we're done visiting, I'm afraid I'm very busy."

Noodles pulled the lid from another of his boxes and delved inside while Daniel stared at the floor. He had never heard of a Mustonen and he'd worked with every known face in the UK. Had his father kept them apart to keep his secret? Was this man still alive? And if he was, what was he doing selling children to high ranking criminals?

He was getting frustrated and needed to concentrate. As usual, there were more questions than answers. It was something he could investigate later. Like Noodles, Daniel was busy too.

"I know you told me that to stall for time, Noodles, but I appreciate it anyway. It might just save your life. Now tell me about my money."

Noodles' papery face crinkled in disapproval. "As stated previously, there are two accounts. The first holds the bulk of your father's funds. Some eighty million pounds. The second is smaller, holding only two hundred thousand pounds. If what you say is true about Scott, then they both belong to you."

"I need ten million by five o'clock today."

"There is no money, Daniel."

"But you just said –"

"Did you honestly believe all that nonsense about proof of competency? I made it up to afford me time to transfer the money to myself. Your father trained you and your brother to be experts in the art of inflicting misery on others. No-one is more competent at being a Dayton than you, but you were never very smart."

Daniel made to leap over the desk, but the lawyer whipped his hands out of the box and produced a gun.

"It's an old Luger, but I assure you it works."

"You sly, back stabbing bastard," Daniel shouted.

"Says the man who abandoned his daughter, only to return and watch the rest of his family die."

Daniel paced the room. "Fairbanks wants that money. If he doesn't get it, he'll keep on killing until he does."

"Not my problem. The money was transferred to a bank account in the Cayman Islands, which in turn invested it in several building firms and logging companies in Brazil. I couldn't give it back even if I wanted to. And I really don't want to."

"Then I'll tell Fairbanks you have it. How long do you think you'll last with him in your life?"

Noodles laughed. It sounded like glass beads falling onto a solid floor. "I have passports in five different names. I have properties in four different countries under names no-one else knows. Fairbanks is uncommonly bright, but without an in-depth knowledge of the law, he has no hope of following a paper trail so complex. The world belongs to criminals like me, Daniel. Not thugs like you."

"And what's to stop me jumping over that desk and snapping every dry bone in your body?"

A quizzical look passed over Noodles' face. He looked at the gun as if to check it was still in his hand. "I'll shoot you if you do anything other than leave the way you entered."

"You won't shoot me. You're a lawyer, not a thug. Remember?"

Noodles smiled and kept the gun aimed at Daniel. "You're right. No-one reads people like you."

The floorboards creaked. Daniel span on his heels to see No Neck in the doorway, his bulk blocking the gap. He weighed a metal baton in his hand and seemed overly keen to use it.

"Who else knows you're here, Daniel?" Noodles asked.

"No-one."

Noodles waved the Luger. "Are you sure?"

Daniel looked between the two men and nodded.

"I believe you." Noodles pulled the trigger, shooting at the ceiling and bringing down a plume of plaster. It was a distraction and it worked. Daniel flinched, coughing as the dust hit the back of his throat. He turned in time to see No Neck advancing, raising the baton above his head. Daniel ducked, but not low enough. The baton connected with the side of his head and he fell to the floor to the sound of running footsteps.

***

"Daniel? Mate?"

He woke to find Bronson shaking him vigorously by the shoulder. It was an effort to open his eyes. When he prised his lids apart, he wished he hadn't. His head throbbed and his stomach churned with nausea. He gingerly pressed his fingers to his head and discovered the wetness of blood.

"What happened?" Bronson asked.

"That twat Noodles happened. He's done a runner with our money."

Daniel pulled himself up on his elbows and waited until the room stopped spinning. He glanced at Bronson and noted the suspicious look on his face. "What is it?"

"Noodles knocked you out? He couldn't tear the skin off his custard without help."

Leaning on Bronson for support, Daniel climbed to his feet. "He had help. Some guy jumped me while my back was turned. That big black No Neck guy."

His voice echoed and he looked about the room. It was empty. The boxes were gone. Noodles had taken his insurance policy with him.

"Have a look through that desk, will you? We might be able to figure out where he went."

Daniel fought the urge to be sick while Bronson yanked open the drawers of Noodles' desk, throwing them to the floor with a crash. "There's nothing here. Oh, hang on. This one's locked."

He patted down his pockets. "My car's outside. I've got something in the boot."

If the drawer was locked, it must be hiding something important, thought Daniel. Noodles had forgotten about it in his haste. Finally, they were catching a break.

When Bronson returned, Daniel expected him to be carrying a kit similar to the one he had used to break into Mosely's house. Instead, he hefted a crowbar in his hand with a grin. "This won't take long."

Bronson jammed the bar under the lock so it protruded outwards like a lever. He stamped down on it and the lock gave instantly. He was showered with splinters of wood, but the job was done and he opened the drawer.

He looked up at Daniel, unsure of himself. "You're not going to like this, boss."

"I'm not your boss." He joined Bronson on the other side of the desk and saw the note Noodles had left them.

It read, 'Just my idea of a joke. Fondest regards, Noodles.'

"Wait till I get my hands on him," Bronson said, hurling the crowbar at the wall.

Daniel walked to the window and stared at the street below. Young men and women hurried off to work, clutching take-away coffees and consulting their smart phones. They'd punch in, punch out and do it all again tomorrow. Daniel gnawed at his finger. If only his life could be that boring.

"He's been planning this for a while," Daniel said. "He had time to play his little prank so I'm guessing he felt all other bases were covered. There is no way we could find him in time. Even if we did, he won't have the money on him."

"We can't just let him go."

Daniel spat a sliver of skin at the window, a habit he had picked up from his father. "How much money did you manage to collect?"

Bronson grimaced. "I went everywhere you told me, but they've gone to ground. There just wasn't enough time, mate."

"How much?"

"Six hundred thousand. I was lucky to get that. People would rather take their chances holding back than stumping up what they owe."

Daniel didn't know how much money the Daytons had on the street, but he knew it had to be more than six hundred thousand. Fairbanks wouldn't even take that as a down payment. Daniel was sure of that much.

Picking up the crowbar, he swung it at Noodles' desk. It landed with a thud and cracked the surface. He swung it again. And again. As if he was chopping down a tree with an axe. His head hurt and his ribs ached, but it felt good to destroy something. Scorched earth, he thought.

He stopped when the desk was reduced to wooden fragments and sweat stung his eyes.

"Fairbanks wants the money by five today," he said, panting. "It's a drop off at Jesmond Dene. What are we going to do?"

"We could tell him we're not going to pay. I never liked the idea anyway."

"He'll pick us off one by one. We might deserve that, but our families don't."

The twitch in Bronson's face stopped. "It's a drop off, you said?"

"Yeah, why?"

Bronson grinned and smoothed down his hair. "How are your sea legs?"

CHAPTER FORTY

The North Sea around Seaburn Harbour was calm, but always cold. Grey waves toppled onto the shingle beach while driftwood dried under a steely sky. Seagulls settled on the orange sandstone faces of the cliffs and squawked incessantly. It was a cool day and only the stalwarts braved the seafront. Parents sat huddled on deckchairs holding cartons of chips for warmth while their children built sandcastles wearing hats and gloves.

Daniel stood and watched their pink skin turn blue.

"I've got the money," Bronson said, fanning a wad of notes in Daniel's face. "Are you sure you want to go ahead with this?"

Pulling his coat tighter, he stamped his feet. "A bad plan's better than no plan, right?"

He followed Bronson down a steep road into the Seaburn Yacht Centre, a private owned harbour where boats and yachts of various sizes were tethered to wooden jetties. As they prowled the floating gangways, Daniel felt the gentle rise and fall of the waves underneath and turned green. Whoever his true parents were, they definitely weren't sailors.

Bronson capered ahead and they found a cabin cruiser on jetty fourteen called the Slippery Eel. Neither men knew anything about boats, but at thirty-two foot and well-polished, they were impressed. It was white with a black streak along the side. The long and pointed bow gave it a predatory look.

Out of the cabin popped the head of a ruddy faced man in his forties.

"Peter," shouted Bronson as way of a greeting.

Daniel followed Bronson on board, feeling uneasy with the bobbing motion of the boat and shook hands with the ginger haired man.

"Daniel, this is Peter Pan Hands."

Peter gave him a wink. "I was a wee thief when I was a nipper. People said my hands were as big as pans and could carry twice as much."

Daniel tried to hide his confusion. Peter smiled. "Maybe it was an Irish thing. You lads said you were in a hurry? Well, I've got what you're after down in the cabin."

The cabin stretched along two thirds of the boat with enough room for a kitchenette and seating area. There were two doors, which Daniel assumed were for the toilet and bedrooms. Peter and Bronson settled easily, but he was forced to stoop against the ceiling, stiffening his legs against the rolling boat. Windows either side of them lent a view of the harbour until Peter closed the curtains for privacy.

"We're all friends here gentlemen, but business is business."

Bronson handed over the cash and Peter counted it swiftly. Satisfied it was all there, he tucked it away in a drawer. He reached to an overhead cupboard and produced a cardboard box, placing it on the table in front of them. "You're lucky I had the parts."

"You made this on your boat? Isn't that dangerous?" Daniel asked.

"Only if you switch it on." Peter's grinning face turned serious when he showed them the explosive inside. "I want you to listen to me now. You get this wrong and you're fish paste. Most bombs have three or four components. That includes a battery, a switch and the stuff that goes bang. Anything else is showing off."

"Did you have all this stuff lying around on a shelf?" Daniel asked. It wasn't just the motion of the boat that was making him queasy. He looked at all the cupboards and wondered what else was hidden behind them.

"Scary, isn't it?" Peter said. "There's no problem getting hold of the explosives. After the Iraqi wars, the black market is flooded with it. Batteries can be bought off the shelf, but the switches have to be made individually, which means, if anything's going to go wrong, lads, it'll be with the switch. The safest way to ensure the bomb goes off right is a manual, but you want a remote switch, don't you? Something that can be triggered from a distance?"

Daniel and Bronson looked at each other and nodded.

"Well, I don't have one. The best I can do is this," Peter said, pointing at a mercury switch fixed to the explosive. A droplet of mercury sat in the centre of a metal circle viewed through a clear plastic container.

"Listen carefully, lads. This'll make the difference between a long life and a wee short one. The button on the side of the switch arms the bomb, right? It won't trigger until the mercury connects with the metal circle. You arm the bomb and walk the fuck away. You understand?"

He looked at Daniel and Bronson, and sighed when they returned his expectant stare with blank looks.

"You switch it on when the mercury is sitting dead centre in that circle. You don't touch it again. When the bomb is moved, the mercury rolls into the metal circle and makes the connection. That's when you get your fireworks and not before."

"How much explosive is that?" asked Daniel. "I don't want to leave a crater."

Peter pulled out a bottle of Bushmills and three glasses.

"It's enough to take off someone's head, but if you're twenty metres away, it'll barely part your hair."

He filled the glasses with dark brown liquor, accidentally spilling some as the boat rolled on a wave. Wiping the bomb dry with a dish rag, he raised his glass into the air. "May the hinges of our friendship never grow rusty."

Peter drained his in a gulp and Daniel and Bronson followed suit. The other two smacked their lips in appreciation, but Daniel struggled to keep his down. He slid his glass as far away from Peter as he could without looking ungrateful.

"Will you stay for another drink?" Peter asked.

"No," Daniel said with a belch.

They took one last look at the bomb and put it back in the cardboard box. Bronson reached for it and paused, looking at Peter. "This definitely won't go off?"

"It will, just not right now."

Climbing out of the cruiser, they tasted salty, fresh air and made their way along the gangway. Bronson carried the box under his arm and a sheen of sweat on his brow, despite cool weather. Daniel was just glad to be on dry land.

This was it, he thought with grim satisfaction. The end was in sight. If they didn't have the money to give Fairbanks, they'd give him something else.

CHAPTER FORTY-ONE

The weather had changed from a sky that promised rain to one that delivered. A murky drizzle descended, coating the world in a film of grey. It seeped into their clothes and chilled their bones. Bronson wiped a drip from the end of his nose. "At least, it will keep the tourists away. No-one would be out in this for fun."

Jesmond Dene was a narrow, wooded valley that flanked the River Ouseburn. Its trees, dells and waterfalls offered a tranquil idyll for residents of the surrounding area. There was a petting zoo, a restaurant and a dilapidated flour mill. The picnic area near the Pavilion was the place people came to sit and no-one liked to stay still when it was raining. It was flanked by trees and plenty of places to hide.

Daniel and Bronson stood by a heavy table set aside from the others. They had transferred the bomb into a blue sports bag and rested it on the surface. Daniel eyed it warily. Once the button was pressed, there was no going back. It couldn't be disarmed, at least not by them and couldn't be moved without dire consequences.

Bronson sucked air over his teeth. The twitch in his cheek jumped erratically. "I'll switch it on."

"No, I'll do it," Daniel said. "Step back a few metres, mate. If this goes wrong, you don't want to be anywhere near me."

Bronson shook his head. "I'll stay."

Daniel thought of Scalper and his devotion to the Daytons. Bronson was the same. He sometimes caught him staring at the hand that had felled Scott. It was as if it had betrayed him and done something unforgivable.

"I never thanked you for saving my life," Daniel said.

Bronson's face darkened. "I don't want to talk about it."

"You've already done things you didn't want to do. I know you didn't want to kill my brother. You sure you want to add blowing yourself up to that?"

Rivulets of rain ran down Bronson's frown, around his angry eyes and perched in his moustache. "I'm not going to get blown up. We're going to arm the bomb. We're going to have a nice little sit down while we wait for Fairbanks. We watch him go sky high and then it's off to the pub. Okay?"

"Nothing we've done has worked so far. What makes you think this will go according to plan?"

"For fuck's sake, Daniel," Bronson said, plunging his hand into the sports bag. "No-one dies today."

He froze while Bronson fumbled for the switch. There was a click and the bomb was armed.

"Now take your hand out. Nice and easy," Daniel whispered.

Any disturbance to the bag and the bomb would be triggered. He could tell Bronson was thinking the same. His face was contorted in concentration and he held his breath. Daniel held his too as Bronson lifted his hand free. And then he stopped.

Daniel looked at him alarmed. "What?"

"My hand."

"What about it?"

"It's stuck."

Daniel peered into the bag and saw only darkness. "What's it stuck on?"

"How am I supposed to know? Why don't we swap places and I'll take a look?"

Daniel saw the mercury ball quiver as he gently pulled back the lip of the bag. His hand shook, but with more light, he saw the problem. "The lining's snagged on your watch. I'm going to have to loosen it."

"There's barely enough room for my hand, never mind yours. Just leave it."

"How can I fucking leave it? What am I going to say to Fairbanks? Here's your ten million quid and guess what? It comes with a free idiot."

Daniel took a deep breath and reached into the bag. His fingers quaked. He rested them delicately on the face of Bronson's watch, waiting until his nerves subsided. The switch and the mercury were hidden from view, but it didn't matter. If the mercury moved, they'd know about it one way or another.

The lining of the bag was hooked over a link in the wrist band. Using his fingernail, he scratched the edge of the metal.

"I've changed my mind," Bronson said. "You arm the bomb."

The rain made the material slippery. Twice he thought it was loose before Daniel eventually freed it from the watch. He pulled his hand from the bag and watched Bronson do the same.

"Fuck," they said in unison.

Jogging to the perimeter of the picnic area, they found a spot behind a thick dog rose and settled in, the drizzle soaking into their clothes.

***

At five pm, nothing happened. Daniel's clothes clung to him like wet rags and his fingertips were wrinkled. The soil under his boots had been churned into a quagmire. He resisted stretching his legs. It might give away their position and although Fairbanks hadn't shown yet, Daniel sensed he was nearby.

Bronson checked his watch. "Is this tart going to show or what?" He eased himself into a more comfortable position, stepping on a pocket of air under the mud. It escaped from his foot to the sound of a fart and he looked at Daniel. "That wasn't me."

Daniel ignored him, scanning the picnic area through a curtain of grey rain. He nudged Bronson and pointed at a path between two bushes. A small figure stood alone, arms clasped to their chest, the rain clinging to its clothing. The heavy drizzle masked their identity, but it wasn't Fairbanks.

"Who let's their kid out on a day like this?" Bronson said. "Should be in bloody school." He settled back down, careful about where he placed his feet.

Daniel wiped the rain from his face, his cold fingers finding the furrows of his brow. Who was that? Why were they alone? He searched the treeline, but there was no-one else around. "They're staring at the bag."

Bronson cupped his hand over his eyes and looked again. "Probably wondering if it's worth nicking," he said.

The kid inched forward, checking over its shoulder, peering into the darkness of the trees. Whoever it was, they were hesitant, scared. Daniel shifted for a better view. As he moved, the kid ran into the picnic area.

"Shit, Daniel. They're going for the bomb."

Frozen with indecision, Daniel watched the child, a girl, running full tilt toward their trap. She was young, dressed in jeans, T-shirt and a cardigan that was too big for her. Water splashed around her feet. Her tiny arms pumped maniacally by her sides. Her pale face was twisted in fear and he remembered the same face staring at him through the window of his car. He vaulted over the shrubbery and ran screaming toward her.

"Eisha, no. Stay away."

She was almost at the table, her hand out for the bag. Seeing her father, she skidded to a stop, leaving tracks in the mud behind her.

"Stay away from the bag," he shouted.

Bronson was seconds behind him.

Eisha ran toward him. His arms stretched for her. His heart thundered, not because he was running, but because of the fear in her eyes. Three more steps and he'd have her.

"Daniel," Bronson shouted. "Watch out."

He wasn't sure what happened next. Did he hear the crack of rifle fire first or the explosion of the bomb? It didn't matter. He was in the air, looking at the ground where the sky had been. A great hand of flame carried him upward and then vanished, leaving him to fall like a raindrop. As he hit sodden earth, his breath was stolen from his lungs. He was drowning. He crawled to his hands and knees, feeling the skin on his back tighten and split.

Daniel raised his head and roared in pain.

There were voices, but couldn't tell where they came from. His strength disappeared and he collapsed, lying on the cool, wet grass.

"Daniel? Mate? Say something."

Two faces pitched into view as Bronson and Eisha peered over him. He reached out and fumbled for his daughter's hand. "Are you alright, Eisha?"

"You shielded her from the blast," Bronson answered. "Lucky her old man's got a fat arse."

His back felt like he'd been given a thousand lashes. His head was raw and cold, and he suspected the aroma of burning flesh came from his hair and scalp.

Daniel cupped his daughter's concerned face in his hand. "I'm glad you're okay."

Eisha started to cry. "I'm so sorry. It was this man. He lied to the nurses and said he was there to collect me. The ward sister said it was okay."

He stirred, staggering to his feet. There was no way the Sister would give Eisha away to a stranger. Not after everything they'd done, but then he remembered telling her he would send someone to collect his daughter. It was a stupid mistake, but not the ward sister's. It was his.

Bronson removed his coat and placed it around Eisha's shoulders. She was shivering and forcing words through her chattering teeth. "He said that you wanted me to pick something up for you. I said I didn't believe him. He said I was being naughty." She looked down to her feet, avoiding Daniel's stare. "Then I really did start being naughty, but then he started getting angry. He said he'd do things to me if I didn't do as he said."

Daniel dragged Eisha to him, pressing her trembling body to his. He hugged her, rubbing her back, anything he could think of to make her feel better until she squirmed out of his grasp.

"You're being too hard," she said.

He leaned down and gently kissed her forehead. The charred skin of his back tore with every movement, but he cast the pain aside. Flexing his hands open and closed, Daniel searched through the rain to the shade of the trees.

"He must be nearby," Bronson said. "He shot the bag when you were getting close. That's what set it off."

"Take Eisha somewhere safe and don't let her out of your sight. Don't go anywhere familiar."

Bronson held out his hand to Eisha. She looked at it and looked back at her father.

"I want you to go with Uncle Bronson," Daniel said. "He's going to keep you safe."

"I'm staying with you." Eisha stamped her foot and her eyes flashed with the anger he'd been warned about.

"Don't worry, girl," Bronson said. "Your old man's tougher than he looks and he looks pretty tough, doesn't he?"

Eisha smiled, but refused to take his hand. "I want you to come back straight away, Daddy."

Daniel nodded.

"I'll be waiting," she said.

He set off for the path circling the picnic area, silently promising his daughter to be the father she deserved. He searched his pocket, pleased to find his Heckler VP70 was where he left it. Jogging onto a track running parallel to the river, he stopped and dropped to his haunches. The river rumbled by. The drips from sodden leaves fell with the clatter of tiny bells. There was that alarm again; the sense that Fairbanks was near.

The bark of an ash tree exploded into splinters behind him. He saw a flash of muzzle fire through the murk. It came from the other side of the river. He lurched forward, keeping low, skidding down an unstable embankment slick with mud. He fought to keep upright and Fairbanks fired again, but Daniel was hidden by the slope. The water made him gasp as he waded through the river, his legs numbing with the cold. Slipping on a rock, he fell. The river, swollen with rain, hauled him under. His burnt back scraped along the uneven riverbed. He cried out, the bubbles of his scream lost in the froth of the water. Jamming his feet against a boulder, he launched himself to the surface, scrambling to the other side, coughing and retching. Daniel gulped down air before pulling out his pistol, hoping it was dry enough to use.

Aiming the Heckler into the trees, he was relieved to hear it sound off. He kept it in his hand and climbed through the brambles, using them to pull himself to the top of the slope.

"Fairbanks? Are you there?"

He peered into a copse of trees. Some of them were old and their trunks over a foot thick. Fairbanks could be behind any one of them, shrouded in darkness and drizzle. The river thundered on toward a waterfall that dropped into a broiling chasm. He could barely hear himself think, never mind detect the approaching footsteps of a killer.

He heard a voice call from nowhere. "Clever idea about the explosives, Daniel. My Uncle would have called it a Trojan horse. I think it was plain underhand."

He was close, thought Daniel. Crawling to the twisted trunk of a buddleia, Daniel rested against it, ignoring the pain in his back.

"You shouldn't have used my daughter, Fairbanks." Daniel continued on his stomach to a patch of high earth. He kept his gun ahead of him, ready to fire at any moment. This was his chance. One shot was all it took. "The last man who did that is dead," he shouted through the rain.

"Well done. I had my suspicions it was Scott, of course. You Daytons are a sneaky bunch. That's why I didn't trust you to make the drop off."

Tracking his voice, Daniel shuffled behind another tree and waited. Fairbanks was overconfident. He had to keep him talking. "How did you know to shoot the bag?"

It came from Daniel's right, closer to the river than he would have liked. "The way you came running out of the bushes like a madman, I knew there was something in there you didn't want your daughter touching. I couldn't know what, but I knew it wasn't money so I gave it a little prod to find out."

Daniel backtracked, placing one careful foot behind the other. He saw him. Fairbanks was about twenty yards away, lying on his front, protected by a fallen tree trunk. He was wearing another Tweed jacket and his moleskin trousers. His rifle was pointing in the wrong direction, but to shoot him, Daniel needed to be on the other side of that fallen tree. His only options were to trek in front of Fairbanks and risk getting shot or slip behind him and risk sliding down the embankment into the river. He tapped his gun against the side of his leg, wishing he could think of a way of finally out-smarting the man.

There was one other option, which in ordinary circumstances, wasn't an option at all, but under the churning of the river and darkness of the trees, it might work. Twenty yards wasn't far and he didn't have to make it all the way. The river and shadows would hide his advance. By the time Fairbanks realised his cover was blown, Daniel would be close enough to shoot over the log and into Fairbanks' spine. Not a kill shot, but good enough.

He leaned against a tree and counted down from five. He got to three and bolted toward Fairbanks. He dismissed all thoughts of failure, all his past defeats at the hands of this man. He concentrated on running and aiming his gun. Tearing through the undergrowth, he made the distance and fired. It was a hit. The bullet ripped between Fairbanks' shoulder blades, but he didn't move. Daniel fired again. He missed, but Fairbanks remained stationary, refusing to return fire.

And then Daniel realised his mistake.

He spun in a circle, his gun waving in front of him, stumbling over the Tweed jacket stuffed with leaves. He lost his footing and fell with a thump, his body crying out its protests. The gun slipped from his wet hand and was immediately lost amongst the bracken. He searched frantically, but stopped at the sound of someone whistling.

Fairbanks loomed into view, his rifle pressed against his shoulder. He stood in his underwear, his wet shirt plastered to his thin frame. He was smiling, but his eyes were deadly serious.

"It was a decoy," he said. "To lure you out into the open. I got the idea from your brother. He lured you back to Newcastle with your daughter, didn't he?"

Fairbanks stopped smiling. "Can you stand?"

Daniel nodded and got to his feet.

"Can you walk to the river bank please?"

He followed Fairbanks' instructions. As he approached, the sound of the rolling water grew louder. The river crashed into boulders and fallen trees, sending dirty spray into an air already soaked with rain. Daniel could see the waterfall further down, drumming relentlessly on the sharp rocks below.

"What happens now?" he asked.

Fairbanks cocked his head to one side, as if Daniel had asked the dumbest question he'd ever heard. On reflection, he probably had.

"I'm going to shoot you. Watch your body wash away. Then I'm going after your family."

Daniel stepped forward, but Fairbanks halted his advance with a warning shot above his head. "I have to do it, Daniel. I can't risk them coming after me for revenge. We both know how destructive that can be."

"You don't have to," he said, wringing his hands. "It's over. There's nothing left."

"What about your daughter? She said some very hurtful things to me. She'll wait, but when she's old enough, she'll come looking, I can tell."

Daniel smiled. His body relaxed. He looked over his shoulder at the grey water flecked with white and turned back to Fairbanks, shaking his head in disbelief. What he had feared most about Fairbanks was his ability to predict another person's actions. He was always right and had been from the start. Fairbanks would be right until the moment of his death, which was only seconds away.

Eisha had come looking. She tiptoed through the woods, moving between trees and slipping through brambles like a ghost. He saw her eyes glitter in the darkness and she pressed a finger to her lips as she drew closer. Picking up a branch half her size, she hefted it behind her.

"I guess this is goodbye," Fairbanks said, staring down his rifle.

Eisha swung the branch, her pretty face scrunched into a scowl. It connected with the back of Fairbanks' head with a crack. His shot went wide. He toppled forward. Daniel scurried to catch him, but his daughter got there first. She lifted the branch again, bringing it down on an arm. It must have broken because Fairbanks squealed in pain, cradling it against his body.

Lifting the branch above her head, Daniel saw her bared teeth, the thirst in her eyes. She was feral and meant to kill him. He hurried forward, snatching the branch from her hand.

She woke as if from a trance and stared at her father. "But I want to," she said.

Throwing the branch to one side, he dragged Fairbanks to his feet.

"Thank you. I thought she was going to kill me."

He looked at his daughter as she gaily pulled leaves from a bush. Her anger had passed. She was the little girl in the hospital bed; the little girl with her hand pressed against his car window. Seeing her now, playing in the woods, holding Bronson's coat against the rain, no-one would suspect how close to madness she really was.

He had glimpsed his daughter as she really was for the first time. Daniel didn't know who his parents were, but Eisha was her father's daughter.

He dragged Fairbanks to the spot where he'd stood waiting to be shot. "I won't let my daughter be corrupted. If there's blood to be shed, I'll do it."

Holding him by his shirt, Daniel shoved him closer to the slope leading to the turbulent water below. Fairbanks' face was blank, as it had been when Daniel threatened him with torture. He looked at the river with mild concern.

"And me without my fishing rod," he said.

Daniel had many precious things in his life – his daughter, Lily, his dream of living a free life. They had all been made vulnerable by the man whose life he held in his hands. As far as Daniel knew, there was only one thing Fairbanks held dear and he nodded toward his earring.

"I know that thing is important to you. Do you want to die with it in or out?"

"In." Fairbanks' answer was fast and decisive, leaving Daniel in no doubt as to what to do. He reached for the earring.

Fairbanks' bulbous eyes glistened with fear. "No, you don't," he said.

He kicked out, his feet striking Daniel's shins in such a flurry of blows Daniel almost buckled. He held firm as Fairbanks wriggled like a dying fish, desperate to escape the hook. He spat in Daniel's face, then clawed at his eyes. He weaved his head left and right.

"Stop struggling," Daniel said.

"I know I have to die, but not that."

Daniel shook him roughly. Fairbanks' teeth banged together. Bloody saliva slipped from his mouth as he bit his tongue, but Daniel wouldn't stop. The muscles in his arms raged and his burnt back screamed. It was the anger he had carried with him for days, his desire for revenge. When Fairbanks went limp, Daniel gasped for breath, feeling his daughter's eyes on him, listening to Fairbanks' groans.

"Not that," he repeated over and over. "Not that."

Looking into his pale face, Daniel searched, seeing the shadows and things no-one else could see. Something clicked in his mind and when he pulled back, he was embarrassed at his stupidity. Fairbanks, his father, his brother, they might never have shown mercy, but Daniel would because no-one was truly evil. At worst, they were simply alone.

Revenge didn't have to end in murder. He could show his daughter the Daytons were kind as well as cruel, that forgiveness wasn't only for the weak. As he caught her watching him, he hoped it might halt the growing violence inside her.

"This was never about a bloody dog, was it?" Daniel said.

Fairbanks raised his head and smiled sadly.

"It was your uncle," he continued.

He nodded and Daniel released him.

"The thing about the dogs ..." Fairbanks said, shrugging and faltering for words. "Well, it helps in this game if people think you're psychotic, but you and your daughter are the real deal, aren't you?"

He looked out over the water and did up the collar button of his shirt. "My Uncle was the only person who ever treated me like I mattered."

"Did you kill him?"

The horror on Fairbanks' face shamed him and Daniel cast around for something else to look at, but his eyes were drawn back to the earring.

"It was a hit and run," Fairbanks said. "Something random out of the blue. Here one minute. Gone the next."

Daniel remembered his father and how his death could be attributed to his choices, like stepping stones along a treacherous path. Every misdeed and crime was a fateful progress toward a brutal end whereas Fairbanks' uncle was snatched from existence through no fault of his own. Maybe that's why Fairbanks needed to control everything. It was an attempt to mitigate his pain, but there was no avoiding what was about to come.

They looked at one another, rain coursing down their faces. Daniel thought Fairbanks might understand that now.

"Do you want to give me a second chance?" Fairbanks asked with a half-smile. Daniel shook his head and when Fairbanks held out his hand, he ignored it. Instead, he stepped to one side, pointing to the river and the path Fairbanks was about to undertake.

Fairbanks nodded slowly and walked backwards to the top of the grassy embankment. He undid the buttons of his soaked shirt and threw it to the ground. The rain sluiced the mud from his skinny torso. He looked cleansed. Perhaps this was some sort of baptism, Daniel thought.

"I always loved the water," he said, "but do you honestly think I'm going to jump to my death?"

His hand snaked around his back. With a wince, he produced a gun. Daniel recognised it as a Colt Eagle, but with black duct tape hanging from its sides like broken wings.

Fairbanks smiled, his dead eyes flashing with triumph. "I'm starting to get used to handguns. I taped it to my back just in case."

Daniel heard footsteps and suddenly Eisha was in front of him, protecting him from the bullet. Her hair hung in wet streaks and she growled like a guard dog, but Eisha barely reached his midriff, giving Fairbanks opportunity to shoot them both. He grabbed her and although she was cold, he felt the warmth of her body.

"Don't do it," Daniel said. "Leave her out of this. Please."

Fairbanks closed one eye and aimed as his earring caught a ray of light.

"Who goes first?" he asked.

The wet mud under his feet gave way. His face froze into a rictus of panic, his bulbous eyes were stricken with fear. And then the mud shifted. His Eagle flew into the air as he tumbled backward with a scream, his arms flaying. Daniel and Eisha ran to the shoreline. He held her firmly, fearful she might fall. Fairbanks splashed into the water and was dragged under by the current. He re-emerged, choking and fighting for breath before slamming against a rock. Daniel found his daughter's hand as they watched

Fairbanks being swept away, his pale form showing signs of red. He disappeared under the surface and the river rumbled on. Like Fairbanks, they held their breath, waiting to be sure of his death.

"There," shouted Eisha, pointing to the waterfall. Above the roar and the spray, Daniel saw Fairbanks pitched over the edge, his mouth agape and his hands grasping for purchase, but the river was too strong. It took him into its embrace and left nothing behind, save for the smile on Eisha's face.

Daniel bowed his head, wondering what to feel. He counted to ten and made it to nine before he led his daughter away through the wood. Finding the track, they trudged back to the picnic area in silence. The table they'd blown up was still smouldering. In the distance, they saw Bronson frantically running from bush to shrub, appearing to have lost something.

The rain stopped and Daniel peered into a grey sky. His carnivorous family were all but gone. His duties were dispensed with and he finally felt a sense of lightness and possibility. Daniel was free to live his dream.

He watched Eisha skip along the track. She was his carefree daughter again, showing no signs of having witnessed a man fall to his death. This daughter hadn't even been there. It was his other daughter, the one who wanted to take a life to protect his. The corruption of the Daytons had begun and he knew it would get worse if they stayed.

"Would you like to live in Scotland?" he asked.

Eisha stopped in the middle of a puddle and cocked her head to one side. He tried to read her thoughts, but her face was blank. Pulling his wet clothing tighter, he braced himself against a cold breeze. The clouds darkened and it started to rain again.

"No," she said. "Better things happen here."

CHAPTER FORTY-TWO

Bronson parked in a bay outside a tower block known as the Devil's Playground. No sooner had he pressed his key fob, beeping the alarm on Ed Dayton's BMW, than he was surrounded by children aged between six and ten. Their faces were grubby and their clothes torn. One young girl wore a T-shirt with 'Pussy' emblazoned on the front while a young boy wore no top at all, preferring to wander the estate bearing his pigeon chest.

"Watch yer car for you, mate?" It was the tallest boy who spoke, though judging by his face, he was also the youngest. He wore a dirty Parka jacket down to his knees and clenched an unlit cigarette between his teeth.

Bronson dug his hand into his pocket and handed over a fiver. He'd just washed and polished the vehicle, as he did every week, but that wasn't why he gave them the money. If he didn't pay the toll, he'd come back to scratched paint work and slashed tyres. It was the same scam he'd pulled as a child.

In the months that followed Fairbanks' death, Bronson set about rebuilding the Dayton's empire without a Dayton in sight. Daniel was keeping a low profile, spending time with his daughter in the empty rooms of Five Oaks. Eisha was ill and he made it clear he didn't want visitors. After what the bairn had been through, Bronson didn't blame him.

As the lift door opened, Bronson shivered. He stepped inside, carefully kicking aside syringes and cotton swabs stained with blood. It was a short ride to the fourth floor, but made longer when the smell of urine was so powerful.

He'd visited Liz in her apartment in Gateshead a few times. She was thinner these days, though it had little to do with diet and exercise and more with wine consumption. The apartment remained in her name, but the income she received from the Daytons had ceased.

"Why has Daniel cut me off? What did I do wrong? And why haven't you found Monica yet?" she'd asked before passing out by the window overlooking her city.

He didn't have the guts to tell her it had been his decision to stop her money. There simply wasn't enough to go around anymore.

The lift door opened and he stumbled onto the fourth floor. He gasped for breath, but the air wasn't much better outside the lift. It was stale and tinged with the aroma of a hundred spoons browning chemicals over a lighter. The bulbs along the corridor had been stolen again, pitching it in darkness. Somewhere somebody was crying while someone else argued for their turn on a pipe. He rechecked the package under his arm and proceeded into the shadows.

A boy of eighteen sat outside room four-one-four. He looked up when Bronson approached and adjusted his clothing so they looked neater on his thin frame. When he smiled, Bronson noted his front teeth were missing.

"He's waiting inside for you, sir," the boy said, jabbing his thumb toward the open door.

The room was similar to the one where Bronson had tortured the long forgotten Enoch; small, damp and furnished with belongings that looked like they'd been scavenged from a skip. He'd insisted on installing a few home comforts however. A kerosene heater and lamp to ward off the nightly chills. A double bed free from lice and stains. And a camping stove for hot meals should the occupant ever feel like eating.

Waiting for him by the bedroom door was Clive Hawk, the so-called king of the Devil's Playground. Clive was taller than Bronson, but thin, like most of the inmates of the tower. He was in his early fifties and wore a mismatched combination of camouflage trousers and a V-neck sweater. It pictured a yellow smiling face popular with ravers in the eighties.

"Charlie," he said, throwing his arms up in the air. "We always look forward to your visits."

Bronson handed over the package and Clive ran a tongue over his cracked lips, a greedy light flashing in his eyes. He might run this tower like a king, thought Bronson, but he was a dirty skaghead just like the rest of them.

"Payment for services rendered?" Clive said.

"You know the deal. He gets his share first and the rest is yours for looking after him. Okay?"

"I've been taking very good care of him, as you'll see. In fact, I've just given him his morning kick. I doubt you'll get much sense out of him, but at least he's happy." Pointing to the floor, Bronson followed Clive's finger to a blackened spoon and used syringe. "Can I go?"

Bronson dismissed him with a wave and Clive scuttled away. He lit the kerosene lamp and ventured into the bedroom.

The curtains were drawn and the room smelled of sweat and take-away cartons. The blankets had been soiled and kicked to the bottom of the bed. Before he sat down, Bronson checked the restraints on the headboard. They were solid, but not too tight. There was no need to make this worse than it already was.

"Are you awake?" he asked.

The figure on the bed moaned and shimmied away until the chains clunked. "It's okay. It's me. It's Bronson," he said, as if it would make a difference.

He lifted the lamp, shining it on the figure in the bed. He checked his arm. Still muscular, but pockmarked with needle wounds. None were infected, thought Bronson with relief, but his head needed shaving again. He didn't want him getting infested with lice. Overall, Clive had made good on his word and Bronson relaxed.

"I've come with the news," Bronson said, settling into a chair. The figure in the bed stirred, but didn't open his eyes.

"We've drawn a complete blank on Noodles. We don't have the money or the manpower to mount a proper search so it's just going to have to wait."

The figure pulled weakly on the restraints binding him to the bed.

"There's no point complaining about it and I'm not here to take orders," Bronson said.

He stared down at his new shoes. They were as bright and polished as his new car. Pulling on his shirt collar, his skin prickled with warmth, though the heater wasn't on. His throat was dry and he wished he'd brought some water.

"I saw Lily this month. I bumped into her at the Mayfair club. Nice girl. We didn't chat long. Got the impression I reminded her of the bad old days."

"Monica?" The name was slurred, but there was no mistaking it.

"I told you to stop asking. I don't know."

His restraints rattled. Bronson stood and paced the floor. "The last I heard she was shacked up with some banker, okay? She should count herself lucky. There's not many blokes would take a pregnant woman on, you know? She's better off."

The room was stifling. He needed air, but the window was nailed shut. Instead he pulled open the curtains and the outside world flooded in. He felt a moment of respite, turning to the figure on the bed who cringed away from the sunlight.

Bronson's stomach lurched at the sight of him. He was as tall as he ever was, dressed in the same suit he wore on the day Bronson had brought him here, engaging Clive as his captor. It was tattered now and dirty. Vomit was encrusted on his chin and his lips were blue. His skin was paler, but when he opened his eyes, they still flashed like frostbitten steal.

It wasn't enough to simply restrain him, Clive had said. He insisted he be hooked on heroin. It was the only way to control a man as dangerous as Scott Dayton. Bronson agreed with his reasoning, but having returned every month since, he worried about his decision more and more.

"I know you hate it, Scott. Maybe it would have been kinder to kill you, but I couldn't so you're stuck here."

Picking up the kerosene lamp, Bronson extinguished the flame. "This is your punishment. For what you did to Eisha. For the betrayal of your father, the Dayton name and all the things I loved. No-one knows you're here. Everyone thinks you're dead. It's purgatory for us both. Christ, if Daniel only knew –"

The mention of Daniel's name roused Scott. He rolled his head toward Bronson, his brow knotted in anger, the tendons in his neck stretched taut. He moved his lips as if he was talking, but nothing came out. Scott continued like that until his strength was spent. He closed his eyes and Bronson watched the ragged rise and fall of his chest as he slipped back into a drug induced coma.

He didn't say a single word, but Bronson was left in no doubt as to the meaning. If Scott ever escaped, he and Daniel were dead men.

Sitting for a further five minutes, Bronson sighed and repeated his apologies like he did on every visit. Checking his restraints, he left Scott to the rancid cell.

Bronson abstained from the lift and took the stairs. With each step downward, the oppression of Scott's room evaporated. Outside, his car was in the same gleaming condition as he had left it, though the children protecting it were gone. Savouring the fresh air, a smile crept onto his face as he climbed into his car.

His future lay ahead like an open road and Bronson started the engine.